The Weight of Silver

The Weight of Silver

E.M. Chapel

For Travis, it would have been impossible to write this without your steadfast encouragement, love, and support—and for my mom and dad who never discouraged dreams of nature and magic.

One

It was an autumn afternoon around four, and the day had already been a purgatorial eternity. Viva, caked in dirt and adorned in a crown of pine needles, willed the ancient printer to spit out tomorrow's rosters, maps, and nature bingo sheets—a little faster, please. How a person could do their job for a few hours in the morning only to be bombarded with twenty fresh emails at lunch was a mystery that Viva would never solve. Email bombardment: the modern equivalent of pitchfork-wielding villagers at the castle door. And even though the former janitor's closet-turned-scarcely-used-office space was the farthest thing imaginable from a castle, villagers were lined up and ready to torch the place.

Unread. Unread. Unread.

The subject line "?" caught her eye. Viva opened the email, and read a message she knew would be a day-ruiner: "Did CeCe bite anyone today?" She sighed, better respond, lest the sender arrive at her door with a newly sharpened pitchfork.

The answer was, unfortunately: "Yes, yes she did." Emphatically in fact. It had been a grand feat, if nightmarish. Viva had never seen a child clamber up a tree, hook her legs over a branch and hang upside down like a rabid bat, then chomp her way through the oncoming line of unsuspecting seven-year-olds. If it hadn't been so horrifying, it would have been impressive. Many of the other kids had wisely dived from the path and taken off running through the woods while Viva coaxed the little monstrosity out of the tree, a tuft of blonde hair hanging like loose noodles from the child's leering, red mouth. The little girl had stared at Viva with unblinking eyes and slurped up the spaghetti strands.

So, Viva responded to the mother's email with a reluctant phone call, praying to the universe for voicemail. The universe clearly had more important things to worry about than Viva. She wasn't surprised.

"Six is fine. Our earliest excursion tomorrow is at 8:30, so six is wide open. I look forward to seeing you." She said into the phone, infusing her voice with artificial sunshine. "Actually, Ma'am, I go by Viva, not Vivian…" After an aggravating line of questioning during which Viva wished she had somewhere to run, someone to run to, to whisk her away, a meeting was scheduled. Viva had surrendered to a morning meeting. She would have to ask Tyree, her best friend and the proprietor of the best coffee shop just outside of town, to open his shop early for her. You couldn't tell a parent that their kid was attempting to manifest as a rabies-infected vampire straight out of Victorian Transylvania without a coffee or four. Tyree would understand.

Viva preferred to let the sun warm up and then greet it with sufficient caffeine and an acknowledging nod, but the mother had insisted, and no one had come to Viva's rescue, no matter how much she wished.

A six a.m. meeting. Only the parents of biters, hitters, swearers, runners, and monsters insisted on meeting with Viva at six in the morning. With other parents, there was no meeting, it was just: Thanks for joining us today at Mancy-led Adventures, here's your Doug back—he knows what poison ivy is now, or Kyra's an excellent tracker, incidentally, we filled out the mountain lion page of our animal sighting booklet.

Only parents of sadistic children scheduled a siege for the break of dawn. They must be toying with her, easy prey to be tossed around until she was sufficiently drained of the will to go on, to concede: all right, your baby angel does not have a blood-lust problem, fine. In her mind's eye, a heap of Viva sprawled in an oily pool, pale and lifeless as narrow-eyed parents stroked glittering pearl necklaces and bared glittering fangs. Viva shook her head and refocused on the growling printer.

It was likely that if Mancy Morrigan, Viva's personal, fully-certified guardian, and the town's official and semi-acknowledged "necromancer"–though no one called them that anymore since the broader and more apt term "mancy" had been accepted over a century before–had been the one on the other end of the email thread or phone line, the conversation would have been entirely different. No one wanted to mess with a mancy, lest they find themselves trapped in that very email thread, forced to flag spam for eternity. But it was Viva on the phone, not Morrigan, and while Viva had dialed, she thought of all the ways she could've failed unceremoniously if she had ever desired to be a mancy too. School, college, men, living on her own, having a career, finding a circle of girlfriends, belonging, life, life, life. At least she didn't have to add mancying to the list of disappointing, if unceremonious, failures.

Viva leaned back in her chair considering the printer, still spewing out her requests.

Once the printer finally spat out the final trail map and hummed itself to sleep, she stood. She was going to make her way back home where no other emails would have a chance to track her down. Maybe she would meet someone on the path, someone new and normal–someone to see her. Viva's heart stung.

The office building Viva exited was a squat brick thing. Morrigan had been the one to rent out the janitor's closet to serve as their so-called office headquarters. Morrigan had even put a small plaque above the door that read: "Mancy-Led Adventures." As a rule, the town mancy had to have some sort of town presence, if reluctantly, so Morrigan had acquiesced to an office on the edge of town in the land of beige. The makeshift office also had the desired effect of not having to allow a computer into their home, which was all well and good, but meant that Viva, mistress of scheduling, communications, reservations, and all other computer-related tasks, had to make the trek into town. She was the one who scheduled six a.m. meetings with parents of demonic children while listening to footsteps and chatter and laughter flow from the other offices. Viva shook her head.

When she left, the parking lot was still full. Viva wondered where the people who worked in the other offices and other people in town for that matter all went after work. Did they go to those places together? Did they laugh together? Walk, chat, smile belong together? She wondered what they all talked about, those groups of faceless people she had never spoken to. Things, Viva thought. Unimportant, but significant things. She felt a pang in her chest. Unimportant.

Viva wove her way in and out of parked cars, a satchel, overflowing with tree branches and trail maps, precariously slung over her shoulder. The back of the full parking lot opened to a wide, dirt path, wise with time and footprints. The way was dusty and overhung with an archway of trees.

When she was younger, the contrast between the dirt path and the asphalt felt significant. Each time she crossed the threshold from one world to the other, from the town to the woods, it felt significant, and she could never describe precisely why. Everyone else exited the parking lot at the front, driving into the town with its buildings and streets and shops and bustle, but the exit at the back was an old forest path that followed a silver creek all the way up through the woods and into the feral hills beyond. Up and up and up, until everything but water and wild disappeared.

Viva

*V*iva was settled into the kindergarten classroom, having placed her sack lunch in an assigned cubby—it was red, which was irritating, as there were empty yellow ones right there, where she would much rather have housed her lunch. She was wishing for her family—Karl or Morrigan. With them, there was no way she would have ended up with a red cubby. She imagined them next to her on the brightly numeraled rug, Morrigan humming floral tunes and Karl sneaking Viva cookies while the nancy wasn't watching. It wasn't fair that she had to be alone. Here. With a red cubby. No Karl. No Morrigan. Viva was alone. She fumed, crisscrossed applesauce on her assigned number on the clown-colored rug. Number nine, the worst number. She wanted to go home.

After an unbearable two hours of homesickness and longing, Viva felt ready to take her chances with a prison break, but as she surveyed the potential exits, the teacher announced: time to play a game. Games were good. Viva was great at winning games, heck, she was great at losing *games too. She would memorize all the rules, so she could play them again at home where games were a lot more fun than anywhere else.*

In the middle of the fourth name game that Viva had convinced herself she was winning, she forgot all about Morrigan and Karl. Though the teacher hadn't been impressed with her Simon Says expertise, Viva was sure she would've won if not for his premature demand for everyone to sit back down on their number and for heaven's sake, be quiet. It wasn't Viva's fault these kids couldn't leap from one desk to another, after all. What was Simon expected to say? Rub your head and pat your stomach? That was not the way to win. One casualty of Viva's brief dictatorship as Simon was a boy who resembled a ruffled scarecrow; he had flashed her a lopsided, bloodstained grin after his nose had smashed against the edge of a desk, gushing streams of red. He had wiped the straw hair from his eyes, smearing it with blood and broken into laughter. Viva grinned. She would have to talk to him again; he might even be able to keep up if Simon was a mancy.

Now though, he was in the nurse's office, and she was confined to the number nine while the teacher rubbed his temples and spoke quietly into the classroom phone. As she waited for something new to happen, Viva's stomach roused like a yawning dragon.

Was someone going to feed her, or what? The red cubby where her lunch bag sat neglected beckoned. After what was a dull eternity, the magic words sounded: "Ladies and gentlemen, get your lunch from your cubby and line up at the door."

Viva bounced over to her red cubby—still, a cruel reminder of the individual wants that had not been met by this new "community" situation that school turned out to embody—and she pulled out her lunch. What would it be? What would it be? Shivering in her grasp, the satisfying weight of the paper bag made her stomach growl louder in anticipation. The beast had awoken.

She joined the single-file line that had formed in front of the classroom door and stood as still as she could manage, her sack lunch held to her chest like a golden treasure. The excitement was building within her, twanging electricity as she bounced up and down on the balls of her feet.

Lunchtime.

The line was moving impossibly slowly, but finally, Viva made it into the cafeteria. Her teacher hustled in the opposite direction as the children all entered a gigantic white room like ants descending upon a discarded potato chip. She wove through various tables, plastic tables with benches attached so that she had to pull her leg up to her chin to insert herself into a semi-comfortable position. Morrigan had suggested she at least try to make friends, so Viva had chosen a table full of other kids and squished herself in between two, whom she recognized from her class as numbers eight and two. Ignoring what they were saying about their names and favorite colors, Viva drooled at the lunches splayed out in front of them. Cupcakes and crinkle-cut carrot sticks, sandwiches without crusts that crackled in protective plastic. Viva felt frenzied. Feverish. Electricity coursed through her blood. What was her lunch going to be? The dragon in her burbling stomach roared.

With shaking hands, too excited to peek inside, she opened the bag, breathed in, and plunged a hand down into the mysterious depths. The wash of anticipation surged through her, and then she took hold of something at the bottom of the bag. She furrowed her brows at the rough, gritty texture her brain was processing.

What was this?

It didn't feel like the thin plastic that housed every decent school meal—it didn't feel like a cardboard box with perfectly cubed, machine-processed meats and cheeses either. Maybe it was something better than both of those, Morrigan was a mancy after all. Her mind spun with static-y ideas flitting this way and that in her twirling brain. Whatever it was, holding her breath, she pulled it towards her. Finally, Viva unveiled the full glory of her first day of school.

It was a potato.

Uncooked, and sprouting, and much bigger than the shaking fist Viva was balling up violently at her side.

The heat behind her eyes deepened. Unblinking. Unfeeling. Unmoving. Her little heart was pounding. The nameless shadows next to her laughing while they stuffed their faces with chocolate, cheese, and peanut butter. Humiliation feels like searing, metal spikes driven through every inch of the body, the mind, piercing with rusted teeth, into the soul. Through this pain, and her hunger, Viva tried to run for the door, but she tripped over the attached bench, and her potato flew out of her hand, rolling chunkily towards the exit.

Tears came now, burning her cheeks, her chin, her nose. Scrambling, shaking, crying, she sprinted away, scooping up the potato on her way, and blocking out the laughter around her. She stumbled toward the door, but a woman with blonde hair cropped severely at her chin blocked the way. "Where do you think you're going?" The woman asked, "Lunch isn't over yet." Viva stammered and sputtered. "Go sit back down, or you'll have to stand at the time-out wall during recess."

This harpy wasn't going to let Viva leave the cafeteria, but Viva would rather square up against an angry Morrigan—Viva shuddered—than go back in that room. Back to the cackling laughter. The hot humiliation. The crushing loneliness.

How quick could this lady be? Viva assessed her chances through tears and hyperventilation. Ready, set...

She made a break for it.

Potato in hand, Viva sprinted, fueled by humiliation, fury, and despair, around the blonde woman, zigzagging down the hall, and toward the exit like a tiny gazelle.

But the woman caught up with Viva in seconds, marched her back to the table that was ringing with hyena cackles. The kids from her class—eight and two—snorted and sputtered at Viva from behind their chocolate rubble.

Viva spent her recess standing in front of a red brick wall just outside of the cafeteria, watching the other kids play tag, swing on the monkey bars, and make friends. All *those happy, grinning shadows. Happy and belonging. They were laughing. She knew it. At her. She was laughable.*

The gnawing growl of her stomach's dragon twisted, and she wept. Viva replayed her humiliation over and over and over; she would spend the rest of elementary school as 'potato girl,' eating, exiled, at her own table with its chemical smell and attached bench, building the dam behind her eyes higher and higher each day.

Two

As Viva neared the arch that denoted the exit from town, she heard a grating caw made of gravel and time. It was a rasping that Viva knew as well as her own voice. She held out her arm, and in a gust of autumn and feathers, a white crow with a wingspan equal to Viva's own flightless arms flapped clumsily down and landed on top of her shoulder–and most of her arm. She grunted under his weight, and he cawed again in her ear as she ducked beneath twisted branches.

"Hi Karl, six a.m. meeting tomorrow. Want to come along?" the dirt of the creek path crunched; walking up the path from the office to Tyree's coffee house was about a thirty-minute excursion. Mancy Manor, where Viva lived with Karl and Morrigan was ten to fifteen more, depending on how many sparkly objects demanded Karl's attention along the way. The crow shook himself indignantly and then nestled one of the many ruffled feathers of his breast back into place.

The sun's sleepy autumn lids drooped earlier and earlier as the season deepened. The air had a dry, wheezing chill, and leaves still clung to shivering branches, while those underfoot crinkled, releasing the scent of earth. A silver creek flowed to Viva's left as she climbed with Karl upstream. "Six a.m. meeting," she said again, "I have to explain to a grown woman that her child cannot chomp on any of our other clients, and I have a feeling that it won't go over well." She paused for response, but when no caw came, Viva restarted, her tone exasperated, "If you would just cater for Mancy-led Adventures like we've asked, the kids probably wouldn't need to bite each other, and I wouldn't have a terrible meeting tomorrow. We could charge more as an all-inclusive package, which would mean all new kitchen supplies for you, sir. Just think about it, please; it would only be chips and sandwiches. It wouldn't take time out of your busy schedule. You already work at Tyree's most of the day, what's a few extra sandwiches?" The creek chuckled between sharp-toothed boulders, foaming at the white-capping tops like the gums of a mad dog. "I need to stop by Tyree's to ask him to open early tomorrow. And I need coffee. Need need, so I'll see you back home." She shook Karl from her shoulder, breathing in relief at the release of his weight as he flapped white wings just above her head. Viva watched the bird fly up the path until he vanished, and she listened to the water running next to her. Running and running and running. A part of her, just a sliver, wondered what it would be like to run along the bottom with the current, silver glass unbroken overhead.

Lost in her thoughts of rushing water, of cool, muted floating, she turned to the creek, taking slow steps towards the water. There was a small patch of green with space enough to sprawl out on a blanket; she crossed the grass and then knelt on the bank, dipping her fingers below the creek's surface, an electric chill shimmied up her spine. She swished her hand back and forth, creating ripple designs as her mind wandered on.

A gust of wind hissing through the nearly naked trees snapped her mind back to the present. She should get going. Tyree would need to close soon. Morrigan was expecting her. She made to turn back to the path when an overwhelming clangor overtook her as a parade of spandex-laden bicyclists stampeded past her on their race down the path. Her heart slammed against her chest, the noise thundered through her, making her bones clatter. She felt an icy shiver, and Viva fell backward. Into the creek.

Bicycle thunder. Rushing waters. Rustling wind. She didn't call out.

She sank.

Down and down. Much further down than a creek should allow. The water caressed her skin. Soft comfort. Cool embrace. Muted nothing silence. The day, the biting child, the phone call, the beige loneliness, every failure, every disappointment, every insecurity washed away as easily as time. All she felt was warm tranquility.

Viva opened her eyes. Not to blurry visions of the green-tinged world above, but to nothing. Nothing was there. What should have been above the glassy veneer had gone. There was only water, only nothing, only silence, but as her sights combed downward, her heart beating fast; before her was an enormous silver castle.

Water flooded into her gaping mouth. There was a castle in front of her. A castle in the creek.

It was the kind of castle that only existed in fairytales. A castle where princesses trapped in top-floor towers let down their hair and kissed handsome strangers.

Squinting through the water, fighting to keep hold of her breath, Viva could see towers, battlements, a keep—all those terms she had collected from grade school storybooks. How could an underwater castle have a moat? But it did. A flowing, silver moat. Her head was fogging without oxygen, the image of the castle wobbled within the moving waters like a mirage. A castle. Beneath the creek. The creek she had lived next to her whole life. Summers inner-tubing, wading, skipping eager rocks. Viva closed her stinging eyes, mind turning around and around, and around, and when she opened them again, the castle had disappeared. There was nothing but dark water, and the empty creek bed. And silence.

She couldn't breathe. Her body was throbbing. She was drowning, and in front of her was nothing. A sharp pain seized her chest, and a gnawing sense of loss, of missed opportunity— another one, but why and what? —held her heart and squeezed, her vision pulsated, and her head throbbed like an aching wound. Kicking her legs frantically, ignoring her numbing muscles, her lungs' pleas for air, she pushed herself downward to the creek bed. She needed to see. Needed to know. Needed something. The aching grew stronger, and her head swam. Black spots peppered her vision. She kept swimming. Kept searching. For silver.

But it was nothing. Just the creek.

Moss and mud, stones and pebbles. Nothing. Until her searching eyes fell upon a silver gleam. It sparkled teasingly on the creek floor, a silver pebble beckoning through her blurred vision.

She picked it up and rolled it over her fingers, and when she studied it more closely, she saw her own image smiling out at her. But it wasn't her. It couldn't be because the Viva reflected in the silver pebble was a Viva laughing surrounded by people she had never met. But there she was and there they were, visions in silver, laughing with her. Not at her, with her. Viva couldn't turn away from the silver pebble. Her eyelids were drooping, her body screaming for air, her muscles cramped in pleading tension. There was no air and no air. No air. The spell fractured. She pocketed the pebble and in what felt like dragging her protesting body through pudding, pulled herself back to the world above. After breaking the surface of the creek, Viva clawed herself out, sputtering lungs of water, and she sank onto the green. Ringing bells of bikers chimed from down the path, or was it the ringing in her own ears, confounded by the release of pressure? Tyree's coffee house beamed from across the path, and the creek burbled in the autumn air.

A silver castle. Pulling the pebble from her pocket, Viva searched with scientific scrutiny, but no. It was just a pebble, small and polished like silver glass. The only reflection was her own, pale-faced and gaunt, dripping and dreaming of silver.

Three

Viva had been frequenting Tyree's since the day they had met in kindergarten, though in those days, Tyree only made cheese sandwiches with the crusts cut off, a process which Karl had supervised like an overbearing mother.

The Daisy House, where Tyree lived and ran his business, was a sweet, pale yellow, trimmed with emerald. The rich green also adorned the front door and garage, giving the place a flowery, living aesthetic. The entrance to Tyree's house was arched stonework, which made Viva think of a cozy village somewhere far away. Sitting comfortably on the right side of the path, smoke poured languidly from the chimney. It was as though it were staged for a pitstop in the middle of an epic adventure. A heroic dragon slayer would stop begrudgingly, finding the town's lack of filthy taverns appalling, but upon encountering the charming, white picnic table; the small, front garden overrun by gnomes; the blanket of seasonal foliage; and the constant aroma of fresh coffee and baked goods, our weathered hero would proceed to bunk with the dragon itself so as not to soften his heroic image before his epic battle. Tyree's house was so charming that Hansel and Gretel would have determined it to be a little too sweet.

When his parents had moved away for their retirement while Tyree was in college, he had converted the garage into his coffee shop, and after years of refining, perfecting, building, his was the best coffee shop in the woods.

Every morning at six, Tyree lifted the emerald garage door like the portcullis of a delicious chateau and flooded the path with a burst of coffee and scones, breakfast, and chocolate.

Viva could see, as she approached, twin cups of steaming hot chocolate as well as a small scone, sugar-dusted, and beckoning—the last of the pastries this late in the afternoon. Viva sloshed her way to Tyree's garage, leaned, dripping against the counter, and smiled as she reached for the two cups waiting for her.

"Have a nice swim?" Tyree's face was all light, warm and crooked, like a joyful scarecrow clumsily, but lovingly sewn together. Like a medical chart, his nose told the story of childhood breakage. His smiling lips twisted up higher on one side of his face, but he had learned to cock his head in the opposite direction when he smiled to provide the world with artificial symmetry. Tyree's clothes could only be described as motley and were never quite right in terms of hue, fit, or weather appropriateness. Ever since they had first met in grade school, he had reminded Viva of a cootie catcher: tiny snippets of wisdom, laughter, or pain folded behind prismatic scribble scrabbles. "How was the water?" His eyebrows tugged together as he cocked his head.

Viva straightened, plucked the cups off the counter, and glancing at the deserted path behind her. "Oh, great. Nothing like a frigid dip in the dead of fall."

Viva stood at the counter, sipping her drink, and allowing thoughts of silver to absorb her. She didn't notice Tyree slip out from behind the counter and walk into the house. He came back out shortly, and Viva jumped when he wrapped a bright orange towel around her before packing the scone carefully into her satchel.

"Seriously, you okay? What happened—wait, was it that biker gang? Bunch of scallywags. We should get Morrigan to have a chat with them. Need a hand up the last hill home?"

Viva tugged the towel around her, a chill passing over her.

"Thanks, I'm okay. I'd better get going. Didn't know I'd be taking a dip on the way home." From behind her, the creek bubbled. "You ever...."

"Do I ever…?"

"I'm not sure. It's a little weird."

"Viva, today Morrigan asked me if she could come in and give a pep talk to the cinnamon in my pantry because this morning's scones didn't taste right. What's up?"

"Have you ever seen anything strange in the creek?"

Tyree thought for a moment, knitting his lips together as though the idea were sour, "Not that I can think of. I haven't been for a swim in a while, but I've never noticed anything in particular. Is everything okay?"

"Oh yeah, I thought I saw...something when I fell in, but then it wasn't there after I blinked, so it was probably just the shock or something."

Tyree grinned, "You sure you need that then?" He nodded at the cups she was holding.

Viva raised one of the cups. "It can only help." She glanced toward the creek again, "Thanks for the drinks." As she began again up the path, she could feel his lopsided smile behind her. The creek's waters burbled innocently downstream, and a sliver of her mind, just a sliver, thirsted for the castle in the creek.

She walked on.

Tyree

*T*he group of children, each in an oversized t-shirt with the words, "Mancy-led Adventures" slapped on the front, marched two by two up the path, the creek babbling beside them as it snaked between trees. Tyree's house was far behind, Viva's was too, and all that lay in front of them was the narrow, dirt path and the encroaching woods. Tyree couldn't remember the time before he knew the Regums, and he didn't want to, though, as his lungs heaved within his chest, he wasn't so sure about hiking.

Since his first day of kindergarten two years before when he had met Viva Regum, Tyree's life had become interesting. Every day, Viva would leave notes for him, telling him which adventures they would partake in that day. Tyree had amassed an army of gnomes and placed them lovingly in the garden, and one, a stout witch that Morrigan had given to him, had become the children's messenger. Viva left notes in the witch's cauldron, and Tyree would respond in kind. One day, he would be asked to become a pirate and board the school rooftop in search of hidden treasure. Another day, he would be asked how many stars he could shout at, and then to listen closely as they shouted back. He and Viva would eat lunch in the branches of a giant oak tree in front of Mancy Manor, Karl always perched nearby in case they fell, which they always seemed to do, but even falling was exhilarating with angelic wings to catch them.

But hiking, he wasn't so sure about. Tyree's legs were searing, and the sun's rays seemed to be going for a skin-sizzling record. He felt like he was going to burst into flame.

He was hiking next to Viva, Karl overhead, and Morrigan was reading a story about goblins at the front of the group as she led the children along the path. He could hear snippets of the story wishing that he and Viva were closer and was making a mental list of information to clarify. Where were these goblins exactly? How could he ensure that they would not wander into his bedroom for a midnight snack? Did they eat little boys as snacks in the first place? All of that would need to be clarified. Thoroughly.

At the thought of boy-eating goblins, Tyree began humming to himself, which he didn't realize he had been doing until Viva slapped him on the back, raised her hands up into the air as though offering her voice to the sky itself, and belted along with his anxious tunes. She laughed after a quick verse and gave him a squeeze. Maybe hiking was okay after all.

The group stopped for a lunch break in a grassy clearing off the path, encircled by dark trees. Without tree cover, the *sun beat harder while humidity swam through the clearing. But Tyree was glad for the break He waited for Viva to get her lunch from Karl as he prepared a spot for the two of them, removing sticks and stones from the area when he heard, "Hey, Scarecrow." A small boy with tiny white teeth and bright blue sneakers stood in front of him.*

"Hi, Chase." Tyree sat down calmly and pulled a peanut butter and jelly sandwich out of his pocket, wondering why he hadn't thought to bring a backpack as he carefully un-ziplocked the crushed mess.

"I like your overalls." Chase chuckled.

"Thanks. I like them too."

"You scared of goblins, scarecrow? I saw you, scaredy. Singing. Like a... Scared. Little, Girl."

"Yeah," Tyree said. The red-faced boy's eyes narrowed in intensity. "I am scared of goblins. I bet they're scary." Flashing a lopsided smile, Tyree turned his attention back to the sandwich disaster.

Chase huffed as though he were about to blow a house down and brought his face to the level of Tyree's attention. Eyes burning rage, so close that Tyree smelled the ham and mayonnaise on his breath. The boy wound up and punched Tyree in the nose. Hard.

Tyree yelped and dropped his sandwich, but before he could check to see if his nose was still attached to his face, a blur of manic fury slammed into Chase. The boy was driven into the ground by a Zephyrus Viva.

It could only have been seconds before Morrigan rushed to the scene, purple shimmers running down her arms as all three parties were driven steadily away from each other, Viva and Chase gnashing their teeth and fighting against the magical force. In those seconds before the mancy had arrived, Viva had, with closed, angry fists, beaten two black eyes onto Chase's face. The boy's hair was now speckled with his own nasal blood.

Tyree didn't remember much about the rest of the day. He remembered the mancy resetting his nose, and afterward, not seeing Viva for an eternity. She hadn't even been at school. Tyree checked the gnome-witch's cauldron day after day after day. But there was nothing. If he walked up the path to Viva's, a deep sense of urgency to leave welled up in him, and he would sprint back to his own house in tears.

The next time Tyree went hiking with Mancy-Led Adventures after a lifetime away, the wolfish boy named Chase shoved him into the creek. Viva Regum had looked down at Tyree from the shore through welling red eyes, her face all resignation and despair, before she walked away with her new hiking partner, Chase.

As Karl plucked Tyree out of the water, he ignored the laughter of the other children. Morrigan dried him off, checking for scrapes and cuts, and at dinner that night at the mancy's house, Viva in full flowing tears, hugged him refusing to let go. Her sorry sorry sorrys filled the space between snot and sniffles and wet kisses all over his cheeks. "Tyree, I'm so sorry sorry sorry. They were all teasing me. I didn't want to be pushed in too. I didn't know what to do. Sorrysorrysorry." They drank hot chocolate together by a crackling fire. But Tyree shivered, recalling the chill of the creek as he watched Viva walk away from him.

Four

Ten minutes until Viva would finally be home. Crunching leaves. Rolling ripples. Blues and browns and oranges. Red. She could feel the spines of fallen leaves crack underfoot. Passersby out for a stroll, some fresh air, or a bit of nature, walked by. Hands in pockets, hands in hands, noses pink with chill. Together. They nodded slightly as they passed her by. Then, finally, there it was: Mancy Manor. Home. At the top of the hill. Unmissable. Unmistakable. Surrounded by thickening woods, which blanketed the surroundings beyond.

Mancy Manor, which according to Karl had always been a mancy's dwelling, but had not always been Mancy Morrigan's, was not a manor in the traditional sense, but was a small cabin sitting on top of a hill nestled in forested land. Mancies tended to perceive the world much differently than average eyes.

Mancy Morrigan, the town's current mancy and Viva's self-appointed guardian, had ensured that her home, her section of the creek, and her path were ensconced within a forest of enormous trees. The cabin resembled an ambitious treehouse that had taken a tumble. It was a one-story cabin painted a deep purple that reminded Viva of midnight, and it was so entrenched in the forest that limby branches adorned the place, so every window heard a skeletal tapping in the nighttime wind. Viva had grown up with thin, boney nightmares.

One gargantuan oak tree, in particular, stood as though it had accepted a position as the cabin's bouncer, and it leaned mightily against the entire right side of the place standing guard. Viva could see the notches in the bark where she and Tyree had climbed up each day for lunch in the summertime. When she was younger.

The creek rolled along to her left. The beverages she was carrying had made her hands sweaty, and her satchel was gnawing at her shoulder. She kicked at the bottom of the cabin's black front door.

"What?" A voice rich and aged came from inside.

"It's Viva."

"Okay?" The voice dragged upward into a sluggish question mark.

"Let me in, my hands are full, and I can't open the door." Viva's satchel fell into the crook of her arm, kicking up a splash of hot liquid that stained her front. With an *umph,* she kicked the bottom of the door again.

The door remained still as if in rebellion before it finally fell open with a heavy sigh. "Was that necessary?" Viva stepped exaggeratedly over the threshold, along which was spread a thick line of mixed eggshells, charcoal, salt, and sage. Viva made sure it had not been scattered after she was through the door, which closed itself behind her. "Did you add more charcoal to the banish?" Viva adeptly avoided a huge saguaro cactus that was immediately to the right of the door. "It's different."

The living room began almost immediately upon entry, and the entire floor was covered in cushions, bean bag chairs, puffy stools, blankets, quilts, and pillows of every size imaginable—a massive pillow fort explosion. From the ceilings hung flowing draperies of silk, taffeta, and velvet. The colors of the room, though assorted, were deeply saturated. Emerald greens, deep mauves, blood reds, rusty oranges; it was not a place for pastels, neutrals, or any shade of white. No taupe, champagne, or ice, no summer lily, and certainly nothing with the word "whisper" in it. This was a room that had never heard a whisper. Rich and potent, it was as though it should be lit by medieval torches or clusters of waxy, dribbling candles, not, as it was, a smattering of hanging wicker lamps.

After weaving through the menagerie, Viva sat on a deep orange ottoman next to Morrigan, who was perched atop a bulbous pouf like a fairy on a mushroom cap. In front of the two women, a fire crackled, lending a supernatural glow to the mancy and her foundling. Viva watched an ember pop and sizzle through the metal grate. Veiled by willowing drapery and a mass of hair, the older woman peered at Viva out of the corner of her eye. "No, the banish is the same recipe I've always used." A pause, and then, "I'm not sure whether to take the cup or your shirt." She raised a skeptical eyebrow. "Where am I going to be getting the most for my money?"

"You mean my money?"

Morrigan snorted and the heaviest cup wiggled itself free of Viva's grip and floated towards the mancy with a small whirring sound and a thin stream of amethyst smoke. "Okay?" She eyed Viva in nonchalant scrutiny as she sipped the remaining liquid from the cup.

Viva waved the question away like an overambitious fly. "Just irritated. I had to set up a meeting with a parent–six tomorrow morning."

Morrigan narrowed her dark eyes, "Tell me what's actually wrong." A grating caw sounded from a large bay window to the left of the fireplace; Karl unfurled himself and rose from his roost.

"Roost" wasn't quite the right term for the place Karl sat himself down after a long day. It would be like calling someone's luxury yacht a boat. It didn't quite get at the spirit of the thing. Karl's kingly roost sat in the deep nook of the great bay window, always warmed by the fireplace. Karl had lined it with his favorite swaths of small quilts and blankets, all of which he had crafted for himself or found over the years, to create a comfortable nest. He had lovingly adorned the roost with collections of pebbles, coins, buttons, soda tabs, all organized around one worn, emerald pillow on which he slept.

Viva shuffled her feet. "Nothing. It's embarrassing."

The mancy's gaze didn't falter.

"Fine," Viva threw up her hand, a splash of her drink escaped the cup and fell like muddy rain to her already stained shirt. "I got spooked by some bikers and fell into the creek and—I don't know if anyone saw me, but either way, it was embarrassing. I should've just set up camp down there."

Mancy Morrigan chuckled; her dark eyes fixed on the glowing fireplace.

Viva glared, "Did you already know I fell in?"

"I didn't know about the bikers," Morrigan conceded.

"How did you know?"

"Viva, you're dripping everywhere," Morrigan's eyes glinted, and she pointed towards the back of the cabin. "Go change and we'll order a pizza. Sounds like you've had a pizza kind of day." The mancy shot a sly wink and as Viva stood, Morrigan asked, a tinge of concern in her voice, "But you're okay?"

Viva smiled. "I'm always okay." She thought for a moment and added, "There was something new when I–Oh, Karl," Viva spun towards the corvid who had descended from his roost, pulled open Viva's bag, and begun feasting on the scone Tyree had packed. Viva pulled the pebble from her pocket, glancing at it again–nothing but her reflection. She held it out to the bird whose silver beak sprinkled crumbs like snow, "I found this at the bottom of the creek when I–anyway, it's a little like the ones in your collection, so I grabbed it for you." Taking to the air again, Karl snatched the pebble from Viva's outstretched hand, bumped her affectionately on the cheek, and made his way back to his fireside roost trailing crumbs as he did.

Viva's room was at the back of the cabin across the hall from Morrigan's. Unlink anything else in the Mancy Manor, Viva's room was entirely white, which Karl insisted made Viva their pearl within an oyster. The walls, furniture, linens, atmosphere, everything was a pristine white, as though Viva had taken up residence in a cloud. She breathed in the quiet. Peeling off her wet clothes, she realized how cold she had been—her skin was waxy, goosebumps rising as she shivered, and pulling a fresh sweatshirt over her head, she thought of the castle she wasn't sure she had seen.

Viva pressed the wet clothes to her skin again, noting how strange the dry ones felt on her now, when she heard voices from the living room that made her return to herself. She tossed the wet clothes into her hamper and rejoined her family.

Morrigan & Karl

M *ancy Morrigan Regum lifted a small piece of Karl's curse on Viva's first day of kindergarten. Of course, as anyone dabbling in magic knows, magic is very particular about curses. Magic, after being convinced of something, is extremely difficult to convince otherwise. It's commonly believed that any frog prince worth his ribbits can kiss someone to turn back into a man, but that of course, is ridiculous. If magic has been persuaded that someone deserves to be a frog, a big, wet smooch isn't about to change its mind, and may merely annoy it, leading to an additional frog. What can be done much more easily, depending on whether magic has had a good day or not, are slight alterations. One might be able to convince the magic that the frog prince should be bright blue and shoot poison darts, for example. A teenager who desperately longs to be cool knows not to ask her parents to forget about the whole curfew thing entirely, but rather asks for a two-hour extension before finally compromising on an hour. Much like manipulative teens, mancies understand stubborn negotiations with occult entities.*

So, after Viva's first day of kindergarten, Mancy Morrigan Regum convinced magic to ease up a tick on Karl's curse. It was time for him to stop wallowing around, staying out late with the other crows, and pull his weight. He could magically help out with cabinhold chores, Morrigan had said, to which Karl rolled his silver eyes and tidied up Morrigan's herbs for the fifth time that day.

The sun had peeped through early morning clouds while the mancy sleepily attempted to prepare Viva for her first day of government-mandated education. Viva sat in the giant oak just outside the cabin. The girl had dressed herself in pink stirrup leggings, a bleach-white sweatshirt, and Mickey Mouse ears. Her ballet slippers sparkled, and she was swinging her feet back and forth in annoyed anticipation of the day. Her mismatched socks grazed the branch below in a swish, swish of "hurry up."

Morrigan was doing the best she could in a kitchen she had only begrudgingly become acquainted with five years prior, when she had adopted Viva after the girl's parents passed. The kitchen had always been unnerving for the mancy, and to her mind, best ignored, even after five years with Viva.

Something was bubbling—what on earth was that again? Should a child's brown bag lunch include something that bubbles? And at what point should something cease bubbling? A pancake on a skillet was rapidly becoming a puck of ash, and Karl was squawking along with the microwave's call to order, creating a cacophony that a brass band locked inside of a bank vault would have a difficult time outmatching.

Then Viva fell.

In a feat of childhood lung capacity, Viva's sudden yelp cut sharply above the smoke detector, the microwave, the bird song, and Morrigan's choice language. Karl and Morrigan both sped out of the kitchen at once and found Viva sprawled out on the grass below the attending oak tree, laughing hysterically.

Breathing a deep sigh of relief, Morrigan held little Viva by one of the girl's bloodied hands, checking for broken bones or lacerations, twisting her this way and that. Morrigan's other hand stretched back towards the kitchen, palm up, as if she were cupping liquid, and the smoke detector, microwave, and bubbling silenced. The mancy called up to Karl, who was at the moment, berating the tree for not having been a better guardian.

"Karl, you had to leave for school ten minutes ago. Bring Viva's backpack down here—it's stuck on that branch. Yes, there." She pointed her foot towards the hanging pack, one hand still working on silencing the kitchen chaos, and the other bandaging Viva's scraped palm. "Leave the tree alone and get down here."

Karl puffed up his pearly feathers and stamped.

"I don't want to hear it. Just get the bag." One of the mancy's hands released Viva's bandaged palm and now cupped over the ripped knee of the girl's pink leggings. Morrigan breathed in focus. "All right little miss, that's

enough of that." Amethyst shimmers zipped and zapped across Viva's knee, like cobwebs, weaving, and threading. The electricity tickled.

Morrigan gave up on kitchen control and brought both hands together as if she were clasping a handful of sand. She began to release her fingers, sparkles bouncing between them in webs of magic. Her breaths were long and deep, and both hands were fiery with amethyst magic. Almost simultaneously, Viva's torn legging stitched back together while a brown paper lunch bag appeared in Viva's lap.

Viva poked at her knee. "Can you tell me how to do it?"

The mancy closed her eyes, exhaustion crashing into her, causing her head to swim. "Focus, persuasion, focus, and lots of energy." Morrigan said between huffing breaths. "I always tell you how. It's just a matter of persuasion. Magic will do what it wants, you just have to convince it that your goals and its are the same." Morrigan opened her eyes and breathed out. Her face had paled and a thin layer of sweat shimmered over her forehead as she lifted Viva to her feet. She winked. "Now you're all set. Do you feel ready?" Morrigan raised a sharp eyebrow at Viva's harumph.

"Karl, let's go." Viva's voice climbed the tree's branches, and he glided down stormily, backpack in beak.

"You remember where it is, right?" Morrigan asked.

Karl nodded with a full-body bob, and he and Viva made their way down the creek path towards town. Towards the girl's first day of real-world society.

"Don't fall into the creek again, there's no time to come back here and change," Morrigan called after them.

Viva would surely be late for school, and Mancy Morrigan had heard all about school blaming parents for every forgotten paper, every knotted strand of hair, and untied shoelace. Another blue wave of exhaustion crashed into her—magical multitasking, dual focus was not natural for the mind or the body. Sighing, she turned to drag herself back inside the cabin. She had a group of birdwatchers to lead up the path in a few hours and she would need a long rest before she could manage that.

Then the kitchen crime scene confronted her. Dripping, oozing, blackened. She stared, wide-eyed. It stared back at her unblinking. Unwelcome memories clawed through her exhausted subconscious, but Morrigan shook them away. This wasn't going to work. Either Viva had to accept that education wasn't the right path for her, or Mancy Morrigan would need to think up a different strategy for the next thirteen years of single parenthood. A white feather floated from the ceiling and dropped innocently into the overflowing sink.

Morrigan closed her eyes. Get out get out get out. Her memories dissolved for the moment. She would just have to not be a single parent. There were two adults in the cabin—technically. And Karl had loved all that kitchen nonsense before… Morrigan flinched and turned around to appraise her cushioned living area, eyes falling on Karl's luxurious fire-side roost; he would need to be a mancy again, and that was that.

Magic is a strange thing, and it has been since the first person found a tantalizing sparkle, and then pointed a loaded finger at a water rat watching in astonishment as it suddenly sprouted a duck's bill, a beaver's tail, and laid an egg.

Oftentimes, God is the one blamed for strange and inexplicable occurrences in the world, but the truth is that people are much more efficient at creating chaos, what with free will, creativity, and cat-killing curiosity, and when a person finds some magic glittering around, all God needs to do is sit back and enjoy the show.

On that fateful evening, after Viva returned home from school, after the mancy's first and last day of scrubbing pancake batter from the ceiling, Morrigan asked Viva to collect herbs from the garden. Once the door had closed behind the girl, Morrigan tapped her shoulder, prompting Karl to perch. The mancy closed her eyes and softly stroked his head. Purple filled Karl's mouth and washed through him from the dome of his head to his longest claw.

"I know you haven't forgiven yourself," Mancy Morrigan said, slowly turning the words over her tongue, "And you know that I won't. Ever. But–" Karl's eyebrows would have furrowed significantly if he still had eyebrows. "We need your help. I–" Her voice broke, "I'm not strong enough to change you back, even if either of us wanted that, but I think you can be a mancy again. Sort of. I asked the magic for a little change, a sort of addendum, so you can help us like you used to..." Her voice caught in her throat. Karl ruffled, sinking his head into his feathered shoulders.

"You can mancy again, but only magic that relates to the cabin, cooking, cleaning, everything you used to do." Despite the shaking in her voice, Morrigan stood up straight and sharpened her expression. "Splitting magical focus worked today, sort of, but since there are two of us here, we may as well use what we have. It's the best I can do. I'm—" She blinked rapidly, shook him off her shoulder, and walked out the door to join Viva in the garden.

Karl hopped toward the kitchen and the oven clicked on. He chirped in satisfaction as the heat coursed through the cabin.

***

Morrigan's incompetence had reared its ugly head once again. In Karl's opinion, the morning had gone as smoothly as month-old milk left in a Floridian attic. The tree out front had pushed the kid off, just for stepping on a sensitive branch. Morrigan, of course, had completely mismanaged the entire ordeal from the get-go and had tried some double magic, which even novice mancies knew was doomed to fail. The woman was out of practice. He scoffed.

The kid had been ruffled, but overall, nothing to call social services over, so Karl flew her to school, backpack in beak, and trying not to notice the rising well of tears behind Viva's eyes as he plopped her backpack at her feet once they reached the front doors.

He had done his part. And now there were brunches to scavenge, shiny treasures to find, garbage to inspect. Images of town swept through his mind as he opened his pearly wings, feathers caressing the cool, fall air in each smooth movement. Images of flaky, golden scones discarded on trash bin rims; sticky, sweet juices dripping from well-seasoned patio tables danced through his imagination; Viva's face reddened with tears; drippings of succulent sausage heated by the afternoon concrete; Viva trembling in a new and foreign place; the cool, earthy drops of leftover coffee; Viva...Oh, hell.

Karl turned from his gluttonous fantasies and flew back towards Viva's school. He glanced into windows, gliding like a rogue cloud. There was no hope in finding her; all he could do was wait. And he did, stomach protesting in sporadic snarls.

Children ebbed and flowed in and out of the building, tides commanded by the piercing shriek of a bell. He watched from his rooftop perch as new children were consumed by and others spat out from the building. The freed children sprinted, leapt, and fell, tiny prisoners released for the day's exercise, the sun imbibed in dregs, causing a drunken frenzy of energy and babble.

For the fifth time that eternal morning, Karl flew down, sailing above the asphalt playground, the soccer field, the sandboxes. Where was she? This was the right place, he was sure of it, this is where he had brought her that morning, and in any case, Morrigan had tasked him to pick her up at the end of the day, and he was sure he wouldn't be rewarded for returning home without her, so it had better be the right place.

Looping around the premises again while devising a repertoire of explanations for where Viva was and why it was, in fact, beneficial that she would never return home, he snuck closer to the children. Perhaps perching at the point of their initial exit would grant him a better vantage point.

As he landed above the cafeteria door where he could see every corner of the playground, he heard choking sobs. Karl squinted his silver eyes. Directly below him was Viva, standing stiffly, back to the wall, tears streaming hotly down her face.

He crowed in a voice that was chunks of barbed salt, careening down an icy mountain road.

Looking up, Viva sniffed wetly, "Hi, Karl."

The girl was piteous. Blue and wet. Karl's heartstrings twanged rusty iron. He hopped down and landed heavily at her feet. She clasped her arms around his thick neck before plopping her rear onto the cement.

"The lunch guard is gonna see you," Viva whispered through choked sobs. "She says I can't move until recess is done." A thin line of snot slipped down onto her lip, and Karl recoiled in horror. "I didn't even get to eat lunch 'cause M. messed it up." Snuffling the mucus back into her nose like a super-powered hoover, she held up a potato, now cracked and bruised from its experience in public education. "See!" The tears flowed freely again. "I can't eat this, and I even tried. It's no good." She pointed matter-of-factly at a small bite mark. "Now everyone thinks I'm weird. I'm all alone." Statuesque, Karl listened to the lamentations of the leaking child, wondering how much more liquid she could possibly produce. "Karl, I'm hungry and school is no good. I got a red cubby, and the number nine is stupid, but I have to sit on that one forever, and—" Karl spread his wings and rocketed away.

A steel door behind the cafeteria stood propped open by a broken slab of concrete. The air coming from the opening was stale and somehow both chilling and unsettlingly warm. Karl descended onto the top of the door, listening, surveying. His cool, silver gaze sailed around the room, noting the only occupant was a small woman in a hairnet and tattered apron. The figure shuffled this way and that, moving objects from one place to another, a dented metallic spoon here, and then back to the oversized and empty sink. He saw it then: a tub-sized cardboard box filled to the brim with bananas that had been cut into thirds by the supplier and repackaged in plastic so that every section was browned and utterly inedible on at least one end.

His mind whirred. He certainly had the element of surprise, he knew his target, and had eyes on the opposition; it couldn't have been simpler. Adrenaline surging through his veins, he rose elegantly, his snowy plumage whispering in the thick, gray air.

He flew in like chaos embodied.

Everybody knows that a bull in a china shop is bad news. The owner of the china shop makes no money on the experience; customers flee without caution, preoccupied with impending impalation; and of course, the bull, who has the worst time of all, suddenly enclosed in a room full of screaming, crashing humans at every turn. Crows in an elementary school kitchen have a similar chaotic effect, though, unlike the befuddled bull, crows enjoy the experience immensely. Karl, having missed breakfast and now coming up on missing lunch, felt he was owed some fun.

Wings flapped rabidly, dust-covered pots and pans crashed to the floor, the hair-netted figure screeched around the room, as gravelly caws reverberated, and banana thirds soared.

Disorder reigned from the kitchen ceiling to the floor, containers of prepackaged food strewn across the linoleum, the breathless lunch lady bent over, clutching her chest in the corner. The ghostly, taloned chaos had vanished as quickly as it had manifested.

Viva, who was now catching banana thirds raining from the sky, grinned wide, her mouth full of mush.

The school day had diminished into pandemonium, and as adults attempted to corral the unbound children, Karl snuck a sufficiently fed Viva from the premises, toward home.

Five

According to Morrigan Regum, mancies did not cook. According to Karl, Morrigan was full of it–to the absolute brim. Morrigan had released the reins of cabinhold chores to Karl when Viva started school, ridding herself of a layer of domestic contention and grumbling corvid phrases such as: "I always used to," "remember when I," and "If I still had opposable thumbs." The day Morrigan loosened the chains of Karl's winged curse and gestured him into the long-neglected kitchen, Viva had seen his eyes ignite. Neither of them would tell Viva the story of Karl's transmogrification, and she was only ever able to pick up abstract morsels of the story over the years, but when he fluttered around the kitchen, sauces bubbling, meats sizzling, and heavy metal blaring, she would see yearning and nostalgia and joy. Sometimes she saw pain.

Viva settled into her dry clothes, and Morrigan, deeply entrenched in a new chair, was humming while gently stroking the petals of a disheveled chrysanthemum. Karl had dozed off in his roost with one silver eye cracked open. In the kitchen a landline waited, fixed to the wall, its piggy tail wound, curling towards the floor "Pizza?" Viva called across the living room from the kitchen, "Oh, I also forgot to tell you–" She lifted the receiver. "–when I fell in–wait… whoops," she hung up the phone and redialed the only number scrawled in haphazard permanent marker on the back of the handset. "M. have you ever seen anything in–Oh hello, yes, we'd like…"

After the ordeal of ordering–Karl's very detailed specifications squawked from across the room while Viva and the man on the other line pieced together nit-picky instructions for each ingredient–Viva hung up the phone wondering what she had been about to say, feeling it peeping out from a bolted corner of her mind.

The three of them ate together at an ancient coffee table in the middle of the cushioned room. The mancy stabbed a cube of pizza that she had cut with architectural precision while Karl nipped at the remaining strands of cheese on Viva's plate. After a few minutes filled with sizzling embers from the fireplace in front of them and the clinking of Karl's beak on Viva's plate, Morrigan turned to Viva and asked, one eyebrow sharply raised, "Ghost hunt?"

Morrigan asked as though it weren't their nightly routine. As though since Viva could remember, she and the mancy hadn't gone ghost hunting after dinner. It was their duty, Morrigan insisted, as the town mancy, to keep the woods clear of anything nefarious, and Viva, imagining the excitement of catching a real-life ghost, had always been eager to join in. Karl stayed home. He didn't believe in ghosts.

As Viva and Morrigan stood to leave, Karl urged their grease-smeared plates towards the kitchen sink and turned his favorite metal album up to full blast.

The cabin had always been overwhelming for Viva, and she remembered Morrigan's pain when she had insisted on moving into her own place during college. Morrigan seemed to take Viva's inability to focus while surrounded by the herbaceous choir of a mancy's collection as a personal affront. Karl's proclivity for punk rock or heavy metal during the cooking and cleaning process was also exhausting, but the woods were tranquility itself.

It wasn't all that deep into the night yet, but as the cabin door closed behind them, the raging cacophony of furious instruments suddenly ceased, and the purple arms of night embraced them. Morrigan led the way out through her verdant garden. Some might protest the use of the term "garden" for what Mancy Morrigan had done with her arsenal of vegetation, Morrigan maintained that to be a good mancy one must be able to find thyme within chaos.

The women wove through the flora-hoard and were out in no time at all. Morrigan's cabin was embraced by woods, which thickened around the parallel creek and path as the hills beyond climbed upward. Walking past Mancy Manor, the path transformed into a thin, hissing tongue that weaved through ancient trees with twisting shadows, the creek puttering alongside, twin serpents. As Morrigan and Viva joined the path, the unmistakable sound of the running waters seeped into Viva's heart. Surrounded by velvet darkness, by twittering bats and twinkling stars, by Morrigan's steady breath, Viva thought of castles.

"When one is hunting for ghosts in black woods at night, a calm manner and some flexibility are required." It was a phrase Morrigan told their clients, and it ran as clearly through Viva's mind as if the mancy had said it to her that very moment. Mancy-led Adventures was Morrigan's business, which she had begun with her semi-unwilling mascot, Karl, many years before Viva had been born and subsequently adopted by the mancy.

When people began to notice they enjoyed being outdoors and the mancy could no longer keep them out of her woods, she was there with a map, an itinerary, and a fee. She scheduled various "adventure-style" outings throughout her woods. Once Viva had started school, a whole new clientele became obvious. Viva suspected that it was all just a way for Morrigan to keep a watchful eye on the goings-on in her woods, but with Karl outfitted in first aid and portable charcuterie backpacks, Viva organizing games and activities, and Morrigan overseeing it all, Mancy-led Adventures had become a huge success. It was mostly teenagers who joined the overnight ghost hunting excursions that occurred once a week. They were similar to pro wrestling: reality was involved, in that the trees and s'mores and campfire did very much exist, but it was a kind of choreographed reality. Not like the real ghost hunts that Viva and Morrigan went on together.

As the women worked their way along familiar paths, stopping to question suspicious new ponds, ruffled mosses, and offset stones, Viva inhaled the earthy fragrance wafting through the trees. Morrigan turned to Viva and fixed her gaze; it was dark and cool as obsidian, and despite herself, Viva's heart jumped, "What?" She asked.

"What's really wrong?"

"What are you talking about?"

Morrigan's gaze sharpened.

"I told you. I fell into the creek. Embarrassing." Viva pulled her best "devastated" face.

The mancy put her hands on her hips and raised a thin eyebrow. "Viva, you've been sulking since you moved back home over a year ago now—was it really that long ago? You know I'm glad to have you. Karl was heartbroken when you left but—"

Viva's heart pounded. The words were there on her tongue, ready to spill out of her. Why doesn't anyone like me? Why can't I be like everyone else? Why couldn't I do it, be a real person, a person with her own job, her own place, some friends, and some…one…Why am I such a fai–But she couldn't say it. No matter how much she willed it to pour forth, it was trapped in her, fermenting. So, Viva, mimicking Morrigan by fixing her hands on her own hips, asked pointedly, "When are you going to change Karl back?"

"Excuse me?" Morrigan's voice cracked slightly.

Viva didn't say anything, didn't move, didn't breathe.

Morrigan cleared her throat and in a strained voice said, "As you well know, that is none of your business. It's also not how it works. It's only because he and I were not careful enough in checking the cabin for nosy child spies that you became privy to–you know he–he doesn't want–we don't–we can't…" Her voice broke and Viva saw a shadow fall over Morrigan's eyes just for a moment, "It's not how it works." The mancy's voice trailed off, but the end of the sentence was heavy with finality.

Viva began to speak, "What did he–" Morrigan's eyes were black ice before she blinked three times in rapid succession and walked away back to the path, stroking the petals of nearby flowers as she did.

It was a dirty trick to bring up Karl and Morrigan's past, Viva knew, though she was unsure why. But she couldn't have told Morrigan what was in her head. She couldn't keep disappointing her. Disappointing everyone.

Leaping lightly onto the branch of a low-hanging tree then swinging her feet back and forth, Viva pasted a smile onto her face and called towards the mancy, "Want to race?" She squeezed her face in mock intensity. "I'll beat you this time."

Morrigan, back still turned, squatted down to a swampy pond that Viva hadn't recalled from the previous day.

"M.," Viva stood up on the branch and leapt spritely to the neighboring tree, "Come on, it'll be fun. I don't think we're going to find any ghosts tonight."

Morrigan had brought her face down to a large lily pad and was whispering something.

Viva hopped to another tree, "Well?"

Morrigan brought her hands down onto the squelching edge of the black pond, eyes locked in focus. She resembled a rusalka, hair curling around her thin face, and like a flash flood Viva saw her mancy, on all fours, a beast, fangs steeled, sharp claws extended into the black, swampy pond, seaweed hair rippling, thin, sallow face peering up from the depths, drowned and haunting, the water spinning silver.

Viva fell hard from her branch.

Morrigan was beside Viva in an instant. "What happened?" She checked Viva all over, twisting her to check every inch. "What's wrong, what's broken, what happened?"

Cradling her elbow and gritting white teeth, Viva shook her head and pushed the mancy away. "Just slipped. I guess I wouldn't have been able to beat you tonight after all. Bad luck with balance today. I think I'm going to go."

Morrigan furrowed her brows and took a backward step towards the swampy pond again. "Yes, good idea. Go get some rest." She appraised Viva again and nodded.

"Do you want to come with me?" Viva wiped a chunk of mud from her pants.

"No–" Morrigan's voice was thin and distracted as she glanced around, "I'm going to keep searching for a while." She turned to Viva again, "Maybe you're scaring the ghosts away with your racket." The mancy's mouth smiled and she winked.

"All right. See you back home." Viva trotted away back down the path. Out of the dark woods, leaving Mancy Morrigan Regum with her elusive ghosts.

Morrigan

*B*efore she was a Mancy, Morrigan Regum was just
that: Morrigan. A small girl, her hair clung in tight
curls to her head. Morrigan and her older sister Lucy
practically lived in the woods. Even though Lucy was
eighteen and Morrigan was only ten, Lucy would watch
from the ground as Morrigan climbed the tallest trees,
leaping lightly from one branch to another and Morrigan
would watch from afar as Lucy swam in the creek, in the
lake, in the rain and in the deepest puddles she could find.
They lived in what everyone in town referred to as the Mancy
Manor, surrounded by deep woods, with their mother, the
town's mancy, which once upon a time had been short for
"necromancer," until the past fell away, leaving only the
shortened term remaining. As a rule, it was the duty of the
town's mancy to give back to the town in some way, so
Morrigan's mother, Mancy Regum, made her living by
giving people very sound advice for a fee. She spent her
working hours in town, often lamenting the fact that people
rarely needed advice during proper business hours, so she

had set up clear woods-based boundaries for the girls. They could explore as far as they liked, as long as they could make it home for what could generously be called dinner. The consequences of breaking these boundaries, the girls refused to discover. The woman who had birthed the girls was even more severe than her youngest daughter Morrigan, leaving Lucy to mediate all interactions in the home.

It had been raining for a full week. The ground had become soft with the moisture so that the girls' clothes were essentially mud. The world was the kind of gray that releases a dead, floral scent from fallen leaves and brown, withering grasses. Soft and freeing, the rain poured down as Morrigan and Lucy clambered through their very own rainforest. Their toes numbed hours before, skin wrinkled under soaked, sagging clothes, but they felt warm. Exhilarated. They laughed as they jumped into piles of fallen leaves, raced along the paths their own feet had made through years of heavy use. Dark eyes glittered with joy as they shook their hair out every so often like freshly bathed dogs.

They were in the middle of a rigorous game of hide-and-go-seek. Morrigan sat perched in a skeletal tree directly above her sister—she enjoyed the audacity of hiding mere feet above the seeker—acting as best she could like a large leaf, listening to her sister count to one hundred as she reveled in the falling drops. The rain pitter-pattered onto the soft earth, shaking the remaining leaves with shushing rustles, filling Morrigan's ears with its calm, steady rhythm. Fifteen, pitter-patter, sixteen, pitter-patter, seventeen, slosh.

That was not the rain.

Morrigan squeezed her eyes shut and strained her ears, willing them to reach the sound.

What was that?

She heard Lucy counting and the backdrop of falling rain. Twenty-four, twenty-five, twenty-six... Slosh. She opened her eyes. Wide. The sound of soggy footsteps. Slow, steady footsteps in the squelching mud. The crunching of autumn leaves underfoot just audible. Something was walking towards them.

Morrigan could barely hear the steps and knew that whatever it was had to be a ways away. There were animals in the woods, and she sifted through her mind's roster of all the wildlife she knew. Last week, she met a silly bear named Roger—maybe it was him. Morrigan squinted, trying to peer through the shield of raindrops beyond her tree. It was too wet, too gray, too dark. She could only make out a large shadow, multiple trees away. Could that be it? Was it moving? Don't blink. Lucy was still counting, eyes closed dutifully.

Slosh.

Lucy would never cheat.

The shadow moved, and Morrigan started. It was a large shadow. Large and inhuman.

Lucy was plugging up her ears with her fingers, and she was shouting the numbers. No cheating. Don't look. Don't listen.

Lucy was counting too loudly, and the sloshing grew louder too; the shadow moved again, and again, forward, reptilian, like an enormous snake, but, no, it had a long sharp snout, spines along its back, and Morrigan thought she heard a hissing breath escape it like steam. Heart pounding against her chest fast and fast and fast, she was sweating, or was it the rain seeping through her clothes to her flesh and chilling her blood, her bones, chilling her, freezing her, her throat was sunbaked desert sand, and her muscles were ice. Morrigan wrenched through the terrified tension of her neck and turned around frantically. Could she make it down to Lucy before the shadow did? The monster. She could fall fast, but could they run home fast enough? Could she land on it? It was big and she was too small. Along its shadowy spine were gleaming spikes, like sharpened stone armor. Could Lucy run fast enough if Morrigan yelled? But her voice stuck in her throat, choking, clawing.

It moved in slithering, steps, slowly. Was Morrigan seeing a glint of claws? Of teeth? Morrigan forced herself to move. She swung herself onto a lower branch and the tree creaked under the weight of her, and a few straggling leaves fell to the ground in front of Lucy's serene face.

The thing stopped in a jerk, what must have been its head snapped up towards Morrigan.

Morrigan's heart stopped. Every hair on her neck stood up. Don't breathe. Don't breathe. You're a leaf. Be a leaf. She could feel eyes, golden eyes trying to penetrate the veil of rain. Searching for her. Be a leaf. She could feel the keen edge of those eyes. The rain was deafening, Lucy's counting barely cutting through.

Morrigan was shaking. Was it the cold? She could feel that now too. Cold wind, biting rain. It was paralyzing. She was frozen. Her fingers clung so tightly to her branch that she thought they would break.

"Sixty-eight, sixty-nine…"

Why couldn't Morrigan yell? Why couldn't she open her mouth? The shadow began to move again. Smooth and slick. It hadn't seen her. How? Was she a leaf?

Be a leaf, be a leaf.

"Seventy-two, seventy-three," Lucy shouted into their empty woods.

Not empty.

Still theirs.

Morrigan took a deep breath, and she could feel the cold terror drip into her lungs. Just scream. She tore her fingers from the branch, the skin flaying off as the bark tore it like tissue paper. And her head pounded and poundedpoundedpounded. She couldn't move or she would fall. She would fall on top of Lucy, and what then? Would they be fast enough to rise? To run. She could hardly breathe, too much, too fast, too shallow. Head swimming in rain and fear and questions and please. Morrigan dragged her hand up towards it. Stop. Don't move.

You.

Stop.

Sneaking. Slow. Stalking. Lucy. Just scream.

Lucy.

Run. The shadow, dripping, watery, oil, so close to her sister now. Golden eyes gleaming. Enormous grinning fangs, claws stretched.

Out of time and options, Morrigan forced the air in her lungs free, the cold and the fear burst out of her in a fire.

She didn't know what she shouted. It emerged from her lungs in fire and ice, bursting forth towards the shape, the thing, the monster. She thought she saw fangs, not bloody but dripping, dripping what? Gold. Flashing in an enormous grinning mouth. Red and jagged like a wound. Bearing towards her tree, she could almost feel them, piercing and hungry. Dripping.

It tried to step towards Morrigan in her tree, but it was as if the Earth turned suddenly upside down. Morrigan saw a burst of what? Of light? Of color? Of movement or sound? An energy burst from her extended arm and hit the monster like a spear, with the force of a raging bull. A golden steam hissed and rose into the sky, falling again in mammoth drops of freezing, silver rain. Rain, rain flooding rain. Morrigan peered down at Lucy and saw water rising around her ankles.

A surge of exhaustion crashed over Morrigan just as she heard a definitive crack through the deafening rain. She swayed. Her head whirled in a cloudy pool. Muscles giving way to gravity. Don't fall out of the tree. Don't fall.

The rain. Beat. Down.

Her limbs went limp.

Muffled, as though submerged under the sea, Lucy's voice counted in the falling rain. Don't fall. Her vision clouded, and through the graying veil, she could hear nothing but water.

Morrigan's body hit the swamping earth with a slosh.

"One hundred! Ready or not, here I come!"

"Run!"

A boy, shaped like a large square emerged from the trees in front of Lucy, lifted Morrigan off the ground, and slung her over his shoulder. "Run!" He shouted again, giving Lucy a push in front of him. Legs flew over rocks and roots as they sprinted full-force, Lucy glancing sidelong in fear and suspicion at the boy who carried Morrigan, but never slowing. Morrigan blinked; her body was still limp and useless. Jumbled, agitated, and muted. Everything subdued. The sound of the rain, Lucy's boots smashing through mud puddles in front of her. Her own feet—.

Morrigan's clarity remained a blinking light in the distance, but it was brightening. She was hovering above the ground, though all she could see was a black swath of soaking fabric, it was soaked. She was bouncing up and down on iron-hard shoulders. Something was coming after them. A monster. She had seen…she had done something…?

Clarity, consciousness, memory. They all flew back to her with the force of a meteor. She started shouting and kicking and hitting. The boy plopped her down and there was Lucy, in front of her. Take my hand. Let's go. Run. They ran, the three of them, two sisters hand-in hand and a stranger racing behind.

Lucy was breathing hard, talking, questions, questions, had she not seen the... the... whatever it was? Not heard it sloshing? It had been almost close enough for Lucy to touch. A step away, maybe two. Morrigan couldn't be the only one to see it. To hear it. To feel it. That fear. She shook it out of her head wildly and ran faster, Lucy's feet pattering beside her.

Run.

***

When the girls burst into the cabin, dripping with rain and mud, their mother sat back in her rocking chair, and asked, "Who is that behind you?"

Acknowledging the boy behind her for the first time, Morrigan nodded. Black hair stuck to his face like paint and dripped over soft, gray eyes. The boy straightened; his full proportions unrolled like a massive stone bear rising to life. If Morrigan had been tasked to create a boy out of giant blocks of wood, it would appear identical to the shivering thing in front of her. He seemed to be Lucy's age, Morrigan thought. Eighteen maybe. Old. This boy, however, could be at least two of Lucy in length and width. How had he fit through the door? Despite the shaking, despite the fear or pain or cold across his paling face, despite his girth, he seemed kind. His square face, slightly chubby from the last bit of baby fat clinging for dear life to his cheeks, and his lips, though he was currently chewing on the bottom one, suggested they were often turned up in smiles. The boy handed Morrigan's mother a soggy piece of paper from his pocket. The mancy read it carefully and nodded before putting it in her pocket. Seeing the mancy's nod, he spoke, a voice like turning gravel. He hadn't seen what Morrigan had seen. No one had seen the monster that she had. That reptilian slithering thing, eyes beating hungry gold. The boy said he had seen a flood of water roaring towards the low clearing the girls had been playing in, and he had raced the rain to get them out of the woods before they were swept away like leaves in a current.

Morrigan Regum told her story after the boy had finished speaking, and after all accounts had been relayed, her mother, Mancy Regum, marched into the forest to see it all for herself.

The mancy found nothing but flooded woods, drowning roots, and swift, rising water. There was no monster but the water.

Six

Growing up with a mancy as a guardian, especially a mancy like Morrigan, Viva had no escape from nature. The creek in particular had always been a particular companion to Viva. For as long as she could remember, Viva was lulled to sleep at night and gently awakened the next morning by soft burbling water. Every walk to school the creek chaperoned, babbling with her along her journey. When Viva was stood up by her prom date, when she flunked out of college, when she didn't get an interview, when she moved back home, the creek had been there. Human friends, Viva found, were much harder to come by; the creek was constant.

Stars had emerged across the sky in an elysian burst. They blinked teasingly, and Viva thought she remembered reading something about celestial movements being casual chit-chat, stars giggling back and forth in the darkness. Twinkling conversations throughout the cosmos about everything and nothing. She longed to be a part of something like that. How did a person become a star?

The air sifted sharply through Viva's hair and gnawed at her cheeks nearer to the water, which rolled along to her right, her eternal companion.

As the path swung around, Viva smiled at the dozens of gnomes in various acts of comradery in the Daisy House garden. She imagined them bustling around at night—what did gnomes do? Cause mischief? Household chores? Some sort of magic? She passed a pink-nosed accountant gnome hovering cautiously over a group of elfish craps players.

The Daisy House, behind the jovial assemblage, sat cookie-like, windows illuminated in frosted light. Stepping off the path towards the house, Viva made for a round gnome clad in star-speckled purple robes. It was the closest gnome to the winding path and had a pointed, black hat; a moon-topped wand; and a large, black cauldron. Morrigan had given this particular gnome to Tyree for some birthday or other, and ever since, the Viva and Tyree had used the cauldron to leave notes, treats, requests, and other small gifts. It wasn't a traditional avenue for misbehavior but sneaking a note to Tyree through the witch's cauldron had always seemed covert and exciting, even if the note merely said: "Dinner tomorrow at the cabin. Karl's making stuffed mushrooms. Seven-ish if the oven doesn't talk back."

It was their childhood secret, almost code, almost rebellion, and more often than not, Tyree's response would include his newest baking experiment, and not much was more magical than that.

Viva checked the cauldron, finding a small bag with two marshmallow fudge cookies. She replaced them with an invitation to tomorrow evening's dinner and trudged back to the path, nodding goodbye to the gnomes—one never knew what kindness would buy. Maybe they would come to her house and fold the laundry she had been neglecting.

Lost in thought and not yet ready to leave the peace of night, Viva meandered away from the Daisy House, over the path, and across the small green patch of grass before reaching the bank. What had the mancy always said about water? Viva couldn't remember; she was thinking of silver.

The creek beckoned with stirring whispers. With an inhale, Viva leaped to the edge, playing with gravity and stability on the bank's mouth. Viva balanced along the edge. Renaissance, she thought, the water was re-birth in the star-smeared night.

Night deepened hard and cold while the light of Mancy Manor and Tyree's Daisy House shimmered like ripples on the surface of Viva's consciousness. Memories of wading with Tyree, competing for who could hold their breath underneath the surface the longest, willing herself not to breathe. You're not cold, you're not drowning, you're okay. Viva always won. Exploring the banks with Morrigan, searching for kelpies and crayfish, collecting pebbles with Karl, Viva's memories wove over, under, around, and around.

Then Viva heard a slosh.

A gasp.

She stopped. Stilled. The Daisy House? It was only a little way behind her–just across the path.

She listened.

An animal? Bikers? Hikers? It wasn't that late.

Silence.

Straightening, both feet firm on the lip of the bank, Viva glanced up and down the creek, back to the path, toward Tyree's. No one, nothing.

Blurp.

There it was again.

An intermittent gasp. A bubble. Air stuck at the top of straining lungs. Viva had seen horror movies before, so she wasn't about to go on a solo search for a choking sound in the middle of nocturnal wilderness. She wasn't stupid. She should get home. She would be tired in the morning. Tired for a meeting she hadn't yet prepared for. She should've gone back earlier or stayed with Morrigan.

A gulp.

A gasp.

A choke.

The surface of the creek was foaming. Rabid, gray, and ashy. Whirling, twisting, her mind willed her to walk away, walk, walk. Run.

Get up to the path, away from the trees, away from the sound, away from the creek, run home. Get off the bank.

Turn, turn, turn your body, Viva. Yes. Now up the bank, across the path, frosted lights still gleamed in the distance, Tyree's place, lit, warm and right there. He would hear you, Viva. He would hear you if you yelled. Morrigan would hear you. If you called for her.

beat

beat

beat

Something pulled her backward, away from the path, away from the Daisy House, away from home. And it was dark. She couldn't think about anything but darkness, and how paralyzed, how numb, how heavy she was. Were her eyes closed? The Daisy House had just been there. In front of her. Or behind? In the distance. Not that distant.

The lemon drop light of the windows. He would've heard her.

But now it was dark.

Something pulled her. Something in her chest was clawing through her and she tried to call out, to shout to–but nothing escaped from her lips, there was only pain and darkness.

Something pulled her. Inch by inch, her body was dripping closer and closer to the water.

A gulp, gasp, choke.

She dug her feet into the ground, trying to make herself heavier, but she still moved, metal strings pulling behind her sternum in a piercing fire of sharp teeth. Her mind reeled in the darkness, pain and paralysis. Her heart beat fire.

Beat.

Beat.

Beat.

Beat.

Slowly as though dragging through quicksilver, the air caught in her lungs. She couldn't breathe.

The stars in the sky drew farther and farther and farther until they had blurred to invisibility. The breeze gnawed at her, hungry teeth on bone. Icey fangs sunk into the deep of her bones, marrow freezing, heart beating glacial gelatin through her veins, tendrils of ice grasping fingers, toes, arms, legs, pulsing white behind her eyes, deep and deep and deep in her skull.

The creek opened around her body, greedily submerging her. She was in the water now. Deep. Each breath shallow, caught. Was she breathing? Hyperventilating. Ventilating at all? She didn't have enough air to hyp, hyp, hyp. As the arctic ripples took hold past her chest, her throat, slithering liquid fingers pressing, piercing through her sternum like talons, air extinguishing, cold seeping, her body leaden, and sinking fast, out of her suffocating control, the world turned to icy black. Sharp and cruel. Viva fell to the unrelenting will of the water.

It was dark. Not as pitch. Not as tar or jet or ink. It was darkness itself.

She couldn't move. Not paralyzed exactly, but as though every muscle in her body was contracted. Lungs empty. No air. Constricted. Watery fingers squeezed. Around her above below and through her. Her mind flashed in and out like television static in the dead of night. She couldn't think, only feel. And Viva felt throbbing, tightening pressure, and then a sudden stabbing pain. As though her sternum had shattered, the shrapnel shooting, piercing. White fiery pain. Icy. Blazing. Burning. Searing. A fire in her chest burned hotter sharper. No longer beating, only a stagnant ball of heat steadily immolating. Then as fast as the watery tendrils had pierced her, they squelched out of her chest, the scorching ball of heat with it.

And Viva felt nothing but the weight of silvering silence.

Silvering

Silver. Silversilversilver. Rippling silver colliding coursing crashing into the walls of Viva's mind.

Shattering.

Silver shards of breaking, metallic waves bounding like the silver spoon that jumped over something. Was it the cow? It was one, and the other. There was no telling. What was real and what was fiction? Dream or waking. It was silver. Silver clanging silver splintering silver fracturing silver.

Eyes. She—she—who was she? She needed to open her eyes, but they were heavy, each lid straining. Heavy silver. She—she— who? She—Viva was laying on her back, and when her lids drew open, she saw silver. Glittering, oceanic. Her vision pulsed. Or was it the silver? Eyes strained to focus. Far above her was shimmering, rippling nothing. Not nothing. Silver. Sitting up, it was as though she were moving through water. Weightless. Floating. Silver.

Muscles tendons joints nerves bones water. Inside out and outside in—she breathed. She didn't choke or sputter, her lungs didn't catch or flood. She could breathe. Or had she become water? After being dragged, stifled, submerged. Is this what death was? She had never been dead before. Her head didn't pound or ache. She wasn't afraid. She was calm in her death of liquid silver.

Considering life, her death, her insulation, Viva wondered— would anyone notice she was gone? Karl and Morrigan surely, but what about the others? Those who worked in the beige land, fleeting acquaintances, anyone?

Time seemed to pass slowly here, but she had always been good at passing time by herself. Every night at Mancy Manor, Karl took to the kitchen, water boiling, spices flying, knives sparring in midair, music blaring. Morrigan would sit in the living room across from the fireplace, herbs meticulously laid out across cushiony surfaces, singing folksy medicinal recipes. The herbs sang in beautiful harmonies, and Morrigan hummed along. In the face of the racket and fetor, Viva had always escaped to the confines of her room. The cool, white room had always been spotless with only a slight hint of lavender, and even that had been insisted upon by Morrigan. Viva's room was an oasis away from the kaleidoscopic cloud of chaos on the other side of Viva's door that—at six p.m. every night—smelled like a bistro cha-cha-ing with a candle shop. So, Viva had become proficient at keeping herself company while color and noise reveled without her. She was an expert in solitude. But this was not her bedroom. This must be death, right? Dead, dead, dead. If she was dead, what would they, the few—what could they say about her? Viva's mind wandered toward an obituary for her soul.

"Vivian Regum. Foundling through the abandonment of unknown parents. Adopted by the town's mancy as an infant.

Known as "Viva" by those few who did know her, lived an unremarkable life on the outskirts of experience. Barely completing high school, she miraculously entered college–due only to the mancy's intervention–and dropped out within the first six months. Never a daughter, a friend, a wife, anyone. Viva was a woman who had no idea what she wanted to do or who she wanted to be, a woman who failed life on her own, and was forced to flounder back to her family, working in the mancy business. Now she's dead. Drowned–tragic, untimely–within eyeshot of her cabin, within earshot of the three beings who acknowledged her existence, within spellshot of a woefully out of practice mancy..."

With that task complete, she pushed herself up, her hands pressed against a thickly graveled ground; she had been laying in the middle of a path. A path paved with silver pebbles, each one perfectly round and polished like glass like those Karl would collect. Pain bit into Viva's chest. Viva picked up a pebble from the ground and raised it up to the silver nothingness. "To Viva," she said to herself, "who was no one." She sank to the ground. Her heart panged.

Glancing at the pebble in her hand as she lowered her toast, wishing she had something a little stronger to celebrate her death with, she noticed a gleam in its silver depths.

In the pebble was a glittering image of herself. She held it tight, gazing into its depths as though into a crystal ball. The Viva in the pebble—skin, clothes, hair all silver—emanated joy. She was smiling wide and walking hand in hand with the most beautiful thing Viva had ever seen. A man, sculpted in pure gold. A man Viva had never seen before. In the pebble's depths, they were laughing, smiling, loving, living.

Viva tore her eyes away from the image and glanced down the path. The pebbles gleamed. Hands shaking, she dropped the pebble and picked up another, trying to understand, trying to think. Her mouth was dry, and she needed to swallow or cough or breathe. Silversilversilver. There in the depths of a new stone was the silver Viva. A Viva she had always pined for—silver skin glittering as she danced in a flowing, silver gown with the same golden man. Enchanted, Viva followed the pebbled path with her heavy eyes, squinting through the wobbling silver atmosphere to see a looming shadow in the distance. A rippling mirage.

Her stomach lurched and she pocketed the pebble and walked down the pebbled path, towards the mirage, mind breaking. Her heart beat. This man. She ran her fingers over the stone in her pocket. This golden god. Maybe she could find him and herself. A new self. Live again, for real this time. In death. In silver and gold.

It was difficult to know how long she had been walking over the pebbled ground before the looming shadow began to take form, but when it did, goosebumps crawled up her arms. Still far away, but recognizable, there was an enormous silver castle.

The pebble path led her to a dark moat of mercurial waters, which surrounded the spectral edifice. Viva stood at the end of the silver path just above the flowing current. A castle. Viva envisioned every fairytale she had ever read: drawbridge, towers, gatehouse, and beyond what must have been some sort of courtyard, was an astral, silver hall. She craned her neck to see into the expansive, watery windows and jumped when a shadow flickered behind the glass. What ghostly fish were trapped within?

Her heart should have been pounding. As she stood in the silver void overlooking the massive silver palace, her heart should have been racing. But it wasn't. Her heart wasn't beating.

Viva, a sculpture of flesh, watched shadows in the windows of the castle flutter around and around until all at once, the pebbled pathway lit up and the shadows scattered. Behind the castle windows and in every pebble on the path, a gossamer figure materialized. Features all in silver. A girl, small and vaporous, movements slow and fluid. Viva wanted to see, needed to see this ghost beyond the glass. She still held one of the pebbles in her pocket; it was ice. Viva's eyes focused; she was close enough to see dark silver chains running up the portcullis, close enough to see the water's steady movement around and around and around. Close enough to see the ghostly figure. The ghostly figure of herself. Her childhood self. It surrounded her from within every pebble along the path, from behind the castle glass. She took her pebble from her pocket and stared.

It was the ghost of her past. Her life lived. Dead memories resurrected in surrounding silver. She watched her child specter fight tears amid classmates' cruel laughter; the memory shivered like ripples over a still lake, and the scene changed. Viva watched herself run home after another invitation passed her by. Another ripple and Viva saw the pain on her past's face as she sat at a desk—another D on another paper. Ripples, and more laughter, trying to ignore hungry stares while walking through her high school hallway, which shimmered into a graduation stage, her specter dropped her cap to the ground and floated away after her name was passed over. Viva's mind spun as she saw herself leave the college campus, the word dropout echoing around and around and around. She watched herself alone and alone and alone, she blinked back tears that wouldn't come and wondered what kind of sick joke this afterlife was playing. In a flash, the images disappeared.

Tears wouldn't flow. She wished they would. Wished she could cry and scream and tear this afterlife to shreds. But she couldn't. She didn't. She wanted to go back or forward or anywhere. Away from her empty past. Away from those pathetic ghosts. But then another figure shimmered to life beyond the glass of the castle walls. The light of the stones brightened. The image was not of Viva, child, adolescent, or adult. It was a man. Golden radiance, a voice of warm honey dripped from his mouth. He held out his hand, "You're nothing out there. There, you're no one and alone. Nothing." Honey. Dripping. Syrup. Dark, soft, and sweet. Viva's muscles eased. Was he talking to her? No one was there but silver. He smiled perfection.

"I—" Viva started, taking a small step backward, but then he evanesced and was replaced by Viva. Not the Viva she had ever known. Not Viva in solitude or lackluster insufficiency. Not herself. It was Viva in silver. Contentedness twirled around her. A Viva all smiles and silver, reaching out to her. Take it. The golden man, divine, mesmerizing, manifested again and grinned, his teeth were white and long, and he was dripping gold. "Take it," he said and held out his hand as well. They, he and the Viva that could be, shimmered like lapping waters, hands extended, reaching. Silver and gold. "You can be something here. Not alone." Shadows shifted from behind the castle windows.

Viva's heart beat.

She stepped forward. Everything was bright and calm, and she was warm in silver and breath, in water and—she could be something in silver. Could be someone. She held out her hand.

The silver Viva dissolved.

He reached gold and long and sharp through the silver edifice, across the moat to Viva watching seeing feeling nothing but empty longing while he reached for her. She wanted to feel his golden hand in hers, longed to smile like the ghost of herself had done, and maybe if she took his hand she would.

He reached past her offered hand and plunged into her chest. He tore. Sharp silver. She felt pain, perhaps, but mostly she felt a tempting possibility, a calm yearning for joy purpose meaning, like everyone else, maybe she could be like everyone else and belong. She tasted the offered maybe maybe maybe. Maybe she wouldn't be alone. In the hollow of her chest, it was echo and echo and echo and echoing. You could be be be. And in front of her he held out in his golden hand dripping silver. Viva was filled by his honey voice you are nothing there but here you could be be be, don't you want to see what you could be if you come to the palace? He smiled gold potential as he held out his hand again, in it, beating dripping yearning, a silver heart.

Viva blinked.

Shadows swam. Around him around and around in a spectral frenzy. Viva was being swept away from the castle away from the shadows and the ghosts away from him away from her heart away from what she could be. She could not fight the current. It all grew small and smaller and smaller, but he was brilliance and gold, melting from her sight, but not before he grinned wide and sank white teeth into her silver heart.

Seven

Her heart beat. The room spun around like a woozy top when Viva opened her eyes. She was ungodly hot and the white sheets clinging to her body were drenched. She shivered. White surrounded her. The desk, the carpet, the walls, the bed: all white. She was in her room. She was in her home. She was alive. A bead of sweat trickled down her forehead along with a wave of, not relief, but something washed over her. She didn't understand it. She thought of silver.

Viva peeled the sheets from her body anticipating a sickening squelch. Why had she thought there would be water splashing over the sides of her bed to the floor? She let the air in the room waft over her, cooling her to goosebumps. Finally feeling more a person than a puddle Viva inhaled, absentmindedly touching the unbroken skin of her chest. A dream, she thought–but–she couldn't remember–she couldn't remember anything. Like smoke, it had dispersed in her return to consciousness.

As she strained her clouded memory, Viva caught sight of the clock: 5:45 a.m. It was early. 5:45.

A thought clunked into place.

Her parent meeting at six.

Nononononono. Viva flung herself out of bed, no time for a shower. Had she showered yesterday? Her hair was still damp with shivering sweat. Gross. Okayokayokay, throw it up, step into clothes, doesn't matter what—no, not that—nope, that's backward. Okayokayokay. She threw on a cap, flung open her bedroom door, the scent of rosemary and bacon greeting her on the way out. She waved it away, hopped over stools and ottoman puffs, swam through multicolored draperies, and she was out the door.

Out the door running, dodging limbs of the oak tree, weaving through Morrigan's jungle of unkempt herbs, and leaping over Karl's small vegetable garden. Her chest stung. Out the gate. Onto the path. Sprinting past the Daisy House, no time. Sorrysorrysorry. This was going to be a bad day. Down the path, kicking up dirt and pebbles as she flew. The creek giggled, flowing along at her right, racing her downward to town. Deep breath in as she ducked under the branching archway, the doorway from wilderness to civilization. The creek flowed. Viva's feet hit the asphalt parking lot.

Keep running.

When she threw open the doors to the greater office building, she stopped. No one asked if she was okay. No one thanked goodness she had made it or offered her a cup of coffee with a knowing nod. No one was there. She was alone. Stillness.

Viva was soaked, sweating under her faded cotton sweatshirt as she walked toward the janitor's office. A few rebellious hairs from under her cap had sprung free and were attempting to lacerate her corneas. Breathe, breathe, and one more breath. Viva straightened the crimson sign for Mancy-Led Adventures and opened the door—she felt a metallic clang in the hollow of her chest.

Before she could cram herself into the desk chair and click on the computer, the closing door flung back open, hitting her fully with a thwack. A woman with unnervingly straight hair marched through and shoved herself down onto the office chair. The only chair in the room. Viva blinked and adjusted her cap again, catching a few of the rogue hairs in front of her eyes. She found a chair from the hallway that was missing half a leg and took an unsteady seat across from the glowering woman.

"What kind of business is this anyway? You're Vivian Regum?" The woman slapped her hands down on the desk as if she were the principal in a low-budget teen drama. The computer snapped on with a bliiiing, illuminating the woman's face with sickly blue light so the lines of it deepened, causing an undead effect.

Viva steadied her voice, while mentally mapping out a potential escape route, "Good morning. It's nice to see you again—we've met during drop-off and pickup time." She smiled in what she hoped was shaped like "nonthreatening." "We've enjoyed having CeCe on our afterschool nature hikes, but we do need to discuss some behavior that myself and the other leaders have noticed."

In terms of conversations, it was not, Viva thought, the smoothest in which she had ever partaken.

"Actually, I go by Viva, but it's, okay, Vivian is fine… Yes, ma'am, we do have a fairly stringent 'no biting' policy, but I can assure you that it is only for the children's safety…Yes, I understand that it can seem a bit militaristic, but many of the kids prefer not to be bitten when they're out enjoying nature…I agree that they are entirely capable of moving themselves away from her biting range, but I think it would be better to eliminate the threat of mastication…Yes, ma'am, we do sometimes see wild animals on our hikes; we walk far up the path, which is in the woods… Unfortunately, yes, we did have a child who was bitten by a squirrel a few years ago, but I'm happy to say that it has been our only incident of animal hostility in the fifty-seven years we have been in business… I understand, and I assure you that we did, in fact, have a similar discussion with the squirrel's parents about his behavior. Our biting policy is consistent across genders, ages, species. We are not singling out your child, I can assure you…I believe you. I'm sure that your child's mouth *is* much cleaner than a squirrel's, but I'd prefer that our hikers not get bitten by anything, no matter how well it brushes… No, no, I'm not saying that your child is in any way like a rabid squirrel–except for her biting compulsion I suppose, but… You know what, why don't I give you my boss's phone number, and you can set up a meeting with her… Just ask for Mancy Morrigan Regum. Yes, the mancy… I hope she will be more helpful than I have been too… Thanks so much for your…"

The door slammed.

"…time."

Viva dropped her head to the desk. That could have gone worse.

It was 8:30. How could it already be 8:30? Viva was dripping sweat again and the oxygen in the room had all but dissipated. Morrigan wouldn't love the phone call she was about to receive, but Viva thought to herself, Mancy M. was good with obstinance. Few people were as well-practiced in it as the mancy. Viva had once been privy to a battle between Morrigan and Viva's elementary school principal. A meeting during which Morrigan, standing tall at just under five feet and bristling with eye contact, had convinced the poor man that Groundhog Day was a time-honored Regum tradition and should be for everyone else in town as well. Did he realize that, if not properly honored, all the groundhogs would up and leave to more appreciative pastures? And what would he do, in all of his misplaced principality, when winter couldn't figure out what to do with itself? Would he be the one to break the news to spring that it would have to come back later? Would he try to convince winter it was time to get a move on? Would he be the one to moderate that storm? Because in her experience, Morrigan had explained, seasons could be turbulent, and she wasn't about to lend out her shadow for the cause. Not again. The mancy had asked the man, who had appeared as though he would like to take a nice walk along the ocean floor at that moment, why the school was open on Groundhog Day, and if it wouldn't perhaps be wiser to give the day its due recognition. Viva had seen the power of a few well-placed periods and rhetorical question marks growing up with Morrigan, but Viva had always been more of an ellipsis person.

Viva sighed, resigned. Morrigan would be able to handle the biter's mom much better than she ever could. Pulling up the day's schedules, rosters, and bug bingo sheets on the ancient computer, Viva put the furious woman out of her mind. Mancy Morrigan would take care of it. Her chest stung.

8:30–this had been an odd morning, an odd morning of rushing sweat and flowing time and running and no Daisy House–maybe that's what she would do–she would stop by Tyree's. She needed to apologize to him for standing him up. He had opened early that morning for her, and she hadn't been there, she thought with a pang. Now it was 8:30 and Viva couldn't remember why that was important, why 8:30 kept blinking up at her from the clock on the desk. What was at 8:30? Oh no. Was that schedule right? Was that today?

Viva flung herself towards the door, vicious threads of hair freeing themselves again from underneath her cap, sweeping this way and that in front of her eyes as she ran again across the parking lot, underneath the arborous archway and up the creek path, gurgling water rolling with her as she worked her way upward. The computer back in the office blurped ill blue.

Schedule:

Mancy-Led Adventures Day Hikes
Meet in front of Tyree's Daisy House 8:30 a.m.

Lunch not provided
Wear shoes, bring crow snacks

Up at Mancy Manor, underneath the oak tree, a group of ten small children was sitting on top of their hands, saucer eyes darting this way and that. As Viva leaped over a particularly ambitious hibiscus, nearly missing a large pumpkin, and sliding into a bed of mint, the kids eyed her with a mix of skepticism and entertainment. Mancy Morrigan eyed her with something more closely related to annoyance.

"I picked them up from the Daisy House. We've discussed rules, safety, the biting policy, et. cetera." Morrigan's eyes glinted, "Karl has the first aid kit. We'll talk about time later–seems to be escaping you today–and Tyree wants a chat. Off you go." The children didn't move but turned to Viva until Morrigan's voice sliced through the morning air: "Time to have fun." The kids jumped and streamed through the garden, avoiding any plants that might snap at them with thorny teeth. The group followed Karl, a small, sequined backpack fitted to him, and Viva brought up the rear, trying to remember what she had done earlier that morning to make her so late. It had escaped her.

The group walked the path that Mancy Morrigan and all the town's mancies before her had patrolled through time. It was the path of

Viva's childhood, along which the mancy carried out her perpetual search for ghosts in the woods and where Karl shared whispers and stories.

"Over here, this bank. Many years ago, this is where the frog, a hungry, tricky frog with sharp teeth and a sharper mind tried to drown the fish. It's how the fish got his fins, you know. See that hollow between those rocks? That's where the frog lives even today, trying to find slow and gullible fish with weak fins…This right here, do you see it? Many years ago, the bees lost their honey. It's true, and this little flower right here, this little yellow one, helped the bees to win it back… Do you see that cave over there where the path forks into the hills? Many years ago, it was Mancy Morrigan Regum who showed the bears how to sleep during the winter. Great, big Roger lives in that one over there; he's sleeping now, so be sure to whisper as we walk past. I'll tell you about seasonal dyslexia in the bear community after we pass…"

Viva knew that these stories were merely methods of teaching: don't get too close to the creek, don't rile up the bees, stay out of bear caves unless you're bringing Roger a new pillow, but in the depths Viva's mind, seeping slowly like a fetid infection wondered why Viva had never been worthy of her own tale. She ignored the thought and continued telling stories while she watched the children laugh their way up the path. In the cool air, by the rippling creek, under the shivering fall leaves, Viva wondered what was happening back in town. Were people swapping stories of their own? Surrounded by friends? Stories they had lived, not heard told by someone else?

Roger

*R*oger, *a massive brown bear who lived in the woods near Mancy Manor, had seasonal dyslexia. It had been a young Morrigan Regum who had become acquainted with the bear, and upon discovering his confused inner clock, began to provide food and company during his waking winters, and surveillance during his sleeping springs and summers. Over the many years the two had known each other, Morrigan, with Karl's begrudging assistance, had created a perfect resort for Roger to spend his long, restless winters. It was a cellar.*

The dark curtain of winter never fell in Roger's cellar. Out of the season's icy reach, it bloomed. The cellar had stocks of various foods on shelves lining sky-blue painted walls. A yellow sun, which Viva had added sunglasses to gazed down upon them in artificial luminosity, and the floor was covered in blooming flowers spanning the colors of the rainbow. Morrigan and Karl had ensured Roger's cellar be even more summery than the season the bear continued to miss.

Between feather and fur, Viva snuggled into a gargantuan roost that mirrored the one Karl slept in at Mancy Manor. Under Karl's puffed wing and the arm of a bear, who was munching on buttery popcorn one kernel at a time held gently between knife-like claws, Viva blustered, "The girl just walked right into their house, Roger." *Viva held up the picture of Goldilocks entering a large, suburban-style house.* "What do you think of that? She's not even embarrassed about it." *Her eyes widened.* "She didn't wipe her feet on the mat." *Viva's small voice squeaked.*

From across the room, Tyree, who was sitting on Morrigan's lap said, "Maybe she was really scared and needed help." *Morrigan smiled down at him and pointed to a vivacious daisy in front of her and sang a high, major note. The flower wiggled in joy and Tyree chuckled, mimicking the note. The flower didn't move. Morrigan sang again, Tyree's laughter squiggling with the daisy's dance.*

"It doesn't matter if she was scared," *Viva said, turning the page of the oversized picture book.* "She should've stopped being scared and knocked. It only takes a second. Then she could be scared again after."

Morrigan pointed to the next flower, a bright pink tulip, and sang a different note, eliciting another dance. "I think it's okay to be scared," *Tyree said, pointing to a drooping daffodil a few flowers down.*

"Breaking into someone's house isn't okay. M., why didn't the banish throw her out like it would at our house? Do bears not use banish? Roger does." *Viva held the next picture up to Roger's face, to make sure he had enough time* to see every detail. "Also, what does it mean for porridge to be just right? It's always gross." Karl squawked indignantly and took a piece of popcorn into his long, silver beak. "Well, it is," Viva continued. "If this girl was so hungry, shouldn't she be happy with any porridge at all?"

Morrigan laughed as another flower bounced to life and Tyree raised his arms in a cheer.

"You're right Viva." She sang, all of the flowers in the room shimmying at the sound. "Why don't you write your version and read it to Roger tomorrow night?"

The winter outside bit with gnashing wind and icy gray, but inside the cellar was light and laughter, and a sea of singing daisies.

Eight

After the allotted four hours of adventure time, the group hiked back down the trail. Children's voices were raised in songs of the day and recitation of the path's tales, in attempts to coerce Karl to perch on their heads, in laughter at his scoffing refusals, and lamentation over sore feet, rumbling stomachs, the heat and the cold.

Viva shivered in the chill of falling evening. It was not yet night, which is a dark and slippery descent, but evening: the gauzy tumble of evanescing color. The sun still shone clear, if weakening. Viva was glad to see her home reappearing, and the Daisy House twinkling not far beyond.

It was customary to end every adventure at Tyree's Daisy House. Not only was it a convenient pickup location for parents, but the incentive of freshly baked cookies spurred the most dragging feet to a prance. And for Mancy Morrigan, it was important not to have people on her land for more than absolutely necessary. As they passed Mancy Manor, Karl veered off from the group to enjoy a precious moment of solitude, the children took to a run towards the scent of melting chocolate, sprinting past their parents' open arms toward sugar.

Viva waved goodbye as groups of two and three and four descended the path, cookie crumbs falling from placated mouths. End of adventure, of trees and water, of bears and magic, and back to the world below.

When all of Viva's responsibilities had departed with an accompanying adult, she turned to Tyree, who was cleaning off the surfaces in the garage. "Hey," she said, guilt clanging in her chest. "I'm sorry I stood you up this morning. I asked you to open early, and then I didn't come. I'm so sorry, I—no, no excuses." Breathe, "I'm sorry."

Tyree handed her a cookie and smiled his scarecrow smile. "It's alright. I figured something happened when I saw you running down the path."

"It was chaos." She sighed. The morning was behind her. "I didn't hear my alarm and was running late, and I had a dream or—I think—anyway… I had to sprint to the office to meet that parent. But I'll make it up to you." She felt a swell of exhaustion. "It's been a long day."

Tyree handed her a cup, the steam rising from its depths. "Since you didn't get anything this morning," he said. "I'll see you after I close up."

She turned back to him, sifting through her memory like a rolodex. "Oh. Okay. Great." Her voice trailed off slightly. Her voice was watery, "Have you ever had dreams you wanted to go back to?"

Tyree squinted a button eye and scrunched his forehead. "I'm not sure. I don't usually remember my dreams."

"I can't remember mine either, not really… but I remember feeling that it…sparkled. I think that I sparkled too. It was like I…" Her voice thinned, and Viva flushed. "Like I mattered. I wasn't alone."

Tyree fixed his black eyes on her. "Maybe you'll dream it again tonight. But I don't think you need a dream to sparkle, and you certainly don't need a dream to matter to me. You're not alone here."

"Maybe," Viva said and smiled at his mismatched, clownish clothes, his shaggy, straw hair. "Maybe. I'll see you tomorrow."

Tyree blinked at her and then leaned down theatrically. "Dinner, Viva. I'm coming over in like twenty minutes. You okay?"

"Yeah, yeah, I just–" Noticing his stooping posture for the first time, she stopped short and laughed. "You're like an ostrich trying to peep into someone's basement window."

Tyree burst into multi-colored laughter and straightened up. "See you in a few. For dinner. That you invited me to. Yesterday." He smiled again as she walked away.

Karl

Rain aligned with Karl's young and crumbling world. How much worse would it be if the day of his grandmother's death had been filled with sun? This was better. He pretended to ignore the tears running rivers down his face as he walked up the creek path, one of his pocketed hands fiddling with the note his grandmother had written so recently. Before.

He was angry. Full of pain. He hadn't argued with the old woman as she croaked her orders to him. Who could argue with a dying woman? And now. Now she was dead, and who could argue with a dead woman? He shuddered. He knew who, and he was on his way to her cabin now. He had been working at a restaurant in town, where his grandmother waitressed, since he was small, first bussing tables, cleaning dishes, floors, countertops, then he learned to cook. His chest swelled as he thought of the delight in his grandmother's eyes when she saw every one of his culinary creations. Then he remembered that minutes ago, he had quit. And his grandmother was gone.

Now he was on his way up the creek path to the town's mancy. She'll have a job for you, Karl, his grandmother had said before she scribbled out the note that was now in his pocket. He had known that his grandmother was acquainted with the mancy—everyone was—but of all the times the mancy had come to their home to advise his grandmother, she had never once glanced in his direction. He had never gotten a sense of friendship between the women, but now, at his grandmother's direction, he was on his way to ask for a job, for a place to stay, for help.

He should probably just turn right around, get his job back at the restaurant where he felt comfortable and safe. But it wouldn't be the same. He could go back and live in his grandmother's house—his chest heaved—no, no he couldn't, but he could find his own place to live, or better yet, he could leave this town and find a new one. He had skills, he had protested. Great, the old woman had said, waving him away like a fly, now go and get more at the mancy's.

How would she know if he didn't go? What could she do to him? A great electric shiver wriggled up his spine. "Okay, I'm going." He shouted into the storm. "I'm going," Karl sighed to himself, shuffling up the path.

Thick mud clung to his shoe, pulling him into the sinking earth, but it wasn't the path that caused his heart to beat faster and his feet to move more quickly. It was the woods.

The trees started all at once just out of town, so that one step was all it took to be in the wilderness. It was as though he had been dropped into a nightmare—dark, jagged shadows looming, only abysmal unknown deeper within. The creek would usually have bubbled kindly on his left-hand side, but it had been silenced in the tumult. He was in darkness. He was alone.

Karl furrowed his eyebrows. There should be leaves shuffling, creek waters gurgling, there should be birds, but it was silent. A subversive nothingness when the mind knows there should be sound, but there was nothing, as if everything had been submerged.

Chancing a glance up from his feet Karl saw a sea of moving shadows to his right, grasping like undulating seaweed under murky water. Great, reaching leaves and petals swelled, height and breadth.

Karl's beating heart throbbed in his throat head fingers toes. He had not seen the small cabin behind the ungodly garden until he was almost upon it. The cabin surrounded by woods. Mancy Manor. He stared at it, tears gushing with each pulsation of his heart. The rain fell hard around him.

He waded through the viscous mud and dipped below branching leaves, over thorny vines and grinning flowers. There was no path up to the cabin, and his eyes stung with focus, rain, and tears, but in time, he was at the cabin, purple as midnight, the door black as coal. He took a breath in, wiping tears from his eyes, and knocked. No answer. Standing at the doorstep, his spirit wavering, he knocked again.

Silence.

Karl sat down on the step of Mancy Manor and wept. Everything hurt.

Then he heard it.

Thunderous shouting through the weather, though it was impossible to decipher any words from the din. The woods were even darker surrounding the cabin. Tree bark on each enormous trunk, almost black, the needles or leaves stood, hackles raised. Shouting continued from within.

Karl pressed fear and pain back into his guts, willing himself to stand, his feet to move towards the blackness. Trembling, he walked into the woods, towards the voice. The trees umbrellaed him from some of the pounding rain, though he still felt his skin wrinkling beneath drenched clothes. The forest closed in like the clasping lid of a music box as he walked deeper and deeper towards the shouts. Maybe he would be lost in the woods. Maybe it was a siren call, their sweet song luring him towards a watery grave in the woods. He was getting closer, but closer to what? With a sudden lurch, Karl's foot slipped, and arms flapping uselessly, he staggered, falling backward in his attempt to save himself. He had unwittingly found the edge of a short hill which fortressed a low clearing below, ringed by trees. He dragged himself back up and squinted through the sheet of rain; he could make out a small shadow standing at the far edge of the fortified clearing.

The shadow was counting in a low, soft voice. A voice like velvet. Karl crawled closer to the edge of the hill and strained his eyes to see the shadow. It was a girl who seemed to be around seventeen or eighteen—his age. She had her fingers shoved into her ears and her chest heaved as she threw her voice as far and wide as she could into the heavy air.

As he scanned the clearing, he saw with a start, in the tree right behind her, its limbs arched just over her head like an umbrella, there was another girl, smaller, dressed in bright yellow, and grinning diabolically. He couldn't help but laugh out loud. What were these girls doing? Playing hide-and-go-seek in a downpour? His laughter was drowned out by a sudden roll of thunder that shook the earth. Lightning flashed, illuminating the two girls, and Karl, not knowing why remained crouched; a shiver of electric fear zigzagged up his spine. The counting girl raised her voice, louder. It was music.

Karl glanced to the opposite hill just behind the girls. His blood froze. A bolt of lightning flashed. Karl blinked. Trees shivered in the blaze of light, sounds of cracking, crashing, splintering, only a little ways off cut through the din of the storm, and he knew: they needed to get out of the clearing. The rain was thick and gray, but as lightning struck and illuminated them again, Karl saw it. He didn't know whether it was in his mind's eye, whether it was a premonition, or whether he really did see the enormous surge coming for them through the trees.

Karl shouted just as another burst of thunder shattered through the trees, then he slid down the bank, waving his arms, willing his voice to rise above the chaos. Lightning flashed. It was coming.

The girl shouted to the universe: "One hundred! Ready or not, here I come!"

"Run!" Karl sprinted towards the two of them; the smaller girl had fallen out of her tree, and he scooped her off the ground and slung her over his shoulder. "Run!" He shouted again, giving the counting girl a gentle push in front of him, helping her climb out of the clearing. *Don't think. Just run.*

They sprinted, full force, over rocks and roots; they were flying.

Thunder crashed and lightning sizzled as the three of them approached Mancy Manor, purple as midnight and black as shadow.

Nine

It was getting dark as Viva made her way back up the path. It was the type of falling night that's dark with lurking shadows, a slow, heavy darkening. Viva took a sip of the drink she couldn't remember ordering, couldn't remember who she had been talking with before, how long before? Couldn't remember. As she reached the cabin, night's soft arms closing around her, she heard a sound, or maybe a shape or feeling. Something calling from the creek. Reaching out from the corner of her eye.

Her skin prickled.

It wasn't windy; the night was still and silent, she couldn't even hear the creek across the path. Ignoring the hairs on her neck rising, ignoring the tiny electric pulses in her veins, Viva fixed her eyes only on the front door of Mancy Manor. Anxiety rose; her blood felt cold. It could be the wind sweeping goosebumps along her skin. Her prickling, clammy skin. But there was no wind. Her chest ached, it wrested and stretched, and she tasted something, something like iron, but it was sweet too—like honey. The door, just open the door. Don't look back.

She was being silly. She shouldn't be afraid of shadows, of the night. Mancies owned the night. But Viva wasn't a mancy. There was a mancy just beyond the door, her mancy. Only a threshold away. She was just being paranoid.

Daring herself to peek out of the corner of her eye, she saw nothing. Viva was holding her breath. Hand on the doorknob, but she needed to be sure. She would not let shadows creep in after her. Breath still trapped in her constricted lungs, she turned her head, careful her hand remained anchored on the knob—did she feel something on the back of her neck? Something wet. Teeth clenched, she squinted through the darkness towards the creek. Though fear crawled over her body on spider's legs, she saw nothing; there was nothing.

She was sweating. Dripping. There was nothing there. Turn the knob. One more time, she looked back.

No movement, no sound. Just shadows.

Mancy Manor was alive with orange light. Viva's anxiety, goosebumps, sweat, the whirring in her mind melted away in the face of Mancy

Morrigan Regum sprawled out on her belly over a bed of living room cushions. The mancy was humming along with a sprig of thyme, which released a heavy brume of aromatics in time. The darkness Viva had felt at the doorstep, in the shadows, the silence, none of it could compete with the sight of Karl, a purse strapped to his chest, overflowing with spices, and a wooden spoon in claw, which he was waving threateningly at a boiling pot of water.

The cabin smelled of food and disorder. There was a crunch as Viva stepped over the threshold. "If you keep putting the banish down before I get home," she shouted over the noise, "I'm going to start feeling like you don't want me here." She crouched down to reorganize the line of crushed eggshells, charcoal, salt, and sage that had been sprinkled over the threshold. She reached to her right toward the entryway cactus and removed a glass jar of the same mixture. "We need to make more, I think. Probably have a week left."

Morrigan shot her a thumbs-up from her cushiony stage.

Shaking the jar before replacing it in the cactus pot, Viva scrunched her face and made her way into the cabin proper. She breathed deeply, letting the incense and the din inundate her and sat down next to a soprano cinnamon stick. She shivered in the heat of the fire. "Why'd you put down the banish already?" Viva wiped grains of salt and charcoal off her shoes as she sank deeper into her seat, savoring the herbaceous music.

Morrigan shrugged. "I put it down after I got back from the office. You seemed frazzled this morning and I didn't want you to forget. Make sure Tyree doesn't shuffle it all around when he comes in."

Viva stared into the fire. "Ty's coming over tonight?"

Morrigan sang her response, swishing a sprig of thyme along Viva's nose, "For dinner. He should be here in a few minutes. Then we feast." She belted in her velvet alto, "Right Karl?"

Karl croaked from the kitchen between reprimands toward various appliances.

Tyree arrived while Morrigan was singing the fourth verse of "Thyme for the Pimply Teen," which was an upbeat tune requiring a complex rhythm from the rosehip section. The day, it turned out had been exciting only for Viva; Morrigan hadn't received a phone call from the irate biter's mom, which the mancy was disappointed about, explaining to Viva– interspersed sporadically with the medicinal chorus–how happily she would have discussed the issue at hand. Oh well, Morrigan had said, maybe tomorrow, before turning the conversation gently. "The group tonight is a teen group, only seven girls. No biters, I wouldn't think, so we'll hike up, stop at each of the spooky landmarks, point out the classic haunts, then get to the campsite. Karl set up camp already. We just need to start the fire once we're done hunting and wrap it all up with the final ghost story and s'mores. Ghosts and stories, easy. I'll take the ghosts; you take the stories." The pause, as Morrigan held Viva in an expectant gaze, hung in the air. Crackling embers sang out as Viva blinked in vacant confusion at the woman whose eyebrows were rising slowly like the moon.

Karl croaked through a mouthful of parmesan.

"Oh, god, M.," said Viva with a sudden pang.

Mancy Morrigan smiled with the satisfaction of a successful huntress.

"You had to go to the office today. I forgot about the overnight and didn't print out the ghost maps. I'm so sorry, I can't believe I forgot. I guess in the rush this morning and the meeting and everything, I forgot it was Saturday. The ghost maps. I'm sorry."

"And the spooky bingo sheets." Morrigan said in her best-vibratoed ghost voice. It was the voice of a ghost that didn't realize donning a white sheet with cut-out eyeholes was unnecessary after actual death. Tyree joined in with spectral jazz hands and a few, "oooo's," and Karl pretended not to know any of them.

Viva deflated. "I'll make it up to you. I'm sorry; I can't believe that I forgot. You had to use the computer, didn't you?"

Morrigan pursed her lips and spooned another mountain of parmesan onto Karl's plate. "I did."

"What can I do to make it up?" Viva was sweating again. "What if I get the hot chocolates tomorrow morning? What if I clean all the gear? What if I–I don't know, give Karl a bath?"

Karl squawked, cheese cascading from his beak and over his white, downy chest.

"I don't need you to lose any fingers. How about the gear and you can be lead for next week's ghost hunt adventure, huh?"

"Okay, yes. Yes. That sounds good." Viva picked up the empty plates from the table, leaving the parmesan puddle that had formed below the crow, and made her way to the kitchen. "I'll take care of all this too."

Morrigan rose from her cushion. "Sure, but he'll just do it again, you know that." She paused and said slowly, "You think you might want to stay home tonight? You may need a little time to yourself. Unwind a bit?"

Viva tugged at a frying pan that was floating stubbornly over the stove. "That's not a terrible idea. It's been a hectic day, that's for sure. Do you mind?"

"Of course not. You rest–I'll take care of this one." She prodded Karl who had started dozing, and said, "I know you've never liked our ghost hunts, but care to make an exception? It's been years since you've... well... and–" Morrigan's voice broke slightly, "–We've never found her– anyone, I mean."

Karl huffed and flapped his wings fervently in protestation scattering cheese over the coffee table.

Viva frowned as she attempted to scrub down a particularly stubborn slotted spoon. "What do you mean her? –"

"I'll do it." Tyree's voice shook slightly, as he cut in. He was attempting to calm the flapping bird while still coming out alive.

Viva frowned. "You hate ghost hunts."

"I just need to be physically present at the campsite, right? In case of emergencies and all that?" Morrigan nodded, and Tyree added, "I don't have to actually try to find a ghost, do I?

Morrigan smiled. "No, you don't."

"Can I be in charge of s'mores?" His button eyes lit up. "I can hike up there right now! I'll need to make sure I've got the perfect s'mores combo. Most people don't realize that the ratios are what matter the most. That's what Karl says at least," he said, now stroking Karl's head softly.

"Yes, he does." Morrigan said.

"Okay!" Tyree stood, almost overturning the table, Karl, and Morrigan in his enthusiasm. "I'm going to get my supplies and get started. I'll see you up there. Um…" He flushed. "Can I be in my tent for the ghost stories part?"

Viva laughed from the kitchen. "Morrigan doesn't tell stories, you know that!"

Tyree shuffled his feet. "I can tell some friendly ghost stories?" The question mark at the end of his sentence trembled at its highest point.

Morrigan said, "I'll tell the stories. I do know all of them after all." The mancy's voice trembled slightly before she opened another box of singing herbs.

Karl snorted and stuffed his head into a powdery wing. His snores sounded almost immediately.

"Thanks! See you up there M., and Viva, I hope you get unwound." He chewed his lip and beamed. "See you tomorrow. You too Karl." Tyree skipped out the door, scattering the remaining banish.

Viva, taking an intermission from kitchen purgation, sat down next to Morrigan and laid her head on the woman's shoulder. "Thanks, M." Deeply etched lines of spindly gladness ran from the edges of the mancy's dark eyes like spiders' webs. The fire was warm. Viva's skin pulsed beneath its heat, and only a sliver of her mind thought of silver.

Karl

*A*fter narrowly escaping the flash flood in the woods, Karl found himself shivering on the floor in Mancy Manor, which despite the townspeople referring to it as a manor, was small. He took in his surroundings warily—it was a sparsely furnished cabin with only a coffee table and one rocking chair. The girls from the woods sat on the floor across from him and stared. The younger girl, Morrigan, appeared no more than ten years old, and the older girl, Lucy, must have been around his age of eighteen.

Karl had handed the soggy note from his grandmother to Mancy Regum, who he learned was the mother of the two girls, Lucy and Morrigan. The mancy had taken it with a nod and invited him in; he would begin working in the morning, she said. Later, at Lucy's direction, Karl had himself comfortable in the large seating nook situated beneath a bay window next to the cabin's fireplace. Though his legs hung down, almost touching the floor, and his shoulders protruded well off the cushioned bench, the fire next to him had offered some comfort. He clutched an *emerald pillow that Lucy had given to him to his chest; she had apologized that there wasn't a better place for him to sleep, but with a burst of pride, had handed him the pillow. "I made it myself," he heard her say through the falling mists of sleep.*

Crushing ocean waves, whitecaps bared like fangs coursed towards him, but in between the darkness, in between rain-soaked woods, the thick, turbid waters, Karl saw flashes of Lucy's face. He heard her voice breaking through the dark.

He woke up alone. The fire had gone out and Karl shivered. What time was it? He pushed himself up, skin prickling from the cold leaking through the window. The main area of the cabin was almost empty except for a short-legged coffee table and a lone rocking chair. Karl snuggled back into his makeshift bed, pressing himself harder to the window and curling up his body to fit onto the bench. He imagined the Regum sisters sitting here on this banquette seat, gazing into the woods. Lucy, calm like blue-infused gray and Morrigan, ready to claw her way through the glass in black ferocity.

After another sleepless hour, Karl walked the perimeter of the room, surveying it again, but there was nothing new to see. Nothing but several wooden boxes stacked on the mantle. He struggled with the fireplace for a while before it sprang to roaring life. The cabin began to warm. His stomach growled.

The small kitchen, which had barely enough room for him to stretch his arms, didn't have much, but Karl thought after searching each cabinet, it was enough. A few old potatoes—already sprouting—eggs, and a large bag of flour. He set to work.

His heart slammed against his chest when he felt a cold hand on his shoulder. Karl whirled around.

Lucy's smile illuminated the kitchen. "Morning," she said, "Did you sleep well?"

Heart beating fire, he said, "Yes." He cleared his throat.

Lucy held her gaze steady.

"I—" Karl gestured around the kitchen, "I started on breakfast."

The corners of her eyes crinkled in a smile and her hand was still on his shoulder. He continued cooking, painfully aware of Lucy's eyes on him throughout. The shade of her gaze was the tranquil graying blue of falling evening and made the hairs on the back of his neck stand on edge. He broke eggs, a few shells escaping his fingers.

Lucy talked as she watched him cook. Twice a week, she said, she was working at the hospital in town. She didn't care what her future title would be, nurse, doctor, leech keeper, as long as she could be something and she could help people after she learned more. She talked about the hospital and her patients, she talked about her mother and the creek, she talked about Morrigan and their adventures. When Lucy learned that Karl did not enjoy the woods, she had narrowed her eyes, and raised a conspiratorial eyebrow; no one could escape her and Morrigan without first falling in love with the woods, she said.

After Morrigan marched in like a storm and found them in the kitchen, the three of them ate together at the coffee table in front of the fireplace. His first morning at the Mancy Manor was fire and food between glances of slate and onyx.

Ten

Before Morrigan left Mancy Manor for the weekly Macy-Led Adventures overnight, ghost maps and bingo charts safely tucked under an impressive layer of clothing, she said to Viva in a tone that everyone recognizes from childhood: "Lock the doors. Turn out the lights." She pointed to the large, glass jar nestled in the dirt alongside the entryway cactus and added, "Thresholds again, please. Windows too. And get some sleep." Morrigan winked before closing the door behind her and Viva was alone.

It took time for Viva to coerce the kitchen clean, but eventually, she left it with the comfortable knowledge that Karl, upon waking, would be only slightly annoyed at the level of cleanliness. She made her way to the saguaro in the entryway and lifted the glass jar out of the pot's dirt as carefully as she could—she was well acquainted with the cactus's version of humor—

and shook the jar, mixing the contents thoroughly. Filled with broken eggshells, charcoal, salt, and sage, the outside of the jar was labeled in Karl's bewitched cursive: *Apply banish liberally to household thresholds and windowsills for full-day protection. Do not eat.* The "Do not eat" had been added for Viva during her infancy, though her not being literate yet had still caused seemingly foreseeable havoc and a trip to the hospital. The Regums had then begun keeping the jar in the entryway cactus: if the label wouldn't deter the girl, the cactus would.

Viva made her way around the house, sprinkling the mixture in each doorway and on the windowsills before locking the door, and turning out the lights. Karl was still perched at the table by the fireplace, his head burrowed between soft wings. Viva left him to sleep peacefully.

It was quiet. And Viva was alone.

Viva's room was cooler than the rest of the cabin, encased in its icy whites, which breathed a frosty calm into her as she entered. She loved her family, but when a person was around Morrigan and Karl, they were utterly surrounded, every sense filled to the brim and overflowing. Viva had always liked the hush, the white, the aromaless state of her room—though Morrigan tried to sneak lavender in once a week.

Allowing her senses to reset from the colorful, the herbaceous, the sonorous, the magic, she finally inhaled nothing and exhaled silence. Alone. Viva's mind whirred. Eyes scanning her room— bed, desk, table, closet—she couldn't find her usual comfort.

Now in an oversized, beige sweatshirt that she had taken from the office lost and found and a pair of old shorts, Viva dragged her creamy down comforter into the living room. Sleep would find her tonight before the fire in a sea of plush. With Karl, whose resounding snores sailed through the cabin on swaying waters of slumber.

Snuggled next to the fire, she pulled her comforter around her like a down taco shell. The sound of sizzling embers met with a clackclackclack as a small, silver pebble fell from a crease in her bedding, smooth and polished to a mirror-like shine. It rolled until it hit the stone base of the hearth with a light "ting."

Viva didn't notice. Karl didn't wake.

Morrigan

"Morrigan!" *A twelve-year-old Viva leaped through the door, managing to scatter banish—a mixture of eggshells, charcoal, salt, and sage that the mancy always spread over the cabin's entry points— through the cabin. Tyree followed behind, hands pocketed, and with a tentative foot, he attempted to rearrange the scattered shells and grains displaced by Viva's youthful explosion. Summer thought Morrigan. She wasn't sure what was worse: the cyclonic energy that came with hot days and free nights or the moribund gray of the school year, but Viva was not about to allow the mancy time to reflect.*

"Guess what we found." The girl had Karl pressed to her like a stuffed teddy, his face smashed against her cheek as he gasped for air. Tyree made his way towards the main room, surveying a place to sit down while Viva detonated. Tyree found an emerald pillow on the floor and took it, ready to turn it into a seat until Karl freed himself from Viva's embrace and snatched the pillow from Tyree's hands,

then delicately placed it in his bay window roost. Karl sat on top of it, cawed, and buried his face in his wing.

"Karl," Morrigan warned. Tyree had deflated. Taking the boy's hand, she led him to a bright yellow seat next to the coffee table. "This one is better. Karl just has…" She peered into the hard, silver eyes, "…issues." Her voice was cold, "He'll apologize for being such an ass, I promise." Tyree laughed.

Viva fumed. Steam building ready to burst, "Listen to me!" She shouted, face contorted in childhood petulance.

Morrigan raised a steady eyebrow at the child. "Excuse me?"

"Guess what we found."

"I don't know," Morrigan sat next to Tyree and handed him a chocolate bar she had found in her pocket, "A snake?"

Tyree's eyes widened, but Viva rolled hers. "No."

"A ghost? Did you find our ghost?" Morrigan's voice thinned slightly as she held out her hand to Tyree until he placed a broken-off piece of the chocolate into the mancy's palm.

"No."

"A spaceship?"

Viva laughed and clapped her hands together. "Yes!"

Karl peeped out from his wing. The mancy lifted her eyebrow again. "You found a spaceship." It wasn't a question.

"Yes!" Viva was bouncing up and down, ready to take everyone on a mission to space that very second. She said as

quickly as she could and, in a whisper, "I know you told us to stay on the path, but we didn't. We wanted to go on an adventure, so we just went off a tiny bit. Just a little! And we found a spooky place. It was spooky, right Ty?" His eyes were fixed on the table in front of him and he didn't move, as though the mancy might not spot him if he stayed as still as possible.

"Where—" Mancy started before the girl cut her off.

"It was so spooky. It was just a black circle and the trees stopped like they can't grow there. I bet aliens won't let them. We walked around—but we were careful! I had my whistle in my mouth the whole time and Tyree had a sharp stick—but we couldn't hear any birds or squirrels or anything. It was—"

Morrigan's blood turned to ice. Crystalizing in her veins, ready to break out of constraints. Her head was pounding, and she knew Karl's eyes were on her—she could feel the cold silver. In the calmest voice she could summon, the mancy spoke. "Tyree." She steadied her voice. "Karl will take you back to your house now." There was a fluttering of wings behind her.

"—But my parents aren't—"

Morrigan's mind spun and spun; the floor the walls the everything seemed to tilt and turn. "Okay. Go into Viva's room and I don't want to see you out here until dinner. Now." Tyree pattered away, tripping over a bean bag as he did. "Door closed," Morrigan said sharply. Click.

"*Vivian Regum.*" *Steady. Steady. Karl landed on her shoulder. He was heavy, claws digging. "Every day. Every day we tell you what?"*

"*But—*"

"*No." Her voice was freezing, throat closing around the chill. "You. Do Not. Leave the path." The blood in her veins was flowing hot now. "You're twelve years old, and you know better." Bubbles formed below her skin, blue and blistering. "Go to my room. You and Tyree will not leave this cabin for a week, and you bet your tiny britches that Karl or I is with you on every adventure from now until you die, and if you ever wander off the path without us again, so help me, I will move this cabin to Kansas, and you will never see the woods again."*

Viva stomped away, tears of fury in her burning eyes, but she said nothing. She knew to say nothing. The door to the mancy's room clicked shut. Morrigan took a rattling breath. Karl's claws dug into her shoulder.

Dinner that night was silent. No herbal tunes. No metal roaring from the kitchen. No fire hissing.

When the mancy got up the next day, Viva wasn't in the room with her. Her heart steeled. Cold fingers, gipping ice. The smell of chocolate chip muffins soared through the air; Morrigan rushed out of her room. Heart pounding. Head swimming. She would have to scour the woods. With a pang that nearly brought the mancy to her knees, she thought lakes, creeks, caves, and snakes, and monsters. She thought of the magic that wouldn't be able to help, magic that wouldn't be able to save her. Morrigan saw herself dredging frigid water, fighting aggressive current, combing over every rock stone pebble as she opened the door to Viva's white, white room. Viva wasn't there. Tyree wasn't there either.

It was empty. And silent. Grabbing her jacket, sprinting out to the main room, ducking, maneuvering towards the door, Morrigan skidded to a halt. Karl was in the kitchen, chirping quietly at the rumbling oven. He cawed and jerked his head towards the living room when he saw the panic in Morrigan's eyes.

Viva and Tyree were asleep in front of the fire, each curled up in a bean bag, each an arm extended toward the other, fingers intertwined, steady breath rising. Morrigan's heart slowed, though tentatively.

She sighed, tiptoed over to the mantle above the fireplace, and took up an old, wooden box filled with various herbs. She sat down near Viva and Tyree, placed the herb box onto the coffee table, opened it up, and hummed honeydew into the new, gray morning.

Eleven

It started. A tap, tapping on the black, cabin door. It wasn't a scratching of claws or a pounding of fists. It wasn't a barge or a crash, but a soft and gentle tap, tapping.

Silence answered. Swelling in the dark of the cabin, a bloated, pulsing silence. Crawling into dusty corners, under bean bags and blankets, engulfing dust bunnies and crumbs.

With a gasp, Viva blinked awake. She was encased in the heavy arms of silence and her thick, white comforter. She sat up and glanced around the room. Sometime after she had fallen to sleep, Karl had recleaned the kitchen and moved to his spot in the bay window next to the fireplace where he now slumbered in his mighty roost.

Gooey silence pulsed in deafening ripples, a quiet that blocked even the moonlight from Karl's open window. Eggshells shivered with the incoming breeze.

Soundlessly.

Mancy Manor, even with only three inhabitants, was rarely silent and Viva's skin prickled as she stood.

The light of the moon of the stars of everything was stifled, was choking as black nothingness leaked in through the window, subduing.

Veiled in the quiet, Viva stepped, pulled toward the door. Over cushions and under tapestries, weaving in the darkness. Each step. Soundless. Only a rattle beneath her sternum breaking through the curtain of silence. Metallic. Louder with each step step step. She walked past the still, lifeless kitchen and stood next to the saguaro, waiting, eyes fixed on the door. Light from the porch lamp cast shadows of the oak's skeletal branches. The shadows were still. They didn't rattle like bones, that was her chest rattling, like a glass marble turning turning turning in a rolling drum.

As Viva stared at the door, she heard a voice. So sweet she could feel it drizzling down the back of her own throat. Ambrosial from within an elusive dream.

The door was only a step away.

His voice trickled over her: "Hello? Anybody home?"

It oscillated dripping honey into a pool of molasses and oozed through the door. Through the black sheet of silence: "Are you there?" It seeped.

Viva's hand was on the knob and her chest was pulsing pulsing pulling and pulling.

Silver.

She longed for silver, tasted it, reached for it, as it reached for her.

Why was someone out there at midnight? Viva turned the knob. Why was she turning the knob? The thought gestured frantically at her through the fog of her mind only after her hand had already turned. Not slowly, she cast open the door.

Her heart beat sharply.

"Ah." The voice drizzled through the door. "Hello there, hello." He was the most beautiful person she had seen–had seen before, before–he stood before her with a smile of glimmering white teeth. Viva had never seen any sort of divine entity, but this was what they must have been like while they were wreaking havoc on the helpless mortals back in time, drawing humanity into nets of chaos through beautiful charms and golden violence. They must have been as indescribably stunning as the man before her, who was ravishing, leaning casually against the oak tree.

Teeth. Dripping. Syrupy words swimming in her daze, in the silence, in the darkness. The color of his skin and the thick waves of his hair seemed to oscillate silver and gold as he shifted beneath the moon's beams, like light-catching foil, but his eyes were a deep pool of gold.

He was an illuminated presence in the silent night.

Clad in a rich suit, hands pocketed, eyes scanning the house with perhaps amusement, he spoke again: "Hello there." The voice stilled the echo in Viva's chest. Was it buttery molasses? Deep, rolling sugar? "May I come in, darling? My car has just broken down, and wouldn't you know it, my phone is dead."

As she turned toward Karl, still sleeping deeply in his roost, from the corner of her eye, she wondered whether the man was dripping silver. He was incandescent. Not dripping; scintillating gold. A cloud smeared over the moon's light, which beamed a cool blue over him like water. He wanted to use the phone? His car had broken down? His smile glittered fixedly on her, golden eyes unwavering.

Why had he come to the cabin? People did come to the mancy for help occasionally. They did come late at night once in a while. Usually women. Usually regulars. Had Viva ever seen him before? Who was he? Did she care? He seemed familiar. Viva's heart beat.

"I tried my luck at the house down the way, but there was no answer, of course, the late hour is my undoing, but I am so grateful that you have answered my call. You are just who I need. Darling, may I please come in to use your phone?" His voice rolled over her in a honeyed wave.

He'd been to the Daisy House then, but of course there would have been no answer; Tyree was at the camp with Morrigan. Why would he lie? Was it impolite to decline to help? It was late after all, and cold. Put yourself in his shoes. Be kind. Just a phone call. She felt a twist. Her breath rattled in her lungs. Her heart stung.

Karl slept deeply beside the open bay window, beside the cold, dead fire, as Viva breathed a soft "Okay."

The golden stranger stepped forward. Watery moonlight washed over the garden behind him. In the sky, the stars held their twinkling breath. The wind picked up and the garden rippled, and Viva breathed in the scent of the creek. Clear waters and wet earth.

Smile unchanging, movements like liquid, the man was seemingly weightless. She stepped back. He moved like his voice as though he were swimming toward her. "Thank you so much, darling, wonderful to see you again. I don't know what I would do without you. To be honest, I almost lost hope of finding someone." He laughed silver bells that were low and resonating. "I promise you, dear, you–" His sticky voice was suddenly pulled taut and strangled.

In a flash of gold, he was thrown backward. His languid voice, his glimmering, lucent eyes, the moonlit man skidded violently through the mancy's garden.

Viva's chest stung as she watched him fly. In a blink, she was launched backward as well, tearing through silk hangings and landing on the floor. Viva tumbled down onto a sea of plush, which proceeded to spurt thousands of foam balls into the air like a pod of whales spouting all at once into the sea breeze.

From the floor, her mind swimming with spinning confusion screeching silence, head pounding, chest echoing, Viva stared at the threshold, the sliver of space between home warm safe fire and the garden outside, where there was a thin layer of crushed eggshells and a dusting of fine granules, and she wondered if she could replace it all with silver.

Viva's head pounded and her lip swelled. Everything hurt.

Her heart beat.

The elysian man had been thrown far from the door—he was sprawled out in the garden within the mancy's jungle of untamed vegetation.

Fighting hard against something welling up in her—something that urged her to go out to him, go check on him, go with him, Viva freed the foaming waves of surging terror and confusion. She pushed herself up and stood. "I don't know who you are. It's late and if you need help, there's a police station in town. Go back down the path. You can't come in." Her voice was a twittering sparrow, but she shook her head and put her hands on her hips, imitating Morrigan as best she could despite the growing sting in her chest. "No."

There was a fluttering of silver in the back of her mind, a siren song pulling her, pulling her where? "No," she said again. Behind the throbbing pain in her head, in her eyes, in her chest, was something sharp and piercing: let him in, walk him to town, go with him. She couldn't feel the blood moving inside her.

Her heart beat.

She needed silver.

The sea of her mind gushed and spun.

From his supine position, he brushed a lock of hair out of his eye, the moon caught it in a passing beam. Glistening? Viva shook her head and tasted blood. Her lip must be bleeding.

This was her house. It was the middle of the night. She pushed the ambrosial voice out of her swimming head. "No." Her voice echoed.

He smiled, and Viva thought she saw water trickling down his open lips, over white teeth. She bit her lip and steadied herself

With an arm like that of Apollo himself, he pushed himself up. Eyes narrow, mouth smiling wide, his entire face illuminated gold, he said, "This will be more interesting than I thought." Something in his voice purled in his thick, honeyed tones. Something glinting.

Her heart shot a beat.

"–Darling–" The word dripped through the air, and dropped, like a smooth pebble into still water. Rippling. "Goodnight."

In a daze, Viva stared at the oceanic garden, uncultivated and swaying under silver moonlight.

Viva blinked.

Why were there shards of eggshell at her feet?

Viva blinked and turned. Karl was sleeping. Snoring in and out and in and out. The dead fireplace didn't crackle, the kitchen didn't blare with music or life, Morrigan wasn't singing with her herbs. Where was she?

The room was silent. It was alone. Alone and alone.

Why was the door open? Viva closed it.

Eggshells? Sweep them up, the shells, broken and sharp, dangerous. It would just take a swish of her hand. To clear them away. It was nothing. It was better. Sweep them away. She sucked her lip. There was blood.

Close the door.

Close the door.

The garden shivered.

Viva closed the door and felt a wave of icy desolation, digging pain, iron, and cold. She yearned for–cold silence crawled, no beating or pulsing or heat surged in her, only hollow silver thirst.

Karl was snoring cartoonishly with a high-pitched "eeeeee" at every exhale. A small fire sizzled in the hearth, and sleeping herbs hummed lullabies from underneath their closed lids. Viva blinked. And listened. For silence.

"Karl?" she called to him across the room, her voice as grating as his ancient croak. "Karl?" She said again, louder.

With skillful and alarmingly paternal quickness, Karl woke. When she couldn't say, couldn't know, couldn't remember why she was at the door where she now stood wrapped in her white comforter, Karl led her back to the living room, ignoring the devastation of foam balls scattered across the floor. He herded the Viva, a lamb lost in a tempest, back to safe, feathery peace before the fireplace. He rolled her gently up in her blanket, tucking her in, and with a whistle and a flourish of white feathers, the fire came alive again. After a brief nod of approval at the hearth, Karl took to the air, and began to tidy up the mess.

Viva fell hard, breathing in and out and in and out in sleep as Karl stuffed the pillowy gore back into wounded cases. Pillows mended, Karl was flying back to his roost, when something caught his eye, something at the foot of the fireplace, gleaming like a laugh. A small pebble. Perfectly smooth and polished like glass. He picked it up in his beak, flew to his bay window roost, and then tucked the pebble underneath his own bedding. He fluffed his feathers and sank down. Karl would not sleep; he fixed his silver eyes on Viva, who dreamed before the raging fire.

Silvering

On the threshold. Standing, staring, waiting at the threshold. Where Viva always found herself: the threshold. Always alone. Viva was within and without. On the threshold of magic: she had never wanted to be a mancy like Morrigan. There was a difference between being surrounded by magic and having to do it yourself; it was like making your own birthday cake. The sweetness not quite balancing out the isolation. So, Viva lived in magic without participating. The threshold of friendship—that had been an enduring threshold, insurmountable. It had been best to turn away, observing from a distance. Wasn't there Tyree? The word twisted in her mind and sizzled. Friendless and wistful, unable to step through.

Thresholds: in and out but neither. Her life was a threshold. But. Was it? She had a family. Morrigan and Karl and Tyree. And that was friendship too, right? An icy, metallic pang shot through her, echoing in every empty space. Teeth. She was at the threshold. As she always was.

Silver pebbles shifted beneath her bare toes as she stood on the lip of a moat. Thick, dark liquid below her gushed. Around around around and around, swirling circles, an arsenical ring around the divine silver castle. She inhaled silver and smiled.

Water flows, Viva thought, over thresholds. Every wobbling in between she had ever known sloshed up the sides of her mind crashing into her throbbing eyes. Waters rising. Viva was always stuck in between, and she could see them all now behind the crystal walls of the castle. Every time Viva had been ignored, every time she had turned away, every slight and failure flashed behind the silver glass. Thresholds. Doors Viva had never walked through. Had she ever–

Silver rushed.

Done anything?

No.

Silver sloshed.

Been anyone?

No.

Silver cleansed.

She watched herself in the castle balancing on tightropes of thresholds. Never moving forward. Never being. Never.

Silver.

Renewed.

In the castle, was herself, her life unlived. Swirling below her, the waters spun.

Water cleansed.

Water renewed.

Viva's chest seared.

Renaissance.

Worth.

Meaning.

The images in the castle windows dissolved and reformed like smoke. Now the manifestation of Viva was laughing. She was in the castle. Beyond the threshold. Joy and light and meaningpurposeplaceself. A silver Viva and, and next to her alight in gold...

You could be someone, he said in a voice like honey. Belong somewhere. You will not be alone. Viva inhaled silver.

Dripping.

Water mesmerized.

The soundless, monochromatic nature of the moat calmed her mind, which she recently—how recently—could not subdue. It would be so different from Mancy Manor. Music. Constant. Colors. Farraginous. Aromatics. Disparate.

You could matter. The waters sputtered below.

Vivian Regum, you could matter. You do not have to be alone. Her mind burned. An iron spark of pain shot through her, numbing her fingers and toes. Her chest burned. Something was coursing through her, something was fighting.

You're Viva Regum. A ghostly whisper floated through her. Viva Regum. Your guardian is Mancy Morrigan Regum. Your father figure for all intents and purposes is Karl. You belong in

Mancy Manor. You're Viva, you're Viva, you're, you're, you're–
you belong...where?

A cold fire behind her eyes seared, and a pain behind her
sternum gaped and wept. Who are you? Pain twisted seared ice
and fire until she couldn't endure it.

Where do you belong?

What, in her fogging mind, sloshing, slamming, was
creeping in?

Dripping.

Come

to

the

Palace

Just step over.

To this side.

Her golden man in the castle, standing next to a ghost of
who she could be, grinned a white smile of teeth.

Worth.

Self.

Not alone.

He held out his hand.

Her heart beat.

Viva slid down the silver bank and into the rushing water. In an instant, she was below the swell and all her pain disappeared.

Not flailing or grasping or contracting or sputtering, only peace beneath the current around and around. It wasn't cold or wet. An oily sheen coated her skin. She was silver. Silver dripped through her and filled hollow places. She had crossed the threshold.

Worth. Meaning. Someone. Something. Saturating.

When she opened her eyes again, Viva was standing on a drawbridge, above the raging, circulating moat. Her silver castle rose before her and beckoned. Only silence surrounded her, and she turned—where had she come from? There was nothing. Nowhere.

She crossed the bridge to the palace's portcullis. Her voice cracked through the empty sky, splitting the encompassing silence. "Hello?" The words slid away into the void without an echo. "Anybody there?" she asked, so brittle.

She had come from nowhere—there was nowhere to return to. She could only wait on the threshold. Before the sparkling edifice, she smiled. Someone had once told her stories of castles like this. A sharp twinge. She wondered who. Viva reached up and knocked on a thick, silver bar of the portcullis.

"Ah." A voice dripped through the grating in thick, malty liquid, "Hello, Vivian."

"Can I come in?" she asked, taking hold of a silver bar across the door; her fingers hands arms dripped silver.

She heard, in the silent expanse, his lips part over teeth in a wide, golden grin as she stepped over the threshold.

Twelve

Viva's eyes were sandy with sleep; she rubbed the grains away. White room, white blankets, white desk, whiteness. This was her room; she was in her room, and it wasn't right, the colors were wrong, and it wasn't enough, she wasn't enough. But it was her room, and it was Morrigan's voice shouting singing laughing down the hall. Her chest hurt.

Viva walked out into the living room where Mancy Morrigan waltzed through the maze of cushions and chairs with a robust bouquet of rapunzel.

Morrigan emerged from her floral partner's nonexistent gaze, muffled hums emitted from a box of herbs on the mantle. The fireplace roared.

"You've been sleepwalking again," Morrigan said before Viva could tell her good morning, tell her hello, tell her something, but what had she wanted to tell the mancy?

"Hmmm?" Viva grabbed the cup of coffee that hovered before Karl's outstretched wing and sipped.

"Karl said you were sleepwalking last night."

Viva sipped while perching herself on a crimson ottoman, roasting in front of the fire. "I was? I was having some… dreams. I think. I'm not feeling great this morning."

"Oh?" Morrigan twirled lightly around. "That would happen before too. Do you remember? One week, you thought you were in the circus. Every night. You'd wake up, put on your clown wig and glittery tights, and head out to the woods. We couldn't convince you that there was no tightrope to walk across the treetops, do you remember? Karl had to snatch you up."

"I–I don't remember. Wait. Did…" She sipped the coffee again, "Did Roger come out of hibernation to jump through flaming hoops with me at one point, or… No. That had to have been a dream."

Morrigan laughed. "That one was real. Sort of. You told him all about one of your previous night's escapades, and he didn't know you were talking about a dream because, well, neither did you, and he was so excited to be awake for the summertime that year and to be involved in the living world. We had to give him one performance with the dreamworld circus. I couldn't say no. But it wasn't flaming hoops, that was the dream. He jumped through a few hula hoops that you held up for him. Karl did ventriloquism, which was… something."

Viva laughed and Karl clicked indignantly from the kitchen.

"But they weren't all amusing. We took you to the doctor—all the doctors actually. As you well know, part of being a mancy is knowing that nobody can fix everything on their own, so it was months and months of doctors doctors doctors."

"I remember that part. Vaguely." Viva watched Morrigan duck spryly underneath a thick, red tapestry. "We did a kind of sleep therapy, right?"

"Yes," Morrigan replied. "I'll find the book for you and all of my journals—notes and things—after breakfast. We can take a look at it tonight too after our ghost hunt—figure out what we need to do."

Morrigan spun gracefully and was dipped low by the leading flower. She chuckled darkly. "The first time you did it, you sleep-climbed out of Karl's window without waking him—I think you were around ten, maybe younger—we were afraid we'd find a little drowned girl in the creek. Luckily, all you did was climb the oak and settle in. We searched for you for hours before we heard you snoring up there. Don't do that again, please. It was not amusing."

"So, we'll go over the strategies, ways to stop it tonight?"

"Yes, we will." Mancy Morrigan dipped again and simultaneously caught a pancake that Karl had flung across the room. "We started to lock everything up tight from then on, spread banish over thresholds, and your sleeping brain seemed to get the message eventually." She took a bite of pancake as the bouquet spun her again, and said, "Not before you managed to steal away our sleep too." She smiled. "We took shifts watching you more closely; one of us sat up just outside your room–you've always been too particular about people being in there–until the sleepwalking just stopped on its own. Why do you think it's starting up again? You're sick? Anything different recently?"

Viva furrowed her brows. "I'm just tired. Haven't been sleeping well. I'm sure it'll stop again soon."

"Well," said Morrigan, bowing politely to the flowers, wiping her brow and taking a seat next to the fire, "We'll keep an eye out, lock up, try out some of the things we did in the past. If you let me, I'll scatter some lavender around–that always helped me–" She cleared her throat, "–But until it's all done, no sleepwalking outside. No sleep-climbing trees, no sleep dips in the creek. Okay?"

She smiled and took another bite of the pancake, crumbs falling lightly to the floor.

Karl wholeheartedly agreed with the mancy from his perch in the kitchen.

Viva nodded. "No sleeping in trees, no breaking out of windows, no drowning in the creek. I promise."

She laughed as Morrigan scarfed down the rest, swiftly stood with an incredible flourish, and held her hand out to Viva, who set down her mug before the crackling fire, and took the mancy's hand. Mancy Morrigan Regum pulled Viva up into a swift waltz while the Rapunzel bouquet watched from a corner and Karl spurred a weathered skillet to hurry up with more pancakes.

In Viva's room, still and sepulcher quiet, a pebble, polished like glass, rested underneath a white pillow, waiting for the princess of the palace to sleep again in silver.

Morrigan

*M*orrigan, Lucy, and the boy named Karl sat in the cabin. Lucy was wondering about the boy sitting across from her, the firelight shadowing his features. Morrigan was thinking about the monster in the woods that didn't exist. The monster her mother, a powerful mancy, had found no trace of. The monster she had imagined. She was thinking about what it meant for someone to see things, things that weren't real. She was thinking: don't think.

The girls' mother, Mancy Regum, had gone into town to "make inquiries" about the boy who had shown up on their doorstep by way of the woods, and Morrigan had not counted the minutes since her mother had left. She had tried; she really had. One, two, three flash. Before her eyes the vision of a shapeless thing. Reptilian. Four. Pause. Five. Nothing. Six. Dripping teeth. Morrigan had stopped counting then. She focused her mind instead on the outside. What she would give to be outside.

Situated in the bay window, listening hard, ignoring the two other people in the living room, Morrigan stared through the rain and into the woods. Her woods. What else have you imagined? Don't think. The trees shivered in the wind, or was it the force of crashing water? Dripping.

Jumping back from the window, she turned. Morrigan shook out her thoughts, filling her head instead with the crackling heat of the fire to her left and the sounds of Lucy and the new boy speaking in low voices.

It was deafening, Lucy's line of questioning: Where are you from? Shrug: town. How old are you? Shrug: eighteen. Where's the rest of your family? Shrug: dead. Don't you have any friends to live with? Shrug. Why'd you come here? Grandmother told me to.

It was infuriating. Morrigan wanted to shout to run, but she sat silent, staring into the heat of the fire, questions and shrugged answers rolling off her back like water. It was too much, and after what seemed like the hundredth enormous shrug, she stood up and walked resolutely out of the cabin's front door, plopping cross-legged in the garden.

Even from the door, even if someone or something— Morrigan shook the thought away—were to stand directly in front of her, boot to boot, she would be utterly invisible. Anywhere in the garden, Morrigan would be umbrellaed by yawning, green arms, adorned in multicolored raiment. She was invisible.

The garden was the perfect place to hide.

Morrigan remembered her mother's surprise when she had first seen her youngest daughter discussing the day's agenda with a giant rhubarb entirely in song. The perennial's growling baritone rolled through the earth like thunder; Morrigan had reveled in the vibrations. The monstrosity was Morrigan's favorite plant in the garden, and it was where she was sitting then beneath its fanned leaves. She listened to its grumbles about the cold weather and the younger plants in the garden. The rumbling song filled her up and she closed her eyes, and every so often hummed a gentle response.

Don't think.

***

Morrigan's nose twitched. The overwhelming smell of thick, sizzling grease, pink meat turning to crispy brown, beige batter goldening in a bath of rich butter woke her. Half of her face was covered in clay earth, which she unsuccessfully wiped at, and pushing the blanket of leaves from her, she crawled back to the cabin, lured by the intoxicating aroma.

There was no one but a dancing fire in the living room. She raised her voice louder. "What's going on?"

"Morrigan." It was Lucy's voice, luminous as the moon on an empty sea. "Come in here!" Swimming with excitement. Excitement from where?

She surveyed the living room again, just to be sure, then she walked to the back of the cabin into her and Lucy's bedroom. Not there either.

"Morrigan, come on!" Lucy's voice again swam through waves of laughter.

"Where are you?" Morrigan shouted, leaving her bedroom behind, checking every corner as she did.

A male voice didn't shout. It grated like a heavy boot shuffling over a dirt road, but somehow, it was also inexplicably soft: *"We're in the kitchen."*

"In the what?" Morrigan's face scrunched. *"What are you doing in there?"*

The kitchen was a small room that was never frequented by the Regum sisters. Of course, their mother disappeared into it for a few moments in the evenings, emerging with that night's life-sustaining substance. It usually smelled of boiled foliage. Morrigan wasn't sure why anyone would choose to go into that room when there were so many more interesting places to be, but when she walked in, she was hit by a burst of smells that made her teeth tingle, as though they were sharpening in preparation for a delectable feast.

Lucy peered over the boy named Karl's shoulder as he flipped and stirred and then with a grin, he clapped, and served up his concoctions onto three plates, handing the first to Morrigan before serving Lucy with a blush.

Karl asked, *"Where do we eat?"*

Lucy and Morrigan both shrugged their shoulders. Food in the Regum house was a way to mark the time at which the girls would not be outside in the woods. They had never paid much attention to the actual eating part, but Lucy led the way to the living room and placed her plate on the squat coffee table in front of the fireplace.

It was incredible. The girls had never experienced food like this. It had all come from that little room that they *avoided. "How do you know how to do this?" Morrigan asked between mouthfuls of scrambled egg.*

"I cooked for my grandmother since I was little. And I cooked at a place in town. She worked there too. It's not hard. I could teach you if you want." Morrigan rolled her eyes, but Lucy's eyes flashed.

Karl asked, "Does your mom not come home at night a lot?"

It was Morrigan's turn to shrug. "Sometimes." She turned to Lucy. "But we don't really notice. We're usually outside by now. She works a lot."

Lucy chimed in. "She's the town's mancy, and works as an advisor, so people call her at all times, and she has to be ready. People don't usually need advice on a schedule. Except for Mr. Walter. He calls every Tuesday at 3:17." She laughed and Morrigan's heart warmed. Warmed with the food—who had known survival could be so delicious? And she warmed with the joy of her sister. And for the new boy, she felt a cool droplet fall from her heart—she was warming to him too. Just a little.

Despite Lucy's protestations, but encouraged by Morrigan's applause, Karl cleaned up breakfast. Not only did he clean the kitchen, which had been well seasoned by dirty pots, pans, mixing bowls, and a startling number of wooden spoons, none of which the girls had ever seen before, he cleaned the entire cabin. Except for the mancy's bedroom, which he tried to enter with a broom before Lucy leaped onto his back and Morrigan threw herself to the ground between him and the closed door. *"You don't want to go in there,"* Morrigan said darkly, pushing at his ankles.

Lucy, still clinging to him like a squirrel on a tree added in her spookiest voice, *"Only mancies in the mancy room,"* before she dropped back to the ground with ghost-like softness. *"Let's go outside."*

As Lucy made her way to the door, it slammed open and Morrigan's mother, Mancy Regum, stepped in. *"Where do you think you're going?"* She scanned the room and sniffed before crinkling her round nose. *"What did you do in here?"*

Lucy attempted to dance around the mancy and out the door, but the woman was everywhere. Lucy conceded with a grin and said, *"Karl cooked and then cleaned. Nice, right?"*

The mancy met his eyes and said, *"I suppose you've found the way to pay your rent."*

Thirteen

Sunday always had the audacity to start early in the morning with a group of thirty adults in their eighties, excited to see what new birds could be spied upon that week.

After their waltz and pancakes, the Regums left Mancy Manor, Karl flapping overhead. Viva and Morrigan were clad in various layers, and each carried a small box of supplies: binoculars, bird identification pamphlets, and bird call whistles. And in case the birds had scheduled themselves elsewhere and couldn't tear themselves away, Karl attended as an avian representative. Along the walk to Tyree's Daisy House, the massive, white crow practiced what could be loosely defined as bird calls. He had allegedly perfected around thirty calls in various genres over the years and was always trying to diversify his repertoire–from Viva's shoulder. Science would declare it impossible, but Viva would swear to anything that

Karl's bird call practice elongated their journey by at least a mile. It was impressive magic.

Squawking, cooing, chittering, and what could generously be called singing hailed their arrival to the Daisy House. Tyree seemed as though he were having a far more traumatizing morning than the woman with a broken crow on her shoulder. The fact that a group of thirty militaristic octogenarians could reduce a man like Tyree to terror was nothing short of hilarity. His motley was strained in his attempts to disappear both into his large shoulders and behind a coffee machine. He resembled a black bear cub clinging desperately to an infant aspen in the naked winter, a camouflage strategy that was more pitiable than effective. Viva stifled her laughter, but Morrigan's eyes lit up as she watched the man twitch at questions like: "But what species do you see most on your rooftop at dawn, dusk, and midnight respectively, can I stay here next week to document the data?" and, "Young man, stand up straight and tell me how many bluebirds were here last May fifth, what time, what did they sound like, exactly, and how blue were they?"

Viva shook Karl off her and he took to the air like an angel, spouting his most shrill call, a supposed nightingale. It probably did sound like a nightingale, one that had gone out on the town the previous night and woke up in an alleyway a mile from home with a splitting headache, a new tattoo, and no pants. Karl's impression was not beautiful, but it was captivating and the thirty men and women who were ready to storm the coffee garage and claim it in the name of discounted movie tickets and four o'clock supper turned to watch Karl glide sensationally overhead.

Taking advantage of brief silence, Viva walked over to the coffee counter and smiled wide. "You had quite the handle on that."

Tyree emerged from the safety of his own shoulders, eyeing the mob suspiciously as they clawed for binoculars out of Mancy Morrigan's box and directed their sights to Karl's aerial ballet. Tyree scrunched up his twisted mouth, his eyes glittering slightly; he tapped on a cup on the counter, as if in deep, furrowed disapproval. "I don't have to give these to you, you know."

Viva, said in mock severity, "Yes. You're right." She twisted her face into what she thought could be construed as contrition, and she began to step backward, fluttering her eyelashes repentantly up at him. "I'll just let M. know that she'll have to live through five hours of birdwatching with old people without her hot cocoa—don't worry though—I'll let her know that it's all my fault for... not being old enough to scare you to pieces?"

Tyree's scarecrow smile unrolled across his face like yarn. He pushed the two cups towards her, and Viva shook out her contrition, skipped up to the counter, and took hold of them, their warmth shooting through her hands, and up her arms–she hadn't noticed how cold she had been.

Leaning against the counter, careful not to spill–especially Morrigan's–she asked, "How has your day been?"

"It's been fine, a little tired, but nothing I can't recover from." He glanced down at his feet.

"Why were you tired? Did you not sleep well?"

"The ghost hunting trip last night kept me up a little later than normal, but I think it went well."

Viva frowned. Last night. What had happened the previous night? Tyree's voice broke through her thoughts– "I made s'mores when they got to camp and hung out in my tent until breakfast and then I made crepes. I think they went over well, but I'd like to make a few alterations to the recipe. Karl said he'll help me out this week." He grinned and wiped at a spot on the counter. "It was alright. I don't really like the ghost ones, but–Oh!" He dropped the cloth he had been cleaning with and whirled to the back of the garage, glancing back at Viva with beady eyes of conspiracy.

"I've got to go soon."

"Okayokayokay, hang on," Tyree muttered, and then louder asked, "Hey, how was your night, anyway?

Viva's mind stalled. She swallowed a metallic taste on her tongue. "It was fine, I think. I don't remember anything in particular. Karl says I was sleepwalking, but I just feel tired. I don't think I'm sleeping well. And," She paused and swallowed again, as Tyree turned and walked back towards the front of the garage, something cupped, hidden in his hands, "I've been having some…dreams, I can't remember them but–I think–and it hasn't been restful. So. It was fine. But you know those dreams where you want to go back and see what happens next?"

"You asked me the same question yesterday. Am I that forgettable?" Tyree said teasingly before his face stretched into another crooked smile, small lines of joy etched around his button eyes. "If you're sleepwalking, it's a good thing you didn't do the overnight tour, right?"

"I'm sure I would've been fine. But if you see me walking around late at night, it'd be great if you'd point me back in the right direction," said Viva.

"Deal."

She added, "It's weird though, I wake up and it's like a pull. I can't remember the dreams, but I know I want to go back. Like I need to be there again."

Tyree opened his cupped hands. "Saved you a s'more from last night. Nothing better right?"

"Good," Viva said, ignoring the sharp pain in her chest, "After five pancakes this morning, it's about time for s'mores. Thanks." She took the s'more, wrapped it up in a napkin, and balanced it on top of one of the steaming cups, "Better go. Thanks again. I probably won't see you on the way back, gotta pop to the office to prep for next week, but I'll see you later."

"I can stay open later, catch you on the way back?"

Viva was halfway to where Morrigan stood tapping an impatient foot. "You don't need to do that; I'll be okay. Thanks though!" She leaped off to find the mancy flinging bird-watching pamphlets into the enthusiastic hands of Karl spectators.

Tyree scrubbed a spot of nothing off the counter and watched the Regums lead the group of thirty shuffling bodies up the path and into the woods.

Viva

The night spread like a thick rug unrolled over the sky. Fifteen-year-old Viva sat in the center of her room, staring out her window. What was this? Apprehension? Nerves? Forced apathy? She longed for the certainty of childhood again; being a teenager was too hard, too scary, too lonely. Childhood was all: do I roll down this muddy hill, hoping it's soft at the bottom: yes. Now though? It was hard to roll herself into friendships, into high school, into normal. Normal, Mancy Morrigan lectured, was not as fun as the hills, the flowers, the trees, me. Morrigan would laugh: don't worry about it because it will fall into place. Don't worry other people. Don't worry about their susurrations, their giggles behind your turned head. Don't worry about your apprehension, nerves, your anxiety.

So, Viva forced apathy. Don't worry.

She tried. Questioning, questioning, questioning her hair, clothes, and tossed a brand-new lipstick from one hand into the other. Viva crawled backward to rest her back against her bed and bit her lip. Surveying. Considering.

Assessing. White bed, white desk, white carpet fresh and cloud-like under her bare feet—she loved her room. Heavenly, calm, and still.

Viva popped the cap off the lipstick and scrutinized inside the tube as if analyzing its place in the rainbow. If she were a mirror held up to the universe, shouting identity, purpose, and place, what would people see in her presentation? The deep purple popped in the blooming whites of her room. She wondered what it would be like to twirl color all over the empty slate. All of it. Swirling and transient purple, moving the stagnant fibers of whiteness around the room like a breath, like blowing out a dandelion. That was the best part of white: with one sweep, its entire identity, personality, being could change, and then with a swipe, it could change back.

Viva pulled her lips to a smile and touched her naked lips, measuring, assessing, predicting, and then popped the lipstick out of its casing again, and with eyes closed, she traced her mouth. Cloaking herself in amethyst.

She felt like a god, drawing herself a smile, beautiful and new, and she smacked her lips together and lightly touched them again; they felt fake to her touch. Like paint or plastic. Was this how artists felt? But artists didn't paint over something that was already there. They created, they didn't trace, but she had created this smile, hadn't she? This new, purple smile. She felt warm and purple in herself.

Pocketing the lipstick after another satisfying pop, Viva smiled wide at the empty room.

"Well, look at you." Morrigan's voice swept across the living room, over cushions, around overstuffed barrel chairs, and beneath hanging papasans; it wove through draperies, curtains, and tapestries that dangled from the ceiling like intricate networks of cobwebs.

Viva flashed her new smile.

"Bold. It suits you," Mancy Morrigan said, leaning back in her puffy chair, making the shape of a camera with her fingers and clicking her tongue. "Where are you and your new friends off to tonight looking so beautiful?"

Viva blushed. "I think that we're just going over to one of their houses to eat pizza. That's what they said yesterday on the phone."

"And these girls are...? Or..." Mancy M. winked and placed her chin knowingly between her thumb and index, "...gentlemen?" It wasn't everyone who could so graphically speak ellipsis, but Morrigan Regum was an expert–she didn't even have to click her tongue or waggle her eyebrows. The implication hung heavily in the air with a wide grin.

Viva scrunched her entire face and ignored the heat rising. "It's just girls, M. They're from my class. I've known them for like ten years."

"Ten years and this is the first time you've gone to one of their houses... Or talked with them? How did they get our phone number?"

"Well, yeah." Viva popped her lips together, "They kind of invited me out of the blue."

"Oh?"

"Yeah, I mean, they asked me if I knew Ty, and then they invited me over."

"Ah."

"What?"

"Nothing, nothing. Do you need any money? How about some valerian, I snipped some this afternoon, it's fresh—very vocal, but smooth, like jazz. How about a snack, Karl cooked up some broccoli tartlets—he also made chocolate truffles this morning with Tyree. Do you want to take some of those with you?"

Viva rolled her eyes as thoroughly as she could muster. "No, no, no, and no. Thank you. I'm good."

Morrigan sighed. "They're very good truffles; you're missing out. Do you know which house you're going to?"

"Bridget's house. I wrote the address down for you, and her parents' phone number." Viva held up a neon pink sticky note. "See? Just like you told me to. Bridget laughed when I asked for it, so thank you for that." She rolled her eyes again, attempting to set a record for teen angst.

Mancy Morrigan pushed herself up from her bean bag chair with surprising agility and grabbed the note. "Teenage girls laugh at everything; I wouldn't spend another thought on it. Don't worry." She waved the words away like a buzzing fly. "Thank you very much for this. I should expect you home, when?"

Viva's eye muscles were becoming sore with the calisthenics. "I don't laugh at everything, and I'm a teenage girl. I wrote it on there: they said ten-thirty, and I'll walk home after that."

"You've got better things to do than to giggle around about nothing. You've got taste and sophistication. Like me." Morrigan continued. "Ten-thirty it is. Karl will come to get you then."

"M.!" Viva's face contorted into pure, teenage outrage. "That's going to be so weird! These are my first friends at school, it's the first time they've asked me to come anywhere—they called me on the phone. They picked up the phone and called me. On the phone! Please, just let me walk home by myself. They're going to think I'm weirder than they already do." Her voice broke at the final word.

"Are you sure you want to go?" Morrigan asked. "Karl and I are going to see if we can set up a game of ultimate monopoly in the woods. Invite Tyree. I'll bring the chocolates. Roger is letting us use his cave as jail." She waggled her eyebrows, "It'll be fun."

Viva stamped her feet like a bull, steam emanating from her flared nostrils.

"Alright then. Ten thirty is late to be walking home by yourself. Karl will be sitting nearby, but no one will see him, I promise. He blends."

"Seriously, M., he does not blend." Viva pleaded, "Tell him, please, please. Out of sight. Completely. So out of sight that the tree he's sitting in won't see him."

"I'll let him know. It'll be like he doesn't even exist. What a fulfilling parenting epoch this is for us."

Viva mumbled something under her breath.

"*Excuse me?*" Mancy Morrigan straightened and raised a threatening eyebrow, which sent Viva quickly to the door.

"*Okay! See you later. Bye!*" Viva dashed out of the house.

She passed the oak in the front yard, and into the snarling, living garden. A lively garden was the mark of a responsible mancy, M. often said. After all, she would add, how could you ever expect the plants to cultivate and clean up after themselves if you always did it for them. No, a real mancy knew how to teach discipline, responsibility, basic life skills. So, Viva, feeling as though she could benefit from a good machete, pushed herself from the yard and onto the path.

Summer was dry; her shoes kicked up puffs of dirt as she walked quickly downward. Don't walk too fast, she told herself—don't seem too excited.

Be cool.

Be cool.

Be cool.

Her mind spun. How did a person walk cool, stand cool, smile cool, laugh cool? She was in the middle of testing out her coolest laugh, "*Hahaha*"—not too many teeth, don't widen the eyes—when she heard a, "*Hey!*" in front of her.

In a pang of horror, she realized that she had been grinning like a constipated hyena at her shoelaces while popping down the path in a cloud of dust—probably not the coolest behavior—but the rising humiliation subsided when

Tyree stepped out from the Daisy House and jog towards her. It was just Ty.

"Hey," she tried out a cool grin.

"What's wrong with you?" Tyree had caught up to her and handed her a fresh cookie. "Just out of the oven—what do you think?"

"Thanks. And nothing's wrong with me. Where are you going?"

"Bridget's. Isn't that where you're going too?"

"Oh, yeah. Yeah, I am. Cool." She tried to incorporate a smooth, iced edge to her words.

"We can walk back together afterward too."

"Yeah, sure. Maybe. Hey, this is good. New recipe? I thought you made truffles today."

"I did both!" He smiled a twisted scarecrow smile and puffed his chest out, causing him to tower over Viva like a golem. "I used the cookie recipe that Karl taught me as a base and added a little of my own flair." He twirled in a clunking spin that resembled something a hippopotamus would have tried during a dance audition. It would not receive a callback. Viva laughed spectacular purple into the warm night.

Bridget lived in town. Historically, Viva thought of town as the place for school and chores, and the more traditionally uninteresting parts of the day-to-day. She and Tyree, and certainly Morrigan and Karl, made it a habit to limit town time because it was boring. Though ever since Viva had learned how to use the computer in elementary school, Morrigan had tasked her with the computer-related work at their office. Viva would go after school to print bingo sheets and bird identification in a khaki shirt and shorts, an oversized safari hat drooping below her eyes, watching the other grownups move about the offices, rarely lending her a glance. Town was boring.

Up the path and in the woods, there was hunting for ghosts in the hill's caves; searching for naiads in the woods around her house; there was tree racing, wildlife viewing, stargazing, campfires, and Karl's experimental s'mores. There was none of that in town. Sure, the sock store could provide a person with a few chuckles, but up the path: that's where real life had always been. Until tonight. Tonight, Viva had been invited to a house, a friend's house…well, a classmate's house, but Viva was fairly certain that friendship was on the table.

As Tyree and Viva turned off the main road and onto a sidewalk that would eventually lead to Bridget's house, they discussed school—had Tyree done his summer homework yet because Viva certainly had not found the time—her summer schedule was full to the absolute brim. Tyree's parents had gone out of town again, so Viva invited him to stay with them at the Mancy House until their unforeseeable return; he grinned and said that Karl had collected his weekend bag that afternoon. They laughed about the large brown bear named Roger who lived deep in the woods. The poor thing had a terrible sense of time and every few years, accidentally hibernated in the spring and fall—sometimes even through summer—and come winter, would go into an apocalyptic frenzy.

Earlier that morning, Morrigan had heard snoring from Roger's cave while she was on her solo peregrination through her woods. After some surveying, resource assessment, and assorted color swatches, she and Viva had begun restocking the bear-sized cellar, that Morrigan had built many years before, for Roger's use upon his awakening. Tyree was remiss at having missed out on the day's activities—he hadn't seen Roger recently and wanted to see the cellar updates, but then his face lit up and he chirped that he should bring some of his new cookies to the cellar. He bet Roger would like that.

The two of them chittered until, appearing abruptly before them, a large, tan house loomed in the darkness.

Levity fell away. Viva was all apprehension: what would happen if she went in there, what would happen if they said this or that? Was she standing wrong, had she stood here too long, how did she breathe again?

Tyree tapped her on the shoulder and smiled his lopsided smile with a cock of the head. They walked up to the large front door. Viva knocked with as much "cool" as she could manage, her knuckles barely grazing the treated wood. Tyree squinted an eye, one brow turned down towards his crooked nose, the other raised in a wordless expression: what are you doing?

A thin face with cheekbones like a freshly shucked corpse sprang into view behind the window. With a coyote squeal, Tyree jumped behind Viva, whose knuckles were still held out towards the door.

"Uh," said Viva, reaching behind her to pat Tyree's shoulder, hoping to coax him out of hiding, "Hi." She turned her fist into an exaggerated wave.

The woman, whose hair was an anemic brown, mouthed something through the window as she gestured madly like a rabid aircraft marshal. Viva grabbed Tyree's arm and led him in the direction toward which the woman was gesticulating: to the left side of the house, where they found an open wooden gate and teenage laughter filling the air in thick, cackling miasma.

"Oh my god, that will look so good, I can't even wait." A twittering voice chirped.

"It will, I know, and then after I get those fillers, I'll have to fix this whole nose situation. I can't believe that I got my mom's nose, what was she even thinking, passing on something like that? What a bitch."

The smog thickened as Tyree and Viva stepped through the gate and into a backyard complete with lounging chairs, cushioned swings, and various small tables laden with a rainbow of fizzing beverages. Three girls sat huddled together, each one studying the others' faces. Viva recognized them as Bridget, the girl who had called her up, Nicky and Nikki, two girls Viva had never learned to tell apart.

"The nose for sure, but for me, I need to do something about my jaw. And my mom said she won't pay until I'm eighteen. Is she serious?" Each sentence ended with an upward inflection like a checkmark.

"Oh my god, Tyree, you made it," Bridget beamed. Giggles rose into the haze like greasy bubbles. "Come sit next to me."

He didn't. He stepped forward, Viva's hand still clasped around his arm, and he led the way to a small bench facing the three giggling girls. Viva nestled herself next to Tyree, whose body took up much of the two-seater, and she watched the three girls who, in between sips of cherry coke, poked each other roughly in the face over and over.

"There, there and there. That's what I would fix. I mean, it's not terrible now, but it's not great. What do you think, Tyree?" Bridget cooed.

He twisted himself to regard Viva, laughter fizzing in his throat. "I dunno. I'd probably go experimental, see if they can give me gills or something." He paused, eyes glinting, "Something classy, but practical. Viva, what do you think?"

Viva snorted loudly and instantly regretted it when the sharp eyes of three harpies turned viciously towards her. That wasn't cool. "Umm," she started.

Silence is not colorless, and in the wake of the girls' sharp eye contact, it seemed crimson. Viva ran through her options, rummaging desperately through filing cabinets in her mind, overturning, shuffling, weighing, what to say, do, think?

"Ha-ha-ha…Obviously, I'm gonna… umm… dye my hair…" She grabbed a fistful of her hair, noting with a sharp pang, that she had forgotten to run a brush through it before leaving the house. Damn Karl's propensity to hunt *for treasure around the creek in matching safari hats. "I mean," She shook her handful of hair with more force than she had intended. She tried the cool laugh: Ha-ha-ha-ha, "Who would want this...right?"*

The harpies calmed, feeding on her offered insecurities, and sank back into their miasmatic giggling. Out of the corner of her eye, Viva saw Tyree raise an eyebrow at her and purse his lips. She let go of her handful of hair.

After what seemed like years of discussing the various plastic surgeries each girl at the table needed and praising Tyree for his flawless features, a comment to which Viva had very nearly choked on her mouthful of cola and asked which instance of breaking his nose had led to structural perfection, inciting a boisterous laugh from Tyree and the second installment of raptor-like eye contact from the girls, the three stood up.

"Let's walk," Bridget said.

Tyree frowned. "Walk where?"

"You live way out in the middle of nowhere, right? I want to see it."

"It's not nowhere," Viva started, and weighing her words, stuttered slightly, "I mean, it's not very far away, it's just a little bit outside town."

"In those creepy woods, right?" asked Nikki.

Viva paused in assessment and Tyree said, "They aren't creepy, and it's our backyard, mostly Viva's though." He took her hands and hoisted her up from the chair after him, and she blushed at the sweaty state of her palms. "The mancy owns those woods, you know. It's awesome there."

Nicky flipped her hair over her shoulder and tisked with a smile, "So." From above her imperfect nose, she surveyed Viva. "You live in the woods?"

Viva puffed her chest out slightly then deflated again. "Yes."

"Okay," the three girls sneered in unison. "Let's go see." Nikki turned to Tyree, placing a delicate hand on his arm, and yanked his hand from Viva's, saying, "I want to see where you live too, Tee."

Tyree shrugged his box-like shoulders and said, "Alrighty." And, freeing his hand again, waved a wayward Viva to walk in front of him, the pair led the way through town and towards the creek path.

Karl had told Viva stories of sound over the years. Sound marked comings and goings, earth's inhales and exhales. The absence of sound, Karl always emphasized in ghost story tones, was ominous. Silence is the sound of a hungry mountain lion. Silence is the sound of a predator stalking prey. Silence is powerful.

There was no sound as the group of five teens walked up the path towards the Daisy House. Silent nocturne broken only by their own footsteps on the dirt path, even those, Viva marked, sounded dull to her ear.

Silence until Bridget hissed, sibilance infused into her voice as though with a syringe, "I would hate to live up here. It's creepy. Why does the town need a mancy anymore anyway? They're so weird."

Viva heard one loud "squawk" from somewhere off to her left and rolled her eyes, but in the depths of her teenage brain, underneath a seething volcano full of molten hormones, anxiety, and angst-driven dread, Viva was glad to hear Karl nearby.

"Woah," said Nikki in a tone that suggested she had either tripped on a stone or found another area for facial improvement.

"What?" Bridget asked, slowing her pace and glancing over each shoulder as if danger could only come up dramatically from behind, "What is it?"

To their left, there was a small grassy area just off the path, ceilinged by large, green trees, and just beyond that, the bank of the creek broke suddenly into rolling water. Nikki made her way slowly off the path, "woahing" again at intervals. She crouched suddenly as if something had swooped down upon her and the rest of the group heard another slow, "Woah."

Tyree's hand clasped onto Viva's as he moved slightly behind her. Viva rolled her eyes again. Really, Tyree? They had been traipsing around the path for years; the only thing that could cause anyone to act like this would be a rabbit nibbling the grass, maybe a bat, or in an extremely unlikely event, Roger the bear. Now, that could be interesting, she thought. Viva tried not to smile, then Bridget and her lookalikes might actually need some cosmetic surgery. Viva reminded herself with a slight pang of disappointment: she wanted friends, preferably unmauled. In any case, they were still much too close to town for any real wildlife encounters, and Roger was in off-season hibernation at the moment.

174

Nicky and Bridget tiptoed off the path, gesturing to Viva and Tyree to keep up and shhhhhhh. Only Tyree and Viva didn't force a squatted sneaking position, which, Viva thought, apart from seeming hard to do, seemed to imply some sort of bowel mishap.

Nikki, still "woahing" was kneeling on the creek bank, gazing intently into the water. The word rolled out of her tumbling over itself and again into the creek followed by her unblinking gaze.

Bridget's face blanched; silence pounded in Viva's ears.

"What?" Viva said. She tried to appear stern. Tyree squeezed her hand more tightly and she tried to pull away from his bone-bruising grip. "What is it? I don't see anything." Bridget pointed a shaking index finger towards Nikki, who was rocking back and forth on the bank in rhythm with her woahs. Nicky squeaked and pulled Tyree towards her with surprising strength—if Viva had not pulled herself from his grasp, she would have lost an arm.

"I don't see anything," Tyree said as he shrugged his trembling shoulders out of the embrace. He walked slowly backwards towards the path, gesturing towards Viva. "Let's just get back. I'm sure it's nothing. In fact, I think I'm ready to call it a night."

Nikki was hunched rocking back and forth above the water. Woahwoahwoah. Her voice was the only sound ringing out. Not a rustle of leaves, not a creaking of branches, not a flutter of bats, hooting of owls, squeaking of raccoons. Woahwoahwoah.

Not a caw or croak from the trees.

Viva walked towards the huddled girl. Slowly, as though Nikki was a hissing, sputtering cat on the side of the road, Viva held out her hand like she was waiting for the girl to press a cold nose to it and determine: friend, not foe. Nikki sprang up, seizing Viva's wrist in a steel clasp. And pulled.

Viva didn't hear the world's nocturnal sounds recommence with flapping wings, or Tyree's wordless shout, or a piercing screech. Viva heard the encompassing silence of submersion as she plunged into the glassy waters of the cold, silver creek.

Not being a novice to swimming or navigating flowing waters, Viva put herself in a seated position, feet before her as rock deterrents before she felt her shoulders in a clawed hold. She was not new to the water, but she was new to attempted drowning, but that couldn't have been the intent. It had to have been an accident. She was making friends, wasn't she? Couldn't she? Karl lifted her dripping out of the water and plopped her lightly onto the deserted green. Deserted except for Tyree. There was a splotch of red blood on the bank, and the sound of cackling laughter from down the path whipped through the night.

Viva huddled herself into a ball and shook with fury, humiliation, desolation. She had just wanted to have a friend's house to go to. That was all. Was that too much to ask? She felt Tyree sit down next to her, then the enormous weight of his arm slung over her shivering shoulders.

Don't talk. Don't say anything. I don't want to talk about it. I don't want to think about it. Throw me back into the creek. I'll disappear and never have to think about this ever again. Just throw me back in.

A blanket dropped onto her from above—Karl must have sped home to fetch it for her.

No.

She would not feel Tyree's heavy arm on hers, Karl's blanket of concern, and what she knew would be Morrigan's footsteps marching down the path. She would not feel any of it. She wanted to boil in choler. Teenage magma rose inside her with bubbling humiliation and rage. Just throw me back in.

"*Wow,*" *Tyree said, breaking the silence.*

She would not answer, though Karl cocked his head.

"*You got a solid kick in, Viv.*"

"*What are you talking about?*" *Her voice dripped fire. Hissing spitting silica and ash, humiliation, wrath, and desperation. Worth. But that had sunken like a stone in the creek.*

"*You've got impeccable aim, Viva. I'll never push you into the creek again, but I think you're usually the one who gets me first.*" *Tyree laughed loud and despite herself, she felt the magma cool slightly. Tyree was fresh sailing air. "If that girl didn't need plastic surgery for her nose before, she sure does now. It looks like mine now.*" *He crinkled his nose, and in a blink, Tyree was up and in front of her, holding his hands out. Take them and get up.*

Tyree lifted Viva to her feet, Karl pushing on her back with his feet. "You got her good on your way down. That's the way to do it, that's for sure." He pointed at the blood shimmering along the bank. "Right in the face!"

A bright, luminous laugh burst out of Viva's Vulcan heart, chilling her. As Tyree turned, leading her away from the silvery creek, she noted a slight clink in her pocket. "Hang on a minute," she said, walking again towards the bank, stomping heavily on the small splotch of blood. She let her fingers roll over the items in her pocket then pulled out a tube of purple lipstick and a single silver pebble, smooth and flawless like glass. With as much force as she could muster, Viva launched the purple tube into the flowing creek and pocketed the pebble again—at least she came away with something cool tonight. She rejoined Karl and Tyree, and they walked back up the path, arm in arm in wing.

Fourteen

For Viva, the best thing about Mancy-led Adventures on Sundays was the complete lack of responsibility. All the hikers were adults who, for the most part, could fend for themselves. They ambled up the flattest part of the path, pausing once a minute for a bird sighting and to debate the observation for twenty minutes only to amble on once more. Morrigan was the lead on the Sunday trips, in charge of safety and bathroom break roundups while Viva followed at the rear, wondering about the goings-on in town. Wondering about silver.

Sundays rushed past, and it seemed only minutes until Viva was waving goodbye to the group as they swarmed Tyree's counter, zombies lumbering towards him, moaning disjointed bird calls and demands for sugar. It wasn't only children who needed to be rewarded with treats–

adults, Morrigan had explained, need incentive to finish a task just as much, if not more.

Viva made her way past the swarming elderly, down the path towards town. All she needed to do was print rosters. Yes. Print out the rosters. And check the schedule. Okay. Print out the rosters and check the schedule. And inventory the snack box. Okay... Print out the rosters, check the schedule, inventory the snack box, maps, yes maps, and. Oh shoot. She'd left the first aid kit strapped to Karl, and she needed to make sure it didn't need to be replenished. She kept her pace. She would do that in the morning. Another early morning. In and out. Rosters, schedule, snack box, maps, and coloring sheets, oh no. She had emerged from the path, crossed the parking lot, and there in front of the office building was CeCe the biter and the biter's mother. Viva inhaled deeply. No turning back now; they had definitely seen her. And exhale.

It was dark when Viva left the offices without anything printed, not knowing the schedule for the week, and having forgotten completely about the existence of snacks and without maps. How could one woman have so much lung capacity and endurance? Viva was exhausted. Dripping anxious sweat–a raccoon emerging from a storm sewer after unexpected rain: confused, angry, soaked completely through, and ravenous.

It seemed to take a year for her to trudge her way up to the Daisy House. It was dark. Of course, it was, Tyree closed at five every day, and Viva didn't want to know how far past five it was. Morrigan was sure to have gone on their nightly ghost hunt without her. What time was it? Inhale. And exha–something fluttered on Tyree's garage door, shivering slightly in the light breeze, pitter-pattering like a leaf. It was a note taped to the garage door. It said in Tyree's scrawling pen: "Missed you this evening."

Viva folded the tape back and pocketed the note, making her way through the front garden. Tyree had lit it up completely, each gnome with its own illumination; some with a roaring ceramic fire, some with a lighted hat or shoes, one with a glowing pond in which he had cast a hopeful line. Viva walked over to a gnome with a long, billowing cape drenched in illuminated stars. The witch in the garden, holding a star-topped wand and shrouded in purple robes. In her large, black cauldron was a plastic bag with two cookies and another note on which Tyree had written, "Chocolate makes everything better. No sleepwalking tonight, Karl says so."

Viva smiled and walked toward a gnome clad in dulled orange, his nose pointed straight to the heavens, a long scroll in one hand, a pen held loosely in the other. Viva unstuck the pen from his grip, took a Sunday morning birdcall pamphlet from her pocket, and wrote: "Thanks for the cookies. See you tomorrow" before replacing the pen and plopping the pamphlet into the witch's cauldron. She then walked her cookies across the path, over the swath of green, and to the bank of the creek.

Inhale. She sat, wondering how it had become so dark, so fast. The creek flowed. Exhale.

People think of night as black, and sure, Viva thought: it was dark–that was the habit of night, but as she sat on the bank of the creek under the stars, the moon, the dark reflecting on the surface of quivering wavelets, it wasn't black. Black had never been the word that came to mind when sitting with the night. Night along the creek, through the woods, around her cabin, in the garden–of course, she had been walking through the hills, woods, garden with an experienced mancy since she could remember, but in her memory, the night was never black. Purple, she thought, that was night. A very deep shade of course, but listening to the cool water trickling by, breathing in, she felt purple calm. Viva opened the package Tyree had left, the smell of chocolate rising into amethyst tranquility.

Her heart beat.

What was that? Viva's muscles tensed. Some sort of rustle? Or shuffle of pebbles over the unpacked trail? Did she hear breath? In low and steady out? Her stomach jolted as she tried to calm her breath so that she could hear. A shadow fell over her. She heard the purling water, the incandescence of twinkling stars, the beating moon across the sky. But she didn't hear him until he spoke. Warm and sweet.

"Oh my god–" Viva clutched her racing heart in the amaranthine dim. "Where did you come from?"

He was standing like a shadow on the path. With amber honey, he said, "I've always enjoyed a stroll in the evening, and to tell you the truth, I heard about a bakery up this way and wanted to explore it–see if I could find something delicious." His voice, hair, skin all of him was glistening gold.

Viva turned back to the creek, feeling a warm, golden glow wash over her, feeling the water pull and pull and pull at her mind. She said quickly, the words rushing from her, "Ty closes at five, but he'll be open tomorrow around six a.m." She felt a sharp tug behind her lungs before another wave of glistening calm. "Here." She breathed, glancing at him. "You can have this–it's from the shop." She tore her eyes away and pulled out one of the cookies, breaking it in half, strands of melted chocolate fell over her hand. Red and dripping. No. She focused her eyes. It was just chocolate, thick and almost black. She held it out to him.

Take it. The creek rolled invariably downward in the black night.

Karl

*I*t had been a week since Morrigan and Lucy's mother, Mancy Regum, insisted that Karl join her and Morrigan in mancy training. He felt silly at times, being outdone by Morrigan—he was eighteen after all, and she was only ten, but he was learning. Lucy had no interest in mancying and spent much of her time at the hospital where she worked. Karl thought he was doing well. It was all about choosing the right words, the right tones, the right incentives to convince the magic floating throughout the world to do as he asked. It was all focus, breath, and focus.

Please, raise the egg, he thought as he stared uselessly at the motionless eggs on the counter. He felt Lucy's presence behind him, her steady eye like radiation; a shiver flashed through him. Focus, he thought, please raise the egg, breathe and focus.

The egg wiggled. Yes. Thank you, yes, he thought loudly. Focus. Focus. Now, just a little—the shell cracked in a sharp, white seam. No, no, not yet. It wiggled faster, rising through the air, yes—oh. Whoops. Lucy moved aside *just in time, as the egg, instead of breaking nicely into the pan below, shot past Karl's ear to where her head had been moments before, and then it spattered all over the wall behind them. Hardly noticing the egg-stained wall, Lucy's eyes hadn't moved from Karl. The blue-gray feeling washed over him.*

Morrigan shot into the kitchen. "You're not good at this," she said, a sharp gleam in her onyx eyes.

Karl shrugged his mountainous shoulders, simultaneously placing another egg in the spot the last one had begun its journey and picking up a rag–damp already with three previous egg casualties. He made to wipe up the latest loss, but Morrigan put up her hand. "Don't," she said, "I want to try." Arms akimbo, she brought her nose so close to the wall it almost touched the egg guts. Morrigan scrunched her face and stared. The egg on the wall slowly came together, the drips crawling upward to the epicenter, sparking purple flashes as it did.

Satisfied with her magic, Morrigan's lips twisted up into a wicked smile, but in a flash, Lucy grabbed an egg from the counter and smashed it–crack! –on top of Morrigan's head. Rich, fatty yolk ran down Morrigan's nose as she stared at her sister with wide, black eyes. Lucy stared back, chewing on her lower lip, eyebrows arched and eyes shining.

They were off. Like lightning. Without washing the goop from Morrigan's hair, face, ears, they raced around the cabin, leaping over the coffee table, dodging and whirling, laughing, breathless and bright. Karl felt, from the kitchen as he watched them, Lucy's laughter fill him up.

Fifteen

Viva opened her eyes. White bed, white table, white walls, white room. Teeth. She ran her tongue over her teeth, feeling the sticky sleep stuck to the roof of her mouth. She turned over and burrowed her head into her pillow. Submerging herself in down. She remembered honey flowing, a conversation of sugar. But—why couldn't she remember?

Viva pulled the comforter up past her ears. Burrowing deeper. Focus. Thick golden laughter and smiles, for her. For her. She had not been alone.

Behind her eyes, the creek whirled and turned, running around and around and around. She had been someone, been wanted. The rolling flows of it. Could be someone. Beautiful and silver. Of the creek. Dripping white teeth. The creek cascaded over smoothed glassy pebbles in her mind. Silver.

But she couldn't remember.

What couldn't she remember?

Oh, shit.

The schedules, the rosters, the snack bin the maps the everything. She had left it all for the morning, and morning was breaking into her room with a vengeance through the open window.

In the last few days—days? She had run up and down the path again and again and again and again. Viva was tired, and frazzled and fraying, and after she threw herself into yesterday's clothes, she sprinted down the path, ignoring calls of what? Of indignation, or concern, or confusion, of scolding from Morrigan as she dashed past down and down and down.

In unabashed beige, the office closed in on Viva, who sunk herself into the ancient swivel chair behind the desk. The computer blinked on, and the clock said six. It wasn't as late as she had thought it was while she was diving into clothes on the way out the door. Why had she thought it was so late? But it was early. Six? What was at six? Was there something at six? Time slammed into her in breaking waves. Her head swam with the last few days. Or weeks months years hours. She gasped for air. Or.

What time was it?

The printer ground with permanence as it spat out schedules and rosters. The sound of physicality. Tangibility. Of thick, black ink.

Dripping. Only a few more sheets and she would be back on her way—on her way up the path. Or down? A wave of exhaustion—or, or something close to it—lost time, lost sleep, lost hunger, lostlostlost—slammed into her like... like what? She couldn't think through surges of... of... of? Above and behind and aroundaroundaround.

What was one sinking soul to the ocean, she wondered, as sleep hit her in crashing waves.

Viva was tired. So tired. The printer ground, and Viva's eyes blurred into a stew of times and names and supplies on the screen. Her head jerked. Bobbing, until something akin to exhaustion—something caught up. Caught her. Consumed her.

Viva fell asleep in the swivel chair, noticed only by the beige office walls. The printer clunked to a halt.

To silence.

Silvering

She knew where she was. Who she was. Where she belonged. She smiled wide, water dripping over her open lips and into her mouth. Sweet or bitter? Thick and greasy. Viva was home.

She knew what to do. Viva would be silver.

She stepped forward and fell into the ring of rushing water.

In soundless submersion below the surface, she no longer felt the exhaustion that had preyed on her in the office. Beige leaked from her pores and was diluted in the waters.

She resigned to the current's hold. How waifish she had been before, stuck in a squeaking swivel chair—she felt an ache—

listening to the incessant whir of a printer. She wasn't tired now. She was renewed.

One more spin around her ethereal castle after, how many, she didn't know. How long had she been turning and turningturning in the water? Placidly floating forever silver.

After time, some time, little time, sands of falling time...she didn't know. The thought of time fluttered in and out of her mind and out again like flapping white wings. After time, Viva maneuvered her body so that it was vertical, and took hold of the castle-side bank. She would climb to her stronghold, emerging from the water renewed, reVivad, and she would finally enter the silver palace.

The embankment was slick and smooth, and Viva pulled herself out of the water and climbed, her fingers searching for hidden crevices, her legs burning as they pushed her up and up and up.

Almost.

She climbed to the castle, heart beating faster and faster as the palace walls grew closer, larger, brighter. Viva's hand grasped the top of the bank, but it wasn't smooth like the rest of the wall; a jagged fang bit through her water-softened hand. Blood poured from the bite, teeth still embedded in her flesh.

Huh.

It didn't hurt. It didn't sting or burn. It didn't anything. The gaping crevice between flesh wept hot and thick.

Empty.

She watched the drizzle slip down her arm—more blood than she would have imagined—but it couldn't be blood because it was liquid silver ooze dripping down her forearm.

She pulled herself up and onto the embankment, avoiding the rest of the bared teeth spaced along the edge in open-mouthed protection of the castle. Viva gazed up at it, heart beating against her sternum so fast, so hard she wondered when the bones would split.

Her palace.

Her heart beat.

With a growling of metal on metal, the portcullis rose.

She crossed the threshold.

The Weight of Silver

From the portcullis was a pebbled path lined by lustrous, silver trees sculpted to perfection. Between the trees, sheeting the courtyard to the edge of each wall was a blanket of manicured gardens. So different from any garden Viva had seen before, every petal, every leaf, branch, and stem in changeless silver perfection. She walked the path, running a finger over the petals of one stretching silver rose. It pricked cold and sharp. Viva pulled her hand away quickly, squeezing her finger tight. Dripping.

The path ended at a kingly fountain before it split off into four directions. Viva reached out to it, the water falling over her open hand. It splashed silently into a bowl of silver pebbles all reflecting a Viva who could be. Her lungs seized; she kneeled, dipping her hands into the bowl, the pebbles running through her fingers like sand through an hourglass. Each silver Viva was in a different moment of bliss. She watched herself and herself and herself. She watched who she had never been. Silver Viva enveloped in gold.

Across the courtyard was an expansive, opalescent hall, everything beyond hidden except for silky shadows, which fluttered behind glass windows that peppered the structure. Shadows like ribbons tossed carelessly to the sky. Ribbons. Silks and hangings. Swinging tapestries. Viva's mind swam with draping fabric lolling from a cabin ceiling. An image of Morrigan flashed behind her eyes accompanied by an icy stab. Silky shadows fluttered. She wanted to swim. To swim in the hall with the other dancing ribbons. Behind the silver glass. She watched herself in the pebbles. Dancing twirling sparkling. She was a shadow. She was silver. She was—

Who? ... Her... her... Viva's... Viva's mind rolled within a fuming bog, and she couldn't remember. Couldn't remember what she couldn't remember. Her hand throbbed as she spun and spun and spun. Until she fell hard to the pebbled ground. She lay outstretched in silver, and a thin, white paper tumbled lightly from her pocket. Picking it up with one hand and holding it far above her face, her body still sprawled out on the floor, she read the untidy words: "Missed you this evening." The hand holding the note dripped silver liquid.

What was this?

Images danced within the pebbles, fulfilled ghosts of belonging and worth. Tyree's face flitted behind her eyes as someone else's had done moments before. A place behind her sternum gnawed with serrated teeth. The paper dissolved into nothingness before her eyes, ashy particles drifting into the stale air. Huh.

She blinked.

She couldn't remember.

In her boggy haze, words and memory and silver whispers swam around and around and around. The void behind her eyes felt sore as she stared up at the silent fountain waters falling falling falling falling.

He materialized then, rising slowly from the fountain's pool, her golden god, his radiance making her eyes sting, while the fountain's rain splashed around him. He smiled at her in a supernovae blaze. Dazzling teeth, golden hair a halo. Perfection.

Viva's mind bobbed, gasping for a breath, then sinking again below the swell, he held something out to her. Tyree's face flashed behind Viva's stinging eyes in a sharp bite. It was a silver cookie, steaming fresh-baked heat. Viva heard the rush of moving water. Enchanted. With a breath, he split the cookie in two, jagged edges like silver teeth, and out of the break poured a stream of silver.

Her heart seeped.

Sixteen

Tyree entered the office that could only have been sponsored by the color beige holding a cup with Viva's name scrawled onto the side. Seeing her head resting on the keyboard, he frowned.

"Hey," Tyree set the drink down and tapped her lightly on the shoulder, "Viva, wake up." The woman shot up like a firework, shivering, her face beaded in sweat. "Woah." Tyree started, "You—" Viva opened her mouth and vomited onto the beige carpet below. Not sure what to do, he bent over her like a vast low-hanging cloud. "Okay, okay. Oh…Viva, what did you do to your hand?"

Viva stared blankly down at her hand through swimming, saturating fog. Her eyes reeling, teeth chattering. Where was she where was–this wasn't right, none of it was right, who are you? —senses gray and hissing with static—in the haze, her hand was thickly gloved in warm blood.

Dripping.

It didn't hurt.

"I need to go home." Homehomehome. The sound echoed silver in the beige chamber. Viva shouldered someone roughly out of her way and fell blindly to the pebbleless ground.

"Hang on, just– I'll help you get home, okay?" Tyree crouched low to support Viva's limp arm over his shoulder.

"Homehomehome," she choked through a mouth full of spit. "Who are you?"

Tyree closed the door of the beige office behind him with a click, and behind the door, a silver pebble, round and polished to perfection, tinkled lightly off the desk and onto the carpet.

Viva's head bobbed up and down, batting his shoulder with surprising force. Tyree shifted his arms, juggling the full drink–why hadn't he left it in the office–in one hand while attempting to balance her enough so as to prevent an unnecessary concussion. In his crouched position, knees almost parallel to the ground, back bent and twisted, he could feel his muscles quivering in protest–this was acrobatics, this was contortion, this was the circus.

Two bikers double-took the scene, and a small woman in running shorts removed her headphones and gripped her pepper spray canister more tightly. Tyree didn't notice. He held Viva upright, shuffling her slowly upward while attempting not to tip over under his own burning muscles. Timber.

It was as though she were half a ghost, still catching up with the idea of weightlessness; he wasn't dragging her at all, she was controlling all of her forward motion. Tyree's shoulder throbbed between twinges of sharp pain. He stopped off the side of the path by a little clearing next the creek. Just for a minute. He'd shake himself out, get a better handle on where things were in terms of weight distribution and begin the march again, but as he untangled his arm from—somehow—both beneath and over Viva's right shoulder, catching her hair in his watch for a few anxiety-ridden seconds, her eyes snapped open.

She babbled like a madwoman about papers and the printer, and being late, late, late. At that point, Viva had sprung back up to her feet. Worried that she would try to run down the path herself and get trampled by a rogue bicyclist, Tyree told her not to worry, she wouldn't be late, Morrigan had taken the morning's group already, and he would get the papers from her office. Just wait here on the grass. Be still. Don't move. What papers again? Okay great. Be right back. Like a bullet swerving through the air in lost momentum, he shot down the path.

Questions, confusion, concern bounced up and down inside of his head as he made his way towards the office again. The morning's events rolled through him like thunder, as he sped downward, his hair falling into his eyes like scattered straw.

When he reached the offices, swinging open the door as though he were busting into a den of nefarious activity–stop right there, you slippery day hike rosters, you won't get away that easy–he was again greeted by all the inglorious beige, and a burst of the creek. The scent of water. Of algae. Of silt and mud. He couldn't wonder at it–he had a job to do–Tyree scooped up the papers, which had fallen to an unorganized clump on the floor and turned to leave, but as he did, he spotted a glitter out of the corner of his eye. Plopping a silver pebble into his pocket, Tyree walked out the door, leaving the land of beige behind him.

Viva seemed to be feeling better when Tyree came back to the green spot on the bank of the creek where he had left her. But she was still pale, her eyes glazed, and Tyree put his arm around her and gently led her up the path.

Viva was quiet on the way to Mancy Manor. She had shaken off his arm and refused his hand and his tilted glances of concern with slight acidity.

She was tired, she said. Just tired. Really tired, it was probably a cold. Hadn't been sleeping well, she said. And she was sleepwalking again, with dreams. So many dreams she couldn't remember. She repeated that she wanted to go home, just go home.

"I get it, but–," Tyree said, attempting to remove any tone of concern from his voice.

Viva cut him off, "Thanks."

They had reached the Mancy Manor. The garden shifted with life, and Tyree glanced beyond toward the door and then at Viva, searching for something. She seemed better, but– "Thanks for walking me back from–" she frowned slightly as he handed her all her papers from the office, then she waved at him.

"Why don't you come to my house tonight for dinner for a change. I'll cook for you, and we can talk. Might make you feel better to get a change of scenery," Tyree said, voice wavering slightly. He handed her the cup that, by some miracle, was still full.

"Okay," she said easily, though her eyes didn't seem focused, as though she couldn't see him. Viva turned towards the cabin, weaving her way through and over boundless vegetation, finally dipping underneath an outstretched branch of the oak tree. They had eaten lunch in that tree every day for years–how many years was that? About twenty, he thought. Tyree, smiling, put his hands into his pockets and felt something smooth, glassy.

"Wait, I forgot," he called, holding out the silver pebble. "I found it in your office, and I think it might be for Karl's collection." He pulled out the stone and jogged through the garden towards her.

"Thanks." She took the pebble from him. "It's…" Her eyes glazed before she shook her head and added, "Sorry." Her voice seemed hollow, echoing tin, as though traveling from far, far away before she disappeared behind the door.

"Nothing to be sorry about," Tyree said quietly as he turned back down the path, towards his Daisy House, legs aching and shoulders pounding.

Viva

Viva was home for the weekend from college. She sat motionless on a cushion, the rich colors of the room washing her out. Sometimes in the cabin, she felt like a ghost, overtaken, overwhelmed, but she couldn't think of that now, now, she was fixed resolutely on his eyes, silver, and shimmering. They were Christmas ornaments in dead night, glinting off nothing but starlight. She should be able to see herself in the silver depths, but they were not mirrors to this world. They were matte and void. Two white lids closed over them asynchronously. Blink. blink.

"What, Karl? What?" Viva broke the stare; her voice was husky in her throat. She pulled at her shirt sleeves uncomfortably. "M., please? Can he just…?"

Karl squawked, his dragon tongue hissing with his gravel cadence.

Mancy Morrigan Regum sat on a ruby beanbag chair, statuesque, but her eyes shined. Without moving her steepled fingers from the front of pursed lips, she said, "No Viva. You haven't been here for dinner in over a week, and we *want to know why. We deserve to meet your friends. Do you remember who kept you clothed and fed all those years? I think we have the right to ask a few questions."*

Morrigan turned to a shifting shadow that was attempting to both find its bearings within its own beanbag chair while simultaneously hiding behind Viva's rigid body. It had, in its fifth attempt to stand and reseat itself, caught its arm in a mauve, drapery hanging above it, and was now fairly horizontal in its struggle. Viva reached behind her to help untangle the pitiable thing and pulled its seat closer to hers.

The shadow, coming into focus, was a young man whose general demeanor was as though he had found himself slathered in barbeque sauce and standing in Roger the bear's cellar–post-hibernation. The boy had thin brown hair. Delicate and brittle. It fell listlessly down his long forehead, stopping abruptly above his eyebrows which were thin as a whisper. He had finally found balance in his seat but couldn't figure out what to do with his lanky, pony legs. His arms, now free of the hanging fabric, hung spiritless by his sides, his knuckles nearly grazing the ground.

Viva glanced at him. He was fine, no problem.

She fixed her eyes determinedly on Morrigan and slowly mimicked Morrigan's steepled fingers, raised an eyebrow of her own, and said firmly, "Yeah, okay. Fine. Let's just–"

Karl cawed again and shot from his bay window roost into the kitchen, his tailfeathers grazing the top of the cowering boy's head, mussing up the wispy hairs so they stuck up as though from electroshock. Morrigan's eyes exploded in laughter. The mancy blinked, and in what she must have believed was a hostess-like voice, asked, "Viva told you about Karl? I apologize for his manners, but he is the man of the house, in a manner of speaking. Does what he wants and all that." Seeing the boy's fearful expression, the mancy added, "We can't lock him outside, or put him in a birdcage, no matter how much we want to. It's a curse..." Her voice trailed off like smoke.

The young man's response was watery: "Yes. Umm. Ma'am—"

Mancy M.'s voice trampled him like a hippopotamus with a vendetta. "I'm not ma'am. I'm Mancy. Mancy Morrigan if you have the time, and I suggest you spare it."

Magma inside of Viva's spirit churned, rising to her throat, and into her cheeks. "M.!" she tried hard to exclaim viciously.

"What?" Morrigan's hippopotamus had found its new target and reared again. "You wouldn't roll your eyes like that at a doctor. You wouldn't roll your eyes like that at a lady knight or whatever you'd call her. Knightress?"

The heat in Viva's face blazed. "You think you're like a knight? Are you serious? Like King Arthur or something?"

Mancy Morrigan moved for the first time; she carefully folded her hands in her lap. "Viva. King Arthur was a king... that's the 'king' part of King Arthur, and I'm much more interesting than he could ever hope to be. Please. It's just manners. Now that's enough. Henry, was it?"

Knees now pressed to his chin, he choked, "Yes, ma'a... Mancy."

Mancy Morrigan smiled. "See Viva, it's easy. Henry, do you go to the college in town too? Are you taking the same classes as Viva?"

Realizing himself to be the center of unwanted attention, the boy denoted "Henry" shifted his legs underneath him, so that he resembled a constipated frog. "Umm. No, ma'a— Mancy. No, I'm working on my degree in meteorology, so all my classes are in different buildings than Viva's... Mancy."

Morrigan eyed him up and down. "How did you two meet if you aren't in any of the same classes?"

He said, "We met when we were both getting coffee from Tyree's Daisy House one day. It's that place that's just down the path from here."

Viva shifted toward the boy, who was now attempting to become the bean bag chair he was sitting in. "So, M., I told you that we can't stay for dinner, right?" Karl squawked indignantly from the kitchen. "I know, I know, I'm sorry," Viva said more loudly than she needed to. "But we promised a few of Henry's friends that we would meet them at a restaurant before the movie, and huh—" she stood up, took Morrigan's watchless wrist in her hand, studied it thoroughly, and clicked her tongue— "We'll be late if we don't leave now, so we're going to go, okay?"

Morrigan didn't move.

Another squawk sounded from the kitchen as something crashed against another something.

The mancy raised her eyebrows and tugged her wrist from Viva. After a few moments of waiting for something that the mancy knew wouldn't come, she sighed. "Yes, okay, all right, but Henry"– she turned to the boy, who had finally managed to dislodge his rear end from the chair, only to fall like a newborn pony, face on the floor, one leg still entrapped in the chair– "You can come over here this weekend."

Henry uttered a "mmmppfhh" as he stood, tugging his leg from the depths of the chair. Hair ruffled fuzz atop his head, a few loose ends clinging desperately to his forehead, he muttered, "Yes ma'a–Mancy."

Viva took him by the sleeve and led him out the door. "Bye."

The door popped closed behind her, and Mancy Morrigan let out a long breath, "Karl, it's just us again, so how about steak?" Karl flapped his wings wide; the kitchen came to life.

***

Viva and Henry were silent as they walked down the creek path, towards civilization. Viva's mind flitted back and forth from apologies for Morrigan, explanations for Karl, and excuses for herself.

She shouldn't have brought him there. She had known it would be a disaster, but Morrigan finding him somewhere on a random Tuesday would have been worse. She should have hired a stranger to pretend to be–well, she didn't know any strangers. She should've convinced Tyree to lose twenty pounds, stand on his tippy toes, dye his hair, wear a fake nose...no. It was always going to be a disaster.

The first guy willing to actually walk into her house, and that was the reception. She should have just snuck him in through the window for a quick one-room tour and pushed him right back out. She should have told him her house was haunted, or on fire, or that she lived alone in a car on the side of the road. That she lived in the woods.

What had she been thinking?

Of course, she'd given him the usual "We're not exactly normal spiel, but it didn't seem like it had been enough.

It was never enough.

Here was to dying alone, buried in a sea of beanbag chairs and tapestries, waiting to rest in peace while Morrigan and Karl argue about the menu for my wake. But no one would come to that anyway.

Henry walked beside her, his arms barely moving at his sides, eyes fixed on his shoes, which she hadn't noticed before, were at least a size too big for his feet.

"Hey," she said softly, so as not to startle him out of his reverie, "I'm sorry for M. and Karl back there. They mean well—probably—they're just..."

"Yeah," his shoes were fascinating apparently.

"They're just odd. Harmless, and M.'s great, you just have to get to know her. I mean—" Viva laughed— "She doesn't get any less weird, just more fun, so it evens out." She tried to catch his eye. "You know, she's taught me some incredible things. We go on adventures all the time—I told

you about her business, right? Mancy-led adventures? You should come with us sometime."

He smiled weakly. "Yeah, no. It's cool. Families, right?"

Okay, Viva thought. Okay, great. It was all fine. Yeah, families. She breathed in and touched his hand, which had begun swinging ever so slightly with his gait. "So, where are we meeting your friends? I'm excited to meet them."

"Oh." He smiled and pocketed his hands. "Sure. They're cool. Nice and all. I can't remember the name of the place we're meeting them though. Some restaurant, I think. I know where it is, just not the name. It's a little farther down the path—next to that store that sells only socks."

Viva smiled. "Oh, I know that one. It's M.'s favorite store. She hates going into town, but sometimes when I go to our office to do some of the computer stuff, she waits for me at the sock store and then we walk around." She chuckled. "I'm pretty sure if she could, she would only wear socks all the time. One time," she said, as her eyes glittered in memory, "We brought Karl with us because M. thought that he would get out of the house more in the winter if he wasn't so cold, and she convinced them to sell her a bunch of single socks with different patterns and designs on them. She told them she couldn't just buy pairs because she didn't want Karl's closet to resemble a psychopath's, and that only crazies buy two of every article of clothing, and she wasn't about to live with a nut."

Henry kicked a pebble as he shuffled forward. Viva continued, "M. cut off the toe of each sock and made holes for his wings, and she let me decorate them all with glitter and beads—this was when I was little. We only ever tricked him into wearing one once, and he looked like the craziest sock puppet you've ever seen. We pretty much destroyed the house trying to catch him to take the thing off. We've still got all of them for the little hikers to play sock puppets with if their parents are late picking them up." Henry's eyes were still on the path in front of him, hands stuffed deep into his pockets. Viva's voice trailed off. "Anyway, I know where the sock store is, and I think that restaurant is called Buon Cibo, but it might be something else."

Henry kicked another pebble, removed one hand from his pocket, wiped his nose, and said, "Yeah." He went to kick another stone but missed. "Cool," he said, "Well, I think you'll like all these guys. It'll be four of them, Tom, Joe, Nancy, and Roy. They're good guys. They're in the same department as me, and we went to high school together."

"Cool," said Viva, mimicking his tone and nodding along with her steps. "And then we're going to a movie?"

"Yep. Should be good." He turned the bend, leading the way under the arboreal archway: the threshold into town. She pointed out their office space as they walked by, and then they were silent. The air transformed from fresh and exhilarating to a bouquet of food, drink, people, and merchandise.

They were in town now, and even though it was still light out, the streetlights were beaming, twinkle lights arrayed the main road and each doorway they passed. Catchy slogans and artsy logos with overambitious company names adorned the storefronts, like apotropaic magic, as if the more colorful and odder the name, the more successful it would be. Talismans and good luck charms.

Henry led the way down the street to a small building that mimicked Italian architecture in a way that implied zero knowledge of the country. Viva thought it was a bit like the oversized oven into which Hansel and Gretel shoved a cannibalistic witch. The light from inside the restaurant shone through the seams of the steel front door. Orange and warm.

Henry opened the door and walked through. Viva had been, not admiring the building, but wondering about it, and had to skip after him to reach the door before it closed.

"Hurry up," Henry said, as he walked forward, deeper into the restaurant. "This way. I see them there in the back. He took her hand in his for the first time that evening and pulled her through rows of empty tables until they reached a dark booth at the back of the place.

The booth was stuffed with four people. Faces were ominously shadowed by a candle flickering in the middle of the table next to a basket of bread and a wine list. "Everyone" –Henry released her hand and squeezed himself onto the edge of the booth and motioned towards her– "This is Vivian Regum." Their eyes snapped up at her, then back to their original occupations. A murmur of "hellos" and "nice to meet yous" reverberated above the table as Viva searched for a spot to place herself.

The woman who must have been Nancy smiled at her from the center of the booth. "Vivian, it's great to meet you. We've been telling this one to meet someone for ages." She smiled, "Pull up a chair. Sorry about that, they didn't have anything else open tonight, so we had to take this table."

Viva surveyed the empty restaurant. "No problem. It's great to meet you all." The hostess yawned at the door-front podium. Viva picked up a chair from a nearby table, "I actually go by Viva, not Vivian. I mean, my name is Vivian, but everyone calls me Viva, so…"

Nancy smiled again as Viva sat down at the newly designated head of the table and turned to Henry. "Henry, since we got here early, we put in our orders already, but don't worry, we ordered your usual." She turned to Viva, "Viva, I'm sure you can still put in your order when the waiter comes back. They took the menus, but just go ask for one. We put in appetizer orders too, so you can have some of that to pick at. So, Henry, what did you do before coming here?"

Viva had questions. Questions like: What do you mean there were no other tables? Questions like, you really couldn't have waited two minutes to order when we arrived? Questions like, so should I just leave? She didn't belong here, and that wasn't a question. But the conversation was flowing now at the booth, swishing back and forth like cool water, and even if she had wanted to interject, to protest, to fight, the current was moving too swiftly.

No one seemed to notice as Viva stood and made her way towards the hostess stand, its occupant hardly able to keep her eyes open, she heard Nancy's full, liberated laughter crack through the room. Just a bad first impression, Viva told herself. Maybe Henry hadn't told them she was coming? Maybe they had forgotten. Maybe…

When she came back, menu acquired, the table was adorned with oversized, oversauced, and over-salted pasta dishes and a few side salads. Nancy's voice cut through the sound of clinking plates and silverware. "Ah! You found a menu, that's great. I'm sure the waiter will be back any minute. Here—she pushed a small dish of olives towards Viva— "Help yourself." Her small teeth shone from across the table in the candlelight.

Henry passed Viva a fork. "I guess you can have a few bites of mine too if you want."

What should she do? Leave? Would that make a scene? Stay and order when the waiter came back? They had a movie to get to, would she be blamed for being late? Should she just ask for an empty plate? Was that presumptuous? "No," she chewed her lower lip, "No, thank you, I'm fine. I had a big lunch earlier. I'm still full, actually."

"Great," Henry said, pulling his dish back towards him and continuing his conversation with the boy next to him—was that Tom, or Joe, or Roy? Or someone else? Viva willed herself to melt into her chair, or at least into the shadows cast by the single candle, flickering weakly.

She wished she was at home with Morrigan and Karl arguing over who got the last piece of whatever it was that Karl cooked tonight. It was probably delicious—food wouldn't dare not be when he was in charge.

Her stomach growled and heat crawled over her neck and into her cheeks. It was too dark for anyone to see her face, blushing like a little girl. Just get through this dinner. Maybe she could just sneak out from the group while they walked to the theater, grab a burger, find a cave to crawl into for the next year? She could hibernate with Roger for a season or two.

Her mind whirred, but nobody asked her any questions. Nobody directed the conversation towards her. Her mind was free to roam.

It seemed like both forever and no time at all before Henry prodded Viva's shoulder and told her that it was time to leave. She noticed for the first time how thin his mouth was, like someone had sliced his face open leaving the wound untreated. Festering. His thin hair. His limby carriage. His weak voice. He was trying to smile, she thought, his mouth was opening at a seam, revealing a black, gaping nothing beyond. "Don't worry," he breathed, "You can just pay me later for the food."

"Oh," Viva said, standing up and putting her chair back at its original table. "Okay."

It had been dark for about an hour. Twinkle lights illuminated the sidewalk, as the six of them walked towards the theater. Streetlights illuminated the concrete path, allowing the many wayfarers in town to pop in and out of shadows like superheroes on an off night. She should have brought a jacket. The cold burrowed through her sweater; every hair on her arms stood alert. The five others continued in conversation, but she was content to walk at the back, a little behind Henry, watching the lights blink and shimmer. Watching the town. Friends laughing together, the couples hand in hand. It seemed that the street was in full bloom tonight. People eating and drinking and sharing stories, jokes, laughter, and love. She smiled to herself. It was nice to see joy outside, meandering through the streets, lingering in doorways, hovering in glances and touch. She missed Morrigan and Karl. She missed Tyree. Viva wanted to go back home.

Henry's wavering voice sawed through her ruminations: "What?"

It took a moment to collect herself, to remind herself where she was. Henry and the other four people in front of her had stopped. They had reached the theater, and they were frowning at her. "Oh." She tried to make her voice soft and light. Make it jingle like bells, benign, lovely, be lovely. "It's a nice night out." Be cool.

Henry pursed his razor-sliced lips. "Yeah. I guess it is. Ready?"

Nancy and the guys entered the theater. "Yep," she said, "What are we seeing again?"

Oh!" he exclaimed, "It's great. It's this movie about a robot who learns how to feel emotions, but he can't stand it, so then he has to find someone to kill him because his programming won't let him kill himself. It's incredible!

That's what Rob and Nancy said. They saw it last week, and I've been wanting to go ever since."

Viva nodded and followed him to the ticket counter.

"One, please," Henry held up his index finger at the teenager selling tickets. He shot Viva a thumbs up. "You need me to wait for you, or can I go get popcorn?"

"Can you wait?" Viva asked, digging through her purse, "I'll just be a second—one ticket for the same, yeah, that one."

The teen poked some buttons on an ancient computer screen. "That'll be ten dollars, miss."

"Sure." Viva started to pour the contents of her purse out onto the counter, "Hang on, it's got to be somewhere."

"Vivian…" Henry shot an uncomfortable glance at a couple who had lined up behind her. "Come on, let's go. You're embarrassing me."

"Hang on a second. I can't find my wallet. I know it's in here. I grabbed it before we left my house."

"I'm going to go get popcorn. I don't want to miss anything." Henry was shifting back and forth like a kindergartener moments away from wetting his pants.

"It'll just be a second. Can I borrow the money and pay you back?"

Henry straightened and turned a bright red. "No, Vivian. You still owe me for dinner. You know what, maybe you should just call it a night."

Viva stopped her search. "What?"

"Well," Henry hesitated, "You haven't really been all that friendly tonight, and I'm going to miss the previews, so

maybe you should just call it a night. Okay?" He began to walk backwards through the open theater doors, his gangly limbs lolling back and forth as he said, "Sorry, Vivian, but I'll call you."

He walked away.

Viva felt her face hot and reddening. Don't cry, don't cry, don't cry. The pressure behind her eyes was building, and she knew she was shaking. Okay okay okay, it's fine. This is fine. Breathe.

Clearing her throat loudly, choking on tears and shame, she packed up her purse as quickly as possible and apologized to the teen, who was still holding a ticket out to her, and to the couple behind her, who averted their eyes as she passed them.

"It's Viva," she mouthed.

It was too much.

She could feel them, the tears hot and intrusive, welling up behind her eyes.

"Sorry," she mouthed. "Sorry."

***

The trip back up the creek was blurred by humiliation, or was it shame? Why couldn't she belong? She didn't know if she had run, skipped, or crawled back, but she was at the front door of Mancy Manor, hearing Morrigan's roaring laughter from within. She couldn't force herself to go further, to open the door, to be met by Karl and M., to see their questioning eyes. Maybe Morrigan would grin. She always knew everything before it happened. She would say: "Should've stayed home. Should've helped Karl with crepes, or whatever he was cooking. Should just accept your spinster fate."

No. Morrigan wouldn't say that, would never think it.

She would say that Viva should've kicked that boy in the shins for being such a jerk. And his little friends too. Morrigan would call the restaurant about the wallet, and Karl would go to the theater to teach those kids a lesson.

Still, she couldn't go inside. She would call the restaurant herself tomorrow about her wallet; she couldn't go back tonight. She wouldn't.

The creek gurgled from across the path, and Viva turned from the cabin's front door. She walked down the path and stopped across from the Daisy House. Clambered down the small slope beyond and sat down on the grassy bank. Shoes off, socks off, eyes closed. She dipped her feet in the water, and let the cold permeate her body. If she felt only cold, she couldn't feel anything else, no humiliation, no shame, only cold.

"What are you doing?" A voice came from the path behind her.

Viva jumped and opened her eyes. "Ty!" She caught her breath. "You almost gave me a heart attack. What are you doing?"

"I was on my way to ask Karl to try my new cookie recipe." He lifted an overloaded plate as evidence and smiled his twisted scarecrow smile, button eyes twinkling. "So... what are you doing?" He made his way carefully down to her, sat on the bank, handed her a cookie off the top of the pile, and placed the plate carefully in his lap, ensuring there was no sugary landslide as he did so.

"Long story. I don't want to talk about it–I lost my wallet." She took a bite of the cookie, realizing how hungry she was–she hadn't eaten dinner, she remembered with a surge of humiliation. She swished her feet in the water again–remember the cold.

"Where did you lose it?" Ty said, carefully selecting a cookie for himself.

"Oh, in town. I left it at that restaurant, you know, the one by the sock store?" Viva swished her feet again. "I'll get it tomorrow; I couldn't do it tonight–but it's okay."

"That place is gross, but I love the sock store. Didn't you guys try to dress Karl up in one once? You came to school covered in scratches and the teacher called the counselor."

"Oh yeah, I forgot about that. That's the maddest I've ever seen Morrigan. Top five at least." Her feet were numb, and the cold had stopped shooting through her.

"Well," Tyree continued as he took a bite of his cookie, "I'm going to the sock store tomorrow, you want me to get your wallet?"

"Really?"

"Sure. It's right there. Easy."

"That would be incredible, but I'll go with you, and I'll buy you a pair of good socks while we're there."

He laughed. "Sure. I'll be moral support."

"Thanks for the cookies." She lifted her numb feet out of the water and crossed them in front of her, rolling a small, *silver pebble on the bank around with her big toe. "Oops, sorry for splashing you."*

"Nothing to be sorry about," said Tyree as he plucked another cookie from the pile.

Seventeen

Deep metallic voices blared from the clamor of the kitchen when Viva walked through the door. She navigated straight back to her bedroom and collapsed onto her bed. She tried in exhausted futility to sleep.

After a few hours of laying in the place between unconsciousness and waking, she walked into the main room of the cabin. Morrigan was staring at her with the intensity of a hawk, rabbit in sight.

"My god," Viva said through a black and industrial soup that seemed to have spattered her brain with an oily sheen. She squinted through the brume into Mancy Morrigan's sharp eyes as she walked through the living room and sat down next to the mancy. "What? Viva said.

"Nothing at all," said Morrigan. They sat together for a long time, listening to Karl busy in the kitchen and saying nothing until Morrigan asked innocently, "Did you see Tyree today?" At

Tyree's name, something gurgled in Viva's mind, swimming through the oily vapors. There was something she needed to do. Somewhere she needed to be. Somewhere out there somewhere not in the cabin. She walked into the kitchen where Karl was heatedly debating the meaning of "pulse," with the blender. The oven clock blinked, blinked, blinked in defense of its electrical comrade.

"I've got to go," Viva said patting Karl on the head as he cawed gratingly at a pot near overflow. She trotted into the living room and crouched down to squeeze Morrigan, whose obsidian gaze followed her movements like the tip of a blade. "I've got to go. Bye. Bye, Karl." The door closed behind her with a soft click. It was a few moments before Morrigan moved.

With a deepening furrow, she made her way to the cactus at the entryway, reached into the pot, the plant's needles parting to avoid her hand. Meticulously opening the jar and scattering the banish mixture at the thresholds of the cabin, Morrigan called out above the din, "Don't disturb the banish on your way back in."

Tyree

A monster at the door! Tyree shot up, his heart pounding against his little chest. The television in front of him blurred black and white fuzz, and he felt the same static behind his eyes. It was a school night. He needed to get back to sleep. As he stretched his arms above his head, a hole in the belly of his lemon-lime t-shirt yawned with the strain. He should have stayed at the mancy's house. He rolled himself off the couch. It wasn't scary there. It was warm, and Karl told him stories to help him sleep. After Viva and Morrigan were fast asleep in their rooms, Tyree would lay on a mountain of pillows in front of the roaring fire, a soft chamomile hum in the air. He would whisper to the feathery shadow in the bay window, "How about a story about wolves," and Karl would tell one. "I want to hear a story about dragons," and Karl would tell one; "I want to hear a story about love." Again and again, until Tyree fell asleep, deep in safe, feathery, repose. In the mancy's house, it wasn't like here.

His parents had been asleep for hours, and as they slept silently at the back of the house, Tyree's stomach had lurched at the midnight sounds beyond his bedroom window, his heart beating faster and faster, imagination wild, so he had walked downstairs, turned on the television, and barricaded himself beneath a large quilt. Now he was awake. The TV screen was fuzzy, and the doorknob was wiggling.

A shriek echoed silently in his head.

The doorknob was wiggling. Tyree's heart leaped into his throat. He swallowed, peeking over the back of the couch—his only barricade—and he wrapped the quilt around him. Every knight needed armor, even the ten-year-old ones. The doorknob jiggled; whoever was trying to break into his house knew how to milk suspense. Maybe the monster trying to get in was scared too, but what would scare a monster? Tyree felt the suspense running down his neck in cold sweat.

The door swung open, and Viva Regum stood in the doorway, illuminated by moving shadows from the fizzing television screen. Tyree screeched. The little girl, hair in serpent-like knots at the top of her head, walked up to the boy, took his hand, and heaved him from his bed and out the door, quilted armor and all.

Outside in the purple darkness, Tyree saw his garden illuminated by thousands of fireflies. Someone had arranged his gnomes around the garden in small groups surrounding various stumps and flower patches as though they were sitting at rustic cafe tables, chatting about the recent goings-on in the creekside town.

Half of the woodland tables were laden with cups and saucers, the fireflies illuminating the tables in candlelight ambiance. There was a flapping to his left. Karl, wings extended, gently maneuvered a teacup in front of a sneering gnome with an eyepatch.

Tyree's eyes met the mancy's. Morrigan Regum had seated herself with a group of stein-hoisting revelers, and she was sipping something from a porcelain cup. She winked one of her hard, dark eyes at him as Viva led Tyree over to her. His fingers tingled in Viva's tight hold. Morrigan motioned to a stump next to her. "Have a seat. Karl will bring you a hot chocolate." The Elysian crow placed a porcelain cup in front of Tyree, and with an inexplicable blue flourish, the cup filled up with thick, hot chocolate, marshmallows rising from the depths like glaciers. He thanked Karl with a sleepy smile and turned to Morrigan. "Viva's sleepwalking," she said, before taking another sip.

"Oh," said Tyree, sipping his chocolate with care. "Should we wake her up?"

"Oh, no." Morrigan slid a plate of cookies towards him. "It's no good waking a sleepwalker. She won't die or anything, but it seems like she's having a nice time, doesn't it? She needs a good night's sleep, and we're right here with her. We'll make sure she's okay." Tyree thought he saw a smile twitch at the edge of the mancy's lips. "I will say, she's more elaborate than most sleepwalkers. Wouldn't leave the house without the teapot and she's been insisting that everything be just right. Karl's been helping to make sure nothing ends up in pieces."

"Couldn't you just mancy it back together if something broke?" asked Tyree, still in awe of the fireflies that were clustering around the gnome tables like luminescent waiters.

Morrigan appeared thoughtful. "Technically, but why waste all of that energy on something so mundane? Better not to break anything in the first place, isn't it?" Tyree frowned, and she must have seen his questions. "Mancying is exhausting, Tyree," she said, "Do you sprint around at full speed to get from your living room to your bedroom? No, because it would be tiring and frankly, useless. So, you walk."

"But Karl does it. He just filled up my cup."

"Karl practices. Do you think you could skip up a mountain tomorrow? Or swim all the way up the creek right now?"

"No." Tyree watched the mancy shift in her seat.

"Correct. Karl regularly does three things: he sleeps, he eats, and he mancies. That's how you become an athlete, and I'm not currently very well-trained, and I haven't scheduled a long nap for tomorrow, so let's just refrain from breaking anything, deal?

"Okay." He sipped his drink. "What do we do now?"

Morrigan watched the little girl carefully tuck a napkin into the shirt of a gnome with a butcher's knife then scold another for not washing its hands.

"We have a tea party," Morrigan said and held up her cup, clinking it lightly against Tyree's.

After two more hot chocolates and twelve more marshmallows, Karl determined all the tea party attendees *to be well taken care of. He landed next to Tyree and Morrigan, nipping at the cookies. Viva eventually sat down with them while Karl told a vivid story about the ghost in the town's only grocery store—doomed for eternity to shift items in the store every so often. The four of them laughed and drank and ate at the tea party at the witching hour, illuminated by fireflies in a garden of gnomes.*

Tyree watched Viva finally curl herself onto Morrigan's lap, breath steadying in slumber. "Well," whispered Morrigan, "Time to go to bed." Her eyes smiled softly as she picked up the girl. "Thanks for joining us, Tyree, Viva wouldn't have been able to rest without you. Come by for breakfast before school tomorrow." Karl croaked in agreement.

Tyree nodded and watched the mancy carry Viva back up the path towards their cabin. "Karl?" he asked.

The crow, three cups held in each clawed foot, clicked.

"If I help you clean up, can you tell me a story about fireflies?"

The two cleared the somnambulist tea party blanketed by stars and stories.

Eighteen

Viva felt a pulsing sensation rush, rush, rush, time, dreams, memory, reality slipping, and when she stepped out the door, Mancy Manor behind her and all in it evaporated above her; she wondered at the hour. She wondered where she was going. Where she was. Somewhere in the back of her mind, behind a sheer veil were the day month year. While she was lost in time and space, a figure came into view.

"Hello, Vivian." He shimmered divine, all of him scintillating gold. He held out a hand to her.

What had she come outside to do? Where had she been going? Wh– "Hi," she stammered. He was gold and reaching out to her. Her mind throbbed and she felt pulled, pulled, pulled. Viva took his hand and followed him out of the garden, towards the path, trying to remember, trying to ignore the clamminess of her hands. Had she met him before? She ran her eyes over his angled face,

his severe cheekbones, his thin nose, and sharp
eyes, all hypnosis. His teeth shone bright behind
golden lips, his luminescent hair, a kingly crown,
rigid even in the autumn breeze. Had they met
before? In a flash, he turned back to her, and she
felt the weight of his gaze in her, as mercury
surging viscous in her veins, no longer thin,
flowing blood. Under his eyes, Viva was sure she
would bleed silver. She would be silver, needed to
be silver. She glanced away clumsily, unable to
keep him in the corner of her eye. "Where are we
going?" Viva asked. He smiled and led her away
from the cabin, from Morrigan and Karl, from all
she had known; he led her down the path, the
creek's consistent babble running alongside, and
when they passed the Daisy House, alight, smoke
pouring from the chimney, Tyree's garden of
gnomes glanced up from their various enterprises
to see Viva descend the creek path, conducted by
blinding gold.

They must have talked about something as they
walked, but Viva couldn't remember. She couldn't
remember. Remember. The descent, crossing the
threshold into town, bowing below the rainbowed
arch. She did not remember where they had gone.
How and when they had left or arrived. She
couldn't remember what she couldn't remember,
and she stared at him. His face that would put
Apollo to shame, into his glinting eyes, and across

his red, startling red, red lips pursed in—pursed in—pursed in something Viva couldn't name. He was enchanting. "I don't remember."

His lips peeled into an open smile. "You were telling me about your life—about, how stagnant and lonely it has become—ah, come this way—" He pulled her forward.

They were in a large courtyard tiled entirely in blue mosaic, creating the illusion of being underwater. In the center was a silver dragon, which encircled a deep blue fountain. Eyes narrowed, it clung to the spitting structure, as though safeguarding treasure within. One of the monster's front paws was dipped into the waters, the other clung to the brim, talons extended and glittering. Spines like sharp stones ran down the creature's curving spine. As the monster watched them pass, fangs bared, flourishes of water spewed from the fountain, feeding the monster with glittering silver.

Her blood throbbed, her skin tingled, and her ears buzzed. "Where are we?" she asked. Letting herself sneak a glance at him and ignoring a shiver coursing down her spine, he seemed brighter now, gold radiated from him, casting the yard in oceanic light and shadow.

"This is just the beginning," he said before leading her through the courtyard and into a structure beyond glass doors on the other side.

It was a dream. Chest pounding, her jaw dropped; the enormity of it engulfed her. It was an eternal hall of glass, and behind every pane were prismatic schools of fish fluttering within their tanks as she followed him further within the pelagic fortress. Shadow and light, movement and tranquility, it was as though Viva were inside of a fishbowl, watching the inverted world swim dreamily around her. The heaviness, the exhaustion, the emptiness that had been so present before—she tried to remember when—had dissipated. Her mind floated with the piscine ballet.

"Come here. Follow me closely." She let the honey of his voice linger on her tongue before it slid down her throat.

They walked through the palatial aquarium. His golden air shifted in silky strands as he guided her through the marine fairyland—suave and liquid. It was a quiet place, the tank walls stifling, perpetual blue. In a flicker of memory, in a movement like the fish behind the glass, darting, she saw them together, silver and gold and a burst of golden smiles, of what could be, then a flicker of someone, someone humming unrelenting to a field of drooping petals, a silver path, a scarecrow face, a snow-white crow, a blink, a silver palace. "Wait, I have to g–" Viva shook her head in a flash of gold. And then Viva didn't feel worry or fear or anxiety or anything. Nothing.

She felt nothing but the watery glass walls surrounding her. There was nowhere else, nothing else, no one else–had she been worried before, afraid or anxious before, wherever, whenever, with whomever, was there before, she couldn't remember, she was with him. Him, radiating golden light. Viva was enveloped by mesmerizing waters.

His red lips curled as he pulled her deeper into the abyss.

She couldn't say how long they had been meandering through the glass fortress before they came to a small bench placed in front of a titanic, unlit tank, behind which danced indistinguishable shadows. She pressed her hands to the glass and her nose gently brushed against it as she squinted into the darkness.

"Seals," he said from behind her.

The shadows rolled; she couldn't make out the details through the murk, but she watched the nebulous shapes, watched bubbles bounce from one shadow to another, shadows passing between and around around around before pirouetting away. A clandestine dance in submerged silence.

Viva was transfixed, didn't remember sitting down, didn't remember, but she was on the bench, sight bound beyond the glass. He must have sat next to her, must have been watching her, and even out of the corner of her eye, he seemed brighter, brightening with each breath she took, with each minute she stayed, could it be that she was illuminating him? Her head spun. Her stomach flipped like the shadows she watched. Her heart beat.

"You know," his voice moved like the dance, slowly as though his words were lacerating the air in fluid strokes, "They have humanity beneath their fur."

"Someone–I don't know who–told me that story," she said, breathing into a searing in her chest. "Men would try to steal the sealskin of the women so that she couldn't change back–she would be stranded with the monster who had taken her skin, which he would lock away forever. One man who did, who stole her skin, trapped her–"

"You're wrong." His voice caramelized. "She wanted to escape the kingdom and the tyrannical queen. She begged the man to save her. She pleaded that he take her with him and hide her skin away, so the queen would never find it and steal her back. It's a love story." He pressed his hand to the glass. The shadows scattered.

Viva stared at a shadow somersaulting around its own nasal bubbles, "I thought," Her mind was static, flickering in and out and grays and whites and, and, and, "Wasn't it a king who ruled the kingdom?" She asked.

"No."

"Do you think these ones can turn into people?" Viva chuckled and turned to him.

"Don't be ridiculous." He grinned, and she felt warmer.

Filling her sight again with the waltzing shadows, it was like trying to see all the stars in the sky at once. Viva laughed nervously.

"Yes?"

Viva thought through all the questions she had been asked the last time she had a date, stomach dropping when she realized that none of those men had ever asked her anything. She stammered, "Are you…" She felt her face reddening but shook it off. "Have you lived around here long?"

"Sometimes."

"Do you have any hobbies?" she asked.

The gold of him deepened as he answered, "I collect."

Viva frowned, trying to remember. "That must be hard. I–" she paused in flickering remembrance, thought trying trying to penetrate the sizzling fog, "–I think I knew someone who collected…things, I–I–It seems like it would take a lot of time and effort. I wouldn't have the patience."

He smiled and said, "Collecting satisfies me as well, it is energizing. It helps one to savor experiences. I used to be far too impatient. I made impetuous decisions without thought, without design. I've learned a great deal through time and experience."

She grasped at gossamer memories, all formless, all fading, farther, farther from her reach. Viva fidgeted, wondering, if she bathed in his golden light, could she turn to gold too? Could she be—the words burst out of her before she recognized the shape of them. "I've been feeling this pull lately, or maybe it's a push—I don't know if it's towards something or away from something, but ever since, since… I can't remember… It's like I'm seeing everything through some sort of film. Like when you open your eyes in the swimming pool and everything is distorted. Like I'm underwater. All the time. And my head hurts, I'm exhausted. But somewhere in the back of my head, something tells me that if I just go to sleep, if I just go back to a dream, it will all be…" Viva's voice trailed off. "But I don't remember the dream, I don't know what it's trying to tell me."

Her mind somersaulted with the tumbling shadows behind the glass. They were like ghosts, slow, swishing fins, in eternal suspense. "Sorry." Her eyes followed the spectral movements. "Lost my train of thought. This room is…" She smiled. "Magical."

"It is."

"What was I saying?"

"You were describing your dreams. The dreams from which you don't wish to wake."

"I think they're… beautiful. Glassy. I only remember silver. And I feel…. Luminous, happy almost." She thought hard and added, "Or beautiful. Or, or someone." She said, mesmerized by the dance, "I used to sleepwalk, and I could never remember my dreams then either."

"Where do you try to escape to when you are asleep?"

Viva laughed a laugh full of absent memory. A silver thread fizzled. "One time when I walked out of the house and went down to the Daisy House." Her heart panged and she wondered why, as she continued, "Of course, I don't remember any of this, but Morrigan and Karl talk about it every time one of us has a cup of tea." She ignored the deepening pain in her chest. "I was little. I walked down the path to the Daisy House. Tyree has a gnome city in his garden, and I set up an intricate tea party for all of them. Asleep! We were young then–I can't remember how old we were–so it must not have been as many as he has now, but it still had to have been about thirty. His parents used to bring one back for him every time they traveled, which was always; that's why he spent the night at our house all the time. Anyway, this particular night, his parents were home for once, so he wasn't at our cabin, and I set up a tea party in the yard. It wasn't an imaginary one–I walked in and out of the Daisy House with tea sets, plates, silverware, doilies. I set all of this up in the middle of the night, dead asleep."

"No one noticed you walking in and out of the house? Don't you find that odd?" His eyes glittered as they brushed over her face.

"I'm sure that I was quiet. Little kid tippy toes, you know."

"Small children do not tip-toe quietly," he said.

"Well, according to Karl–"

"The domesticated crow."

"I'm not sure he would call himself domesticated, but he does make a pie at least once a week. According to him, once I had unconsciously decided that everything was perfect, I went back into the house–"

"This family did not lock their door at night? How did a small child get into a locked house?"

"I"–he furrowed her eyebrows tight– "I'm not sure, actually." Uncertainty collared her, its cold fingers tightening around her throat.

"That is unbelievable, isn't it?" His lips curled up again.

"I... I had a tea party outside. All of the gnomes were placed perfectly around the yard, everything was beautiful, so I went back into the house, walked straight up to Ty's bedroom, woke him up, and marched him outside for the tea party."

"His parents never heard you?"

"Nope."

"And your family never noticed you were gone?" His smile didn't waver.

"I don't think so."

"No."

Viva blinked. "What?"

"No," he said matter-of-factly, golden eyes glinting, "I don't believe you. This seems to me like childish delusion or another fabrication your guardians fed to you. There is no possibility that a mancy would not notice her charge's absence. No chance parents would not hear children romping around their house. It does not fit. It must have been a dream. Or a lie."

Viva said nothing.

"You told me that you did not have friends when you were young. That the other children ignored you or bullied you, so I do not believe a boy who was not your friend would have done this. Do you?"

Viva's head swam, silver ribbons tightened, doubt wrapping around and around and around, the writhing fins of shadows swim before her eyes. "He was my friend." What was his name? Her heart beat. She said it slowly, each word acidic on her dry tongue. Bitter. "It must–"

"I'm sure that his parents discovered you sleepwalking–running away from home perhaps–and brought you back, then your dear Morrigan told you a lovely fiction. Or," his voice flowed over Viva, "Did you merely wish someone would have a tea party with you? Not only a garden of lifeless gnomes? The boy had his own friends, his own family, the mancy off somewhere with her hikers, and you ran away to have a tea party alone. Poor Vivian, always alone, the only company, the stories in your head. You don't have to be alone, you know." He peered into the tank where shadows twirled.

"I–" Viva felt dizzy.

"Do you like the palace?"

"What?" The shadows were swimming faster and faster behind the glass, bubbles trailing behind like wrappings of the dead.

"The palace. In your dream."

"I–" Her mind strained silver wrappingwrapping, tightening, cutting, her eyes transfixed by the umbra before, above, and behind her. Around and round and round. "I don't–I don't remember–"

He stood up and pulled her to stand as well.

"Take my hand."

Viva did, senseless fog taking her, head swirling around and around around.

She stumbled.

She followed.

Her golden man became more scintillating with each twist and turn, brighter, sharper, stronger, as they walked deeper into the watery abyss. Viva held to him more tightly, her breath short and shallow, her muscles strained, fingertips numb, chest hollow. He glowed lustrously through the darkening halls. He led them around another curve, and Viva couldn't have begun to say what underwater life stared back at her from the other side of the glass. Shadows. Viva shook her head and water sloshed between her ears. "We walk the creek every day together," she heard herself say. "I suggested hiking classes for kids. Before that, it was Morrigan following people around if they came up the path, making sure they didn't do anything foolish on her land."

"You've only ever followed the town's mancy around and around and around. A lost animal, Vivian. Here, you don't have to be lost. Belonging nowhere. Useless and alone. Nobody. You belong in the palace."

"Yes, I–" She couldn't think. Everything sloshed and sank. Gasping, reaching, sputtering, memories stranded in the sea, clinging to a plank, calling out. Unheard. "I can't think."

His voice surrounded her like midnight. "Would you like to no longer be alone? Never alone? To belong somewhere?" He emanated potential in the blue of the aquarium, his eyes brightening and in them she saw herself all in silver. He emanated everything she had ever wanted.

"I–" She stumbled; she couldn't keep her feet below her. Almost numb, insensible and weakening. "I should get back, it's already–it's late."

"It is."

"I think it's time to go." She breathed dryly and walked herself towards where? Where had they come from? Where was she?

She was in the courtyard, even more stunning under dark night, radiating blue, the water splashing over the kingly fountain. Bits of opal sprinkled over the dragon's golden scales, his spine, his grinning teeth. All was ablaze with the light of the moon and stars overhead.

Viva couldn't breathe, her lungs constricted, her head swam as the world swirled all around her. She was hollow but heavy. He reached out to her and in his hand was something small, something smooth and silver. Through her haze, she took it and held it up to the moonlight. In it, as though within a crystal ball, was her face, beaming back at her, from behind the glass, all in silver. "Toss it in and make a wish," he said, or had it been the reflection of herself. Someone said it. Someone said to make a wish. A wish she had always wished.

Viva's chest heaved, and another wave of exhaustion crashed into her. She tossed the pebble into the fountain, and it seemed to hang just above the surface. Waiting for her.

"Wish." Warm honey dripped from his mouth, over white teeth, and deep amber lips, over the beaming, golden skin of his face. Dripping. He held his hand out to her.

Take it.

The pebble rotated above the entrancing fountain waters, sharp, metallic, slicing behind her ribs. Laceration. What did she wish for? What did she, Viva Regum wish for? Every day alone in the beige office. Outside of town. Every day alone. Every day watching everyone else. Waiting and wishing and hoping, despairing. What did Vivian Regum wish for? The silver pebble fell into the water without a sound and sank. Viva watched it disappear below the depths.

***

Beyond the arboreal archway, his smile lit up the path, more gold than ever. She crossed the threshold and took his hand. A sensation like tin foil working back and forth over a set of front teeth shot up her arm, an electric shiver sizzled down her spine.

Nineteen

That night, sleep descended upon Mancy Manor, ravenous, all teeth and edges.

All silver.

Silvering

They dreamed. Viva, Karl, and Morrigan, minds tumbling through crazed unconsciousness, a grotesque tandem bicycle spinning, toppling toppling toppling. They dreamed of jagged metallic cliffs and of water, of demented, gushing whirlpools, walls of water sputtering, closing in, crashing, rising, engulfing. The shrapnel of a waterfall sputtering onto faces until each being stood, soaked, shivering, unseen, and lost to the others.

Karl's feathers drooped over spectral arms and legs from a time long past. His thick, black hair, entangled in white feathers all encased a sodden, nightmarish face. A face reflected in a funhouse mirror, now sharp and beaked, now boyish and square, framed in feathers and soggy black locks.

Drowning.

Endless whirlpools gyrated beside the three of them, cliffs turned to ravenous, twirling waves, above them, now in front and now behind. An abyss below them speckled by watery teeth that foamed and slobbered. Falling and twisting together wings hair feathers limbs, choked and flailing in a riptide battle. Between stinging eyes and drenched eyelashes, Morrigan saw waterfalls devouring Karl 's flapping wings, arms, clawing, screeching, drowning. She did not see Viva swallowed by the hungry waters. She could not. Morrigan was drowning too.

The water that bled over Karl and Morrigan's hair and feathers, into their eyes, nose, mouth, was arsenical silver. Glittering and thick. Both fought gushing waves when they heard a cutting scream through the impenetrable cacophony of crashing waters. From somewhere. They heard lungs filling with oozing silver liquid, emptying shrill cries to nothing.

The Weight of Silver

Steeped in pain, they heard it above the surge: Silver. They were spinning faster and faster now. Ringing clanging, raging waters, spinning whirlpool, choking cries, and chaos.

Karl felt, Morrigan felt, or both felt the other's hand. No earth or grass or cliff or dirt in reach to grasp so they held each other, choking and drowning.

Above it all, the echoing drops of stones dripping into silent water. Morrigan and Karl watched through sputtering breaths as the silver walls broke apart, crumbling into colossal silver boulders, polished and smooth like glass. They pushed each other, pulled each other, grasped desperately to each other. Sank with each other.

***

Viva, entirely submerged, felt the thought skipping up her ribs, like a devilish staircase: you're alone. Her heart beat. It ricocheted off her sternum into her spine: you're alone. Her heart beat. A thousand jagged stones dropped from a high tower, smashing through her skull: you're alone. Her heart beat. Bouncing sharp teeth over her bones. It beat so loud, alone alone

alone alone, it drowned out the splashing, the shouts, the agony. Alone, clanging, shattering, metallic din. Echoing off the cliffs, bubbling in the flooding waves, whispers in silver nothing. It filled her, its clanging reverberations echoing like strands of lightning.

She shouted again. Pain. Unheeded. Unheard. Still. Alone.

It was in her beating beating slicing beating—serrated—throbbing and beating. She drove her fingernails, her claws, across her chest, shredding, tearing.

Stop beating. A-lone. Stop beating. A-lone.

An offering.

It crashed against the walls of her shattered mind with every throbbing beat. That heart in her chest. That sound coursing through her. Alone.

And beating.

Red and dripping.

Stop. Beating. Beatingbeating. Viva clawed at her chest. Alone. Open, open. Gaping empty screeches of pain, of desperation, of submission. And a shadow, a winged monstrosity, flew toward her. It resembled Karl, but it wasn't feathered. It was pearly, scales adorning a twisting, turning body. Water slid from scaled wings, golden claws poised, katanas. Talons large enough to slice through a body, the flailing water ting ting tinged off them like hot, sizzling rain on a tin roof. The monster's silver beak was sharp metallic. Its eyes glowed silver and she saw herself in them like a mirror. Like a crystal ball. The her what she had been and all that she could be.

A surge.

Splashing water, blood, clangor. The water. Where was she in this liquid purgatory that smelled of rosemary now sage now chamomile or rose? Herbaceous music fell from the silver sky with whirling pools and crumbling boulders. Noise fell, cascading smashing into the next or the last.

Viva clawed, screeching to open the doors of her chest, beating alone, beating alone, clawing at skeletal hinges. Clothes shreds, flesh tearing off in strips, and the monstrous, scaled, taloned, beaked thing was there. Rapier talons glinting, beak a sickle steeled for harvest. It cleaved through her chest in a flash of gold. Her flesh splayed like a butterfly's wings, and now, now she could make it stop. Make it stop beating. Alone. She took either side of her ribcage in slippery fingers, blood dripping down her arms, over hands and fingers, hooking them underneath bone, and she heaved while the monstrosity watched her hungrily while she splayed open her ribs, a cadaverous armoire. The monster's silver eyes shone, unblinking, blood dripping from the serrated teeth of its curved beak. It gaped inside her open chest. Cocking its drenched head with a jerk, scales shimmering, it dipped low and sank its teeth into her red, beating heart. A flash of gold a flash of silver struck Viva. She was alone—

Stillness fell. The noise, aromas, falling crashing chaos ceased.

Viva sank further into still water.

Not a ripple—not a sound—not a beat. Only Silver.

***

The Weight of Silver

Morrigan and Karl dripped hand in hand on the silver shore of a frozen lake. A lake they both knew too well. Fingers woven together one course and weathered, the other downy— both held tight. Spitting wind tore at their faces with sharp, white teeth. It smelled of nothing but iron. They walked towards the edge of the lake each gripping tightly to the other.

A crack like lightning.

Out of the ice broke a thin, bloodless arm. Tissue paper flesh sliding airily over tender bone. It had been underwater for a long time. The skin on the hand had sloughed off like the cocoon from a dead caterpillar. Then a shoulder throat head.

Lucy's glazed eyes brushed over the two, who had begun to run across the ice towards her, breath puffing clouds into frozen air. She, Lucy, Lucy there, steps away, leaning a gray cheek on her decomposed palm. Gray lips and clouded eyes. Morrigan and Karl sprinted through ever-expanding ground, stretching themselves out to her. To Lucy. She tore her eyes from them, twisting her rotting neck, slate gaze surveying the silver landscape, the lake, the shore, the nothing.

In her silhouette, she was not Lucy. Eyes still clouded, taut lips pulled over white teeth like packed ash. Viva. Each spectral movement, kaleidoscopic —Lucy, Viva, one rotting ghost or the other.

Karl and Morrigan ran.

Ran.

Ran, stretching longing willing to reach. Lucy Viva Lucy Viva the woman in the icy lake laid eyes on the desperate pair again, watching their breath rise in silver threads, their legs flexing in vain, watching them futile and frozen. She smiled sharp, white teeth, threw her hands up into the frozen air, and slipped back down below the lake's surface, now iced over like living crystal.

Morrigan and Karl halted on the frozen lake, feet frozen to the ground, struggling to free themselves and run, hand in hand staring at nothing. Forced to surrender.

Between their entwined fingers, silver liquid poured from their connected palms over their fingers, staining the place below fingernails, dripping onto the ice, dark and warm.

Silence fell to nothing.

Twenty

The following morning, Mancy Morrigan Regum overlooked a grassy clearing full of young, lunching adventurers, and she felt a twinge of impatience. Though, as she watched a small blonde girl with a wicked grin tug one of Karl's tail feathers out of his ruffled body, it was probably closer to concern than impatience. She had not woken Viva to lead the adventure, instead leaving her to sleep, surrounded by a thick layer of banish and lavender. When Karl had first told her that Viva had begun sleepwalking again, the floodgates of memory had crumbled. Morrigan was drowning.

Where was her Viva?

She hadn't appreciated having to pull Tyree away from his work to check for Viva at the office the day before, but with a group of—how old were these kids? A mancy couldn't just take off. And later that evening, Viva had sprinted out the door without a word. When she had returned shortly after, face like a ghost, she had gone straight to her room without a word to Tyree who had been waiting patiently for her. Morrigan had seen his heart crack before he blinked quickly and smiled, asking Karl whether he needed any help in the kitchen. Morrigan had shaken her head and gone out on her ghost hunt.

Best to keep a close eye, lock doors, windows, block up the chimney, just to be safe, she might even suggest some sort of night watch to Karl, who was now flapping furiously in white, hot rage, away from the blonde girl who—what on earth— "Get those feathers out of your mouth and give them back," Morrigan shouted from her overlook. Ten sets of wide eyes shot up towards her, then towards the girl with a mouthful of feathers. Her impatience bubbling, the mancy stood up like a spring, plopped down onto the clearing towards the little girl who was now all teeth and narrowed raptor eyes.

"Give those to me." Morrigan took the damp, white feathers. "Don't even think about it—crying will not work on me." She raised her eyebrow in what she calculated to be exactly one tick upward. The little girl dropped her maw open and another three feathers fell soggy to the ground. Good god. "Pack it up," she announced to the silent spectators, "We're heading up in two minutes." A crash of thunder boomed through the air and the rain started. A liquid curtain. Morrigan sighed, she could hear the children up in arms already. A flash of lightning cracked through the sky and illuminated an idea. Morrigan smiled. "Have any of you heard about a bear named Roger?"

Karl

*T*he corner of Karl's mouth twitched as he stood over the loaf of pumpkin bread he had just removed from the oven—his chest swelled with pride because he hadn't really taken it out of the oven, had he? It had been three months since he had come to Mancy Manor, and he was finally learning. He knew how to do all of this now, he knew the herbs, though Morrigan was much better than him with those; he knew the woods, though he always lost every game they played; and now he had, after forty-five minutes of magical back-and-forth, convinced the bread to take itself out of the oven, to sit still on the counter as a serrated knife, poised moments before, sliced through bread's steaming flesh. Karl watched in satisfaction, calmly asking the magic to continue slicing. He was breathing, he was focused, and then Lucy walked in and said, "Hello."

The knife clattered sharply to the floor ensnaring a corner of the bread in its teeth as it fell. Karl's breath hitched as he turned, careful, very careful to set eyes only on the fallen knife, but as he crouched down to pick it up, her hand was *on his shoulder—please don't feel his heart beating beating beating. Karl strained his ears—Morrigan slept heavy and late, but sometimes she would come in early to steal food under the guise of helping him with breakfast, but all he could hear now was her heavy snoring from the back of the cabin and the skipping footsteps of his own heart.*

He glanced at Lucy in what was supposed to be only a flash, but her sprite-like smile snagged him. His chest was sore, while the corner of his mouth tugged harder upward.

"Shouldn't you try to mancy it?" Lucy asked with a flourish of her arms before placing her hands out in front of her, palms up. "I'll help," she said, her face pulled in mock severity as she peered at her empty palms. "Go."

Karl's head swam. Focus. He crouched down to the knife. Just focus. He didn't hear her chuckle at the strained face of concentration he knew he was making. The knife shivered on the floor. Focus. She was tapping her foot as though Karl was wasting her precious time and the knife, he thought, was shaking in tittering laughter at him too. Focus. It finally floated up, still quivering in the air and Karl rose with it, guiding the knife to Lucy's ready hands, until it hovered just above them. He breathed and Lucy winked at him.

The knife fell fast, teeth exposed, but Lucy was fast too and even as Karl stood, still wrapping his mind around her around the knife around the heart attack he was sure he was experiencing and around the concept of inconvenient gravity, she saved herself. Mostly. The knife's teeth nicked her on its way down, and eyes glittering, she threw her head back and laughed, one sparkling burst before she pushed him out of the way, and wrapped her finger in a towel.

"That wasn't very good," she said, laughter dancing in her eyes, "You'll just have to keep trying."

Karl opened his mouth, sure his heart would leap from it and wrap her in a bloody embrace, but Morrigan's voice shot to the kitchen. "What's going on? How's a girl supposed to sleep with all of this... nonsense?"

Karl could feel Lucy's eyes on him, and he couldn't breathe.

Twenty-One

It was still light out and not at all cold as Morrigan walked up from dropping off the day hikers at Tyree's Daisy House. Karl fluttered grumpily in front of her with a number of damp, reclaimed feathers in his beak.

As a rule, Viva was usually the one to greet the parents and wait with straggling kids whose supposed adults had managed to forget the pick-up time for the fourth week in a row, but today, Morrigan was alone for the job.

She watched Tyree closely as he distractedly withheld conversation, just playing catch up from opening late he said: very busy, lots to do. Morrigan had an idea of what was actually bothering him.

She had never known Tyree to sleep late or neglect his customers, even at his first business in the lemonade game when he was knee-high, wearing oversized clothes like an unsolved Rubik's cube and a bright intensity that had warmed Morrigan's heart. Over the years, she'd seen more than one customer walk away from young Tyree's crooked smile in a daze and with a much lighter wallet, confused as to why they had purchased a case of creekside lemonade to be delivered to their doorstep within the week.

But his normal spark was now barely a sickly glow. The man was distracted, and when Morrigan pointed out that, though very ambitious of him, she couldn't entirely see the purpose of trying to force coffee into a cup while it was upside down, he frowned at her, head atilt. Blinking button eyes, he flipped the cup with an "Oh" and handed it to her with hardly a glance. She had a hunch that it all might have something to do with the absence this morning of one Viva Regum.

When the mancy finally arrived back home, the cabin was still, but her mind spun. It was silent, but for Karl's wings flapping as he and Morrigan made straight for the back of the cabin towards Viva's room. Morrigan cracked the door and spied Viva on her bed in a deep, purple sleep. Everything was quiet.

Viva needed the rest. Needed the time to herself. She was listless and jumbled in a way Morrigan only recognized from times of illness and stress. This befogged Viva bared little resemblance to the Viva Morrigan knew most days. A Viva who had always been disturbing in her resolute chaos, certainly not flighty about which tree to leap from, whether or not to dive into a cave, or how long a midnight walk should take. No. Viva had always been decisive. Morrigan had set Tyree's arm at least four times because of Viva's assuredness that of course, he could make it from that treetop to this one, and how else did he expect to chase sneaky dryads anyways–just jump. Never: Should I jump? Never: Which foot first? Never: To which tree? Never: What if I fall? But now? Now, Viva seemed to Morrigan like lace tossed into the air, floating waywardly, and the mancy felt utterly helpless in the face of it. Morrigan left her to rest. To heal and return to the Viva she recognized.

Morrigan didn't enjoy silence; it left too much empty space for stuff. Stuff that noise did a good job of blocking out. Too much empty space for thought to seep in like sticky, red sap. Empty space was just that: empty. Gaping. Too much silence and anything could squeak itself in.

She went back to the main room towards the fireplace–Morrigan breathed in the crackling sputtering sound of flame–on the mantle were her boxes of herbs. The ink on the labels was dim and washy, her mother's fine handwriting put to the test of time. Like everything. She opened the lid to lilac, allowing the aroma to fill up space. It hummed delicate, staccato tones as Morrigan navigated her way to a mustard-yellow bucket chair and hummed along with the sprigs into the quiet space.

She watched as Karl carefully placed the three manhandled feathers in a tidy corner of his roost and shook himself out, he then lowered his head into the soft feathers of his wings. Perched, seated upon his dais, warmed by the rich heat of the fire and ruffling under a sporadic breeze that slipped through the window behind him, he closed an eye. The cabin, filling slowly with sensation, reposed.

Karl

*K*arl hunched himself further into his shoulders. *Focus. Just focus.* The plate laden with cinnamon bread, now slathered in honey butter, framed by sliced fruit, tottered only slightly on its journey through the air and onto the coffee table. Karl, following the plate, blinked at the fireplace, and it flashed into orange life. He huffed at Morrigan's manic applause, but Lucy—had she just smiled at him?

The fire flashed brighter just for a moment. Pocketing his hands, Karl tore his gaze away from the girls, though his mind lingered. It was a brisk morning that brought up imagery of crispy, red apples, juice dripping sweetness, and though Karl was warm from cooking, an electric shiver coursed through him as he fluffed three overstuffed pillows that were placed around the coffee table where Karl, over the past year, had noted their three habitual seats.

Karl had mancied the pillows himself, and his chest puffed with pride at the room, which was becoming more and more like a home and less like an abandoned shed. In his *bay window, over the deep banquette bench where he slept, a few tapestries hung from the ceiling. Multicolored quilts and a growing collection of pillows filled the surface. While Lucy was in town at the hospital—which seemed to be more and more often these days—he and Morrigan would wander around town, now buying fabrics and groceries for Karl to practice with, now stopping in gardens where Morrigan would sneak snippets of her favorite things to plant in the mancy garden, but they wouldn't be going to town today. Lucy didn't have to work today, Karl's face flushed. Maybe they could lounge by the creek or race up the path further into the hills. Maybe they could camp out—it had been a few days since they had been blanketed by the open night together, counting stars and sharing stories. Karl's thoughts turned over all the days' possibilities until Morrigan's fingers snapped hard in front of his clouded eyes.*

"What are you doing?" Morrigan's eyebrow tipped up suspiciously as she snuggled herself onto the mustard cushion across from him.

"Nothing," He began to spoon food onto three plates. "I was just thinking about what we could do today."

Morrigan snatched her plate from him and inhaled deeply, eyes glittering. "We already decided."

Karl tried not to notice that Lucy moved her cushion a few inches closer to his as she reached for her plate, her fingers brushed against his. "What are we doing?"

Morrigan spoke, her full mouth of buttered bread. "You'll see," she said mischievously before reaching across the table and patting him on the hand. "It'll be okay, don't worry."

It took a long time for them to leave the cabin. Karl cleaned up from breakfast, straining to hear the whispered conversation near the door, and when Morrigan shouted at him to hurry up, the damp rag he had been conducting through the kitchen crumpled lifelessly onto the counter.

They walked up the path in casual conversation. Conversation about Lucy's nursing. Conversation about a bear named Roger the three of them had become acquainted with—they should stop by in the evening, Lucy said, give him a little company because he seemed lonely. Conversation about nothing and about everything.

He didn't realize that they had left the path until he stumbled over a crawling branch, his knees skidding along lush grass, palms slamming to the earth. The girls turned to him, both the same snickering lighting up their eyes, before they whipped back around, but Lucy stopped walking, letting Morrigan make her way ahead, just a little, and she held her hand out behind her back, fingers extended. He took it. She walked forward mightily, pulling him up with her as he stared at the back of her head. His legs turned to warm jelly.

For what seemed like miles, Lucy's hand was wrapped in Karl's; she pulled him forward, guiding him around tricky stumps, outstretched branches, and her hand was in his, her hand was in his, her hand was in his, Morrigan glancing behind at them sporadically and when they reached *a clearing leading to an expanse of scintillating aquamarine, Lucy squeezed his hand and his heart jumped.*

Trees framed the lake—a picturesque scene—the space was void of humanity, except for the three of them. There were no footprints anywhere, though Karl knew that not many people traversed the creek path except the mancy and her children. He didn't have much time to think about why before Morrigan and Lucy pulled him to the water's edge. It was a chilly day, and the water must have been prickling cold, but Lucy opened her arms wide, shouted out into the open air, and she leaped toward the smooth surface. The water broke. Ripples undulated towards him, and he realized, as he watched the blue roll over her that his hand was shaking. He dove in after her.

During their time at the lake, Morrigan sat, uncharacteristically calm, at the edge, watchful of the water's every movement. She laughed and chatted at Lucy and Karl who swam nearby until Karl thought his fingers and toes were going to fall off, icicles dropping off a door frame, and only then did he drag himself out of the lake and lay down on the shoreline next to Morrigan soaking in the crisp sun. He stared up at the cloud-spattered sky and felt full.

"Happy one-year manciversary," a velvet voice said close to his ear. Karl turned his head and Lucy's face was so close to his that he jumped.

"What?"

"You've been living with us for a year." Morrigan said as she attempted to convince a particularly stubborn tree branch to sing a tune with her. "Congratulations to you."

Lucy was very close to him, and Karl couldn't remember what he usually did with his arms—did they usually hang at his sides like limp laundry? Was his breath always this shallow? "I have something for you," she said. She placed, gently on his chest, a small silver pebble, flawless and smooth, almost like glass. "One of my patients gave it to me last week; he found it by the creek, and I thought that you could use it for your crafts somehow."

He smiled, picking it up and rolling it between his fingers, noticing only the heat of Lucy's hand on his shoulder before she stood up in a flash and sprinted back into the water. He put the pebble into his pocket and took a deep breath.

Twenty-Two

Morrigan rested her chin on the back of her hand. Viva had left her bedroom to join them at the squat coffee table; she was gray and sallow. Clearly the lavender cleanse of her bedroom had done nothing for the girl's insomnia. Orange light from the fire emphasized deep shadows beneath her eyes. Afternoon waffles stacked one on top of another; Viva stared unblinking into the fire, letting the tower transform into Pisa with every addition. Morrigan placed three on her plate, drizzling thick maple syrup into each divot. One by one.

Viva was disappearing in front of Morrigan's eyes. After filling in the last divot of her top waffle, Morrigan tipped it with her fingers, watching the syrup fall onto her plate in a pool of warm, sticky sweet. She took a bite and asked, "So you weren't able to sleep?" Viva didn't blink. Had her eyes always been that cloudy? The fire hissed. Morrigan continued, "Even after getting to bed early?" It was too quiet, she thought. "Karl," she shouted into the kitchen, "Can you turn that up?" Heavy metal rattled into the living room and Morrigan breathed. "Viva?"

"Hmm?" Viva focused the flames. "What do you mean 'went to bed early?'" Viva's voice dragged like tar.

"What?" Morrigan took another bite.

"What do you mean I went to bed early?" Viva asked.

"I mean that we were glad to see that you got to bed early last night and that you skipped the adventure this morning…What do you mean what do I mean? –Karl, just a bit louder. Two more notches, please."

A squawk sounded over electric guitar.

"I was out until late last night," Viva said.

"You were what?" Morrigan put the waffle down and wiped her hand on the hem of her own dress.

"I was out with…" she paused.

"What are you talking about?" It had been years since Viva had been out with anyone other than Tyree–as far as Morrigan knew. Who was the last one… Harry or Henry or Hank? Maybe Paul. Morrigan didn't remember, but she certainly remembered the fallout. Had Viva met anyone since college?

"I left–I said goodbye to you and Karl–" Viva trailed off as if the story had ended. Though, there seemed to be a page or two missing.

"Yes. You did. We thought you went to see Tyree. He came over just before you got back asking where you were. He told me to say he was sorry he missed you, and then you walked right past us all ten minutes later."

"What?"

"Tyree was over to find you then helped Karl with dinner while I hunted ghosts. You were still dead asleep when Karl and I got back from the adventure this morning, and we didn't want to wake you. You have been in your room since early last night." Morrigan paused briefly. "I want you to be careful about the banish, just be sure you replace any that's scattered if you see gaps. I am glad you got some good sleep, but Viva–"

"No, I was out with–I didn't get home until–I can't remember, but it was late. I think." She still hadn't torn her gaze from the fire.

"With whom?" Morrigan pushed away her plate.

"I told you about him, M…. come on."
"Come on what? Viva, you went to the office yesterday morning, Tyree brought you home, and you were asleep in your bed all night. I made an appointment with the doctor in town for later this week for your insomnia and sleepwalking, but–"

Viva cut her short, "–But. I was out." Her voice was hollow.

"Viva. I haven't heard you mention anyone recently. You were in your room all night. We locked everything up after Tyree left. I slept outside your room and Karl was in his roost. We would have seen or heard if you had gotten up and left, let alone come back in with someone."

"I–No–I was at–at…somewhere… It. It was like a giant castle, a glass fish tank. Rooms and rooms and rooms of water and fish and sea lions. I told the story about the selkies, you know, where the man saves the selkie from the sea queen."

"That's not how–well, it's not important." Morrigan placed the back of her hand on Viva's forehead; it was damp with cold sweat. "You remember your somnambulation when you were younger? We would have dream competitions, remember? Whoever had the most vivid, far-fetched dreams won. Do you remember? Usually, Karl won, but not when you were sleepwalking, you won every time." She tried to soften her eyes amid Viva's unease.

"I– no– but–" Viva stood up and wavered slightly before walking out the front door, slamming it behind her. The waffle tower on Viva's plate fell.

Ear pressed against the front door, Morrigan waited until she heard the branches of the oak outside crack under Viva's weight before walking back to the coffee table, where she stuffed three waffles in each pocket and sat in Karl's roost by the bay window.

Dirty dishes had already begun floating from the table and towards the kitchen. "Karl, she's up in the tree. I know you're going to Tyree's soon but check on her before you go. And after you get back. Maybe in between. I'm going to try to find something to help her." Morrigan had plenty of room to maneuver herself in the roost. She placed a hand on the windowpane and focused.

Morrigan

*W*ith a crack, she was awake. It wasn't a literal crack, but the unconscious crack of the mind. The crack that says. Get up. Now. Morrigan got up.

She flew from her room, a chill shivering down her spine, despite her heavy flannel pajamas. The fire in the main room had been out for hours; there was no sizzle or pop of embers. No glow. Morrigan didn't light it. Didn't wake Karl, who was snoring in his roost, protectively incubating soda tabs he had found in the creek that morning. Morrigan walked to the back of the cabin where Viva's white room was and pressed her ear to the door. This girl—so sensitive about people in her room. Morrigan knocked lightly. "Viva?" Listened. "Viva, are you okay?"

Silence. Strangling silence.

Morrigan pressed the door open as quietly as she could, and her heart stopped. Her blood froze. Not just cold. Not like cool gel squishing through her veins. Frozen. Freezing, veins expanding, about to burst from red toothy icicles. Her head throbbed as Morrigan shouted across the house, "Viva?" Voice trembling.

The window was closed, the banish still spread evenly across the sill. Morrigan checked under Viva's bed, threw off the blankets, thrust open the closet door, ripping open boxes and books, and nail polish bottles, just in case, she was searching anywhere, everywhere. The child was small after all. She could hide anywhere. Was this a game? Please be a game.

Karl soared into the room, sleep in his eyes, but registering the empty bed and Morrigan's pale face, bulging eyes, shaking hands, he streamed back out of the room, and Morrigan heard crashing from the main cabin.

She wasn't there.

Shewasn'tthereShewasn'ttherewasn'ttherewasn'tthere.

Morrigan's heart was in her throat and the cold was overwhelming. Or the heat. Or both.

Where could she look? Where could she be? What could she do? After checking everywhere twice, and maybe just once more, Morrigan checked again and againagain. Karl had turned over the kitchen and living room like a tornado.

Viva wasn't there.

For a heartbeat, their eyes met. Breathless, they flew down the path to the Daisy House. Tyree wasn't at Mancy Manor, so his parents were home. The door moaned under Karl's furious knocks. Tyree's parents hadn't seen her. They hadn't seen her, they said, and couldn't a mancy just wave a wand or something to find her—oh and please take Tyree next weekend. Morrigan blanched, and when they suggested she keep a better eye on her daughter, especially being magical or whatever—like they did with their son. Morrigan had turned away from their house, her eyes burning hot rage and despair.

Morrigan walked to the creek. Every piece of her mind, her body, her existence begging. Begging not to find Viva there. Hours. Hours of scouring the creek. Hours of searching the woods. She searched Roger's cave, his cellar. She had broken his hibernation to ask for his survey of the woods. Hours. Hours until Morrigan made up her mind to go into town—they must have some sort of police there. She was sure they would not be nearly as thorough as herself, as Karl, as Roger, but she was out of options. Out of wishes. Out of hope.

Morrigan, with Karl perched, trembling, on her shoulder, his claws sinking into her skin, walked out of the densest part of the woods and towards town. As they passed Mancy Manor, Karl's eyes flitted up. He took off, tearing Morrigan's pajama sleeve as he did, the fabric hanging loosely from his claws. He flew like an explosion towards the large oak at the front of the cabin. Morrigan sprinted after him, her legs searing fire.

When she heard the snores, Morrigan leaped into the tree, disregarding branches scratching at her skin. Karl was already huddled next to the sleeping girl, a wing over her curled figure. Tears flooded freely from Morrigan. Her breath short and quick, mind whirling, tears breath thought all a spinning vortex.

The three of them stayed in the tree for a long time. Morrigan and Karl caught their breath and tried to chase away the darkness that bared its teeth that night. But of course, their new fears would remain always in the shadows, hungry and waiting.

Twenty-Three

Tyree had always loved the unbroken morning. With its scent of fresh serenity, there was something about being up before the sun, something rhapsodic in it; it made him feel like he was supporting the earth's preparations for its flourishing commencement.

Stretching himself awake, Tyree got out of bed, crumpling the sheets and bedspread as he did. The room was dark, aside from the glowing, plastic constellations on not only the ceiling, but the walls and door as well, but his eyes knew this room in darkness. Knew this house in darkness.

It was a single-story, and he only had to walk out of his bedroom to enter the kitchelividiningroom, as he had grown to call it. After his parents had moved out, Tyree had clung to change. His world needed color. He adored color; what better way to distinguish his place in the world? So, he had covered the kitchen and dining area with a juicy Valencia orange paint, striped with pale gray. His table, almost entirely decorative, was covered with a bright yellow cloth, table settings one a deep jungle green, another a luscious pomegranate, and flowery pink. The living area held a deep, blue sofa and shaggy rug, and he had painted it a cool, icy blue on the top of the walls, and light sand at the bottom. Every day, Tyree imagined he was traveling from the tropics to the sea in a single step.

The morning was breaking, and it was time for him to prepare. As his livelihood cooked and baked in the tangerine kitchen, Tyree went out to his emerald garage to warm up the beverage equipment.

The morning seemed to flash by. The sun rose and people congregated outside of the garage. The mornings were always busy, and his thoughts flew from one order to the next in between small talk– the how are yous; the it's a beautiful days; the it's just on the main road in town, right next to the cat barber's.

Mr. Hanson, Mrs. Pine, the Jones twins came by at their usual hours, minutes, seconds, timed like choreography. He thought that a person could certainly know a lot by observing, as he watched the cream and sugar station outside the garage door where Ms. Nelson had just picked up a wayfaring ladybug in the palm of her hands, whispered a sweet comfort to it before tossing it up gently into the air. He wondered what he had never noticed. What he never would. Ms. Nelson took up her tea, sugared to perfection, waved goodbye to Tyree, and walked down the path with the whispers still on her lips.

He hummed as he prepared hot chocolate for Viva and Morrigan–Viva would be by soon. But time ticked on with faces strange and familiar. Jimmy Summers came around with a new boyfriend and a knock-knock joke. Paul Smith tapped his foot and checked his watch as Jimmy delivered the punchline, and even in his rush, Paul couldn't help a stifled chuckle from escaping pursed lips. Opal Pierce mentioned her four granddaughters–very successful, all, and so pretty, and then slid Tyree a piece of paper with four different phone numbers on it. Tyree couldn't help his appling cheeks as he handed a coffee to her, thanking her, and when she had disappeared down the path, dropped the paper into the trash.

The blustering arrival of Karl broke his reverie. The line outside had all but dissipated, the only customers remaining were sipping their beverages on the small picnic table in the front garden overlooking the diverse community of gnomes that Tyree had collected over the years.

Morrigan had told him years ago when she had given him the one with a witch's hat and black cauldron, that gnomes helped care for their household, but only if given proper appreciation and respect. She had taught him to leave a little treat at the picnic table each night–just a little something from his lunchbox. He hadn't believed her. How was something made of ceramic supposed to watch over his house, he had asked? Morrigan had fixed him with her deep, black stare; it's a strange world, she had said, something will appreciate a snack, I'm sure. He was pretty sure it was just squirrels who enjoyed his appreciation and respect, but who would say no to the potential of being looked after a little bit more closely?

Tyree turned from the garden and followed Karl into the house. Within seconds, wings flapping, claws flourishing, voice croaking rough commands, Karl had the oven bursting, batters and doughs mixing, folding, rising, and heavy metal blaring.

"I'm going to take my break up at your place today," Tyree shouted over the baritone roars and screeching guitars. "Viva didn't come by, so I'm going to bring the order up and check-in." He waited for a reply in the flurry. "That okay?" He yelled, trying to float his voice over the rest of the noise in the room. Karl cawed in affirmation, and Tyree, stuffing two muffins into a paper bag, skipped out the door. As he passed his garage, he scooped up the hot chocolates, closed the door, stuck up the "back in 30" sign, and was off.

There had never been a gate to the mancy's garden because no one would have ventured into it without a very good reason to do so. Tyree navigated the place with difficulty. Even after having been a frequent visitor and often short-term resident of the cabin, Tyree still felt as though he should be wearing khaki shorts, a tactical button-up, a safari hat, and wielding a machete as he journeyed through. It was not easier with a bag of muffins and three sloshing, hot beverages. It was a leg lifted here over rose bushes while dipping one of his shoulders under a twisted and deceptively solid series of vines–and how did those have thorns too? He scrunched his scarecrow face when his foot pressed down on a particularly juicy something, but he kept moving forward, one cup balanced precariously under his chin as the others served as weighted balance in his hands until he finally reached the door. In the oak to his right, he heard a rustling in the branches.

"Hey Viva," he called up the tree, the cup beneath his chin plopping heavily to the ground... he was sure M. would find it. "I've got some provisions; I'm going to toss up a bag, so be ready to catch." He threw the bag of muffins into the tree with measured force, and when they didn't come falling back onto his head, he began making his way up branch by branch, setting the cups on steady, wooded arms before each pull of his own body. It didn't take long before Tyree reached his branch—the one Viva had assigned to him so many years before. Viva had taught him, during one of his first visits to Mancy Manor, where to put his hands and feet along the oaken climb. Tyree stretched out along the branch and wiggled himself comfortably in the crook of it; he sipped on one of the hot chocolates and held the other above his head.

"Thanks." The voice was gray.

"What's wrong?" Tyree sipped again and breathed in the woody aroma.

"Hmm?"

"What's wrong?" A thin stream of air flew through the tree's thick branches and hissed.

"Did we used to be friends?" The leaves shifted slightly in a breeze.

Tyree frowned. What did that mean?

"Were we ever friends?"

His heart seized in his chest. "What? Of course. What's going on?"

Viva's voice was steady and dry, as though she were speaking with stale air. Tyree stood up on his branch, careful not to tip his cup over. She was sitting motionless on the branch above, staring, brows furrowed, at… what? Her eyes were watery, and he thought they appeared slightly glazed, a thin silver sheen in the afternoon light.

This skeletal, vacant figure perched in unblinking silence. He had seen her yesterday, asleep at her desk. Sick on the floor. Dragging up the path. She twisted her head towards him and the image, the gray cadaverous sight of her disappeared and she was Viva. Tyree blinked. The light breaking between branches must have shadowed her strangely because now she was her, but… she didn't seem to see him. But she was searching.

"What do you mean, 'were we friends?'" His straw hair fell into his eyes.

"I can't remember."

"You can't remember what you mean?"

Viva didn't respond.

"Or why you asked?" Tyree continued.

Silence.

"Or whether we were friends?" His voice scraped its way through his throat, but he tried to laugh it off. It was a striking match—a dry "tschhh."

"Thanks for this." She held up the cup. A drop slid down the side.

"Sure. You didn't come by, so I figured I'd come to you. Hey, did your day get better yesterday?"

"Hmm?"

"You had a pretty rough morning yesterday. And," his voice broke slightly, "–I didn't see you last night. Did you get some sleep? Are you feeling better?"

"I think so." Viva blinked hard. "I think I went on a date. Or I dreamed it. That was good. I think. I'm not sure."

"You did." Tyree tried not to shatter. "With who?"

Her eyes seemed to clear slightly as she gazed at him. "Gold."

Tyree frowned, one eyebrow squeezing just higher the other, creating a slight zigzag across his forehead. "Ah."

"It was like being in a giant fishbowl and the fish are the ones watching you. Really seeing you. Always there with you. You should go. And see the selkies around and around around."

"I'd love to. Where is it?" Tyree ignored the build-up of saliva in his mouth.

Silence swam through the air. Had she heard him? Had she fallen asleep? No, she was there. Sitting, eyes open, though unmoving, a veil of silver glinting again over them.

"Where… is it?" He asked again, sipping his drink.

"Hmm." Shifting slightly, she said, "I don't remember." She laughed like bells and sang, "I don't remember." Viva then climbed down from the tree and went into the cabin, leaving him behind. Something cracked as his feet found the soft earth again. *Were we ever friends?*

Shuffling back through the garden, Tyree heard the commotion of customers coming from his house down the path; there would be a line forming and Karl would be aggravated at his tardiness. Glancing back towards the tree he thought he saw a shadow of Viva, lounging along her branch in the sun's broken beams. But she wasn't there.

Tyree

"R eady?" *Viva shouted, "Set? Set? Se–et..."*
"Yes!" Tyree yelled back to her.
"Go!"

Tyree pulled himself up branch by branch, feet scrambling below him searching for the next branch. Go go go. He could win this. Snapped twigs rained down on him as Viva climbed just above.

Focus.

He reached his long arms upwards. He had reach. Strength. He could do this. Small bells of ringing laughter sounded above him. Oh no, she couldn't be at the top already. In a last desperate attempt at victory, Tyree braced his legs and sprung himself upward as forcefully as he could, forgetting completely about other branches lying in wait above his head, one of which struck him fully with the force of ancient oak.

Tyree's vision blurred as his grip slipped and he slid into gravity's forceful embrace, but with a painful wrench around his neck, only his head jerked backward. Something was clutching his shirt collar, maybe he had gotten stuck on a branch on his way down. The throbbing, cutting pain of his neck ran down to his shoulders, arms, fingers.

"Ty. Tyree. Open your eyes. Come on, you're fine."

He blinked his eyes open only to see a blurred smudge. Focus. Viva was holding tightly onto his collar; she was bracing herself on the oak's trunk while desperately trying to pull him back up. Don't fall.

"You're making me do all the work, and I don't know how long your shirt is going to hold. M. will kill me if we break your nose again, and I don't know what she'll do if we break your skull. The one day Karl decided to do his grocery run during lunchtime…"

Tyree took her arm, and a branch, finding his feet again, and he pulled himself up until he faced Viva. She was in front of him, and suddenly his face was sandwiched between her cool palms as her eyes searched his—probably for potential brain damage.

"Don't. Do that. Again." She jostled his face with each word. "You can't win if you die. Not even from sympathy, so don't try it." She put her forehead against his and shook her head roughly, her hair brushing against his face as she did. In a second, all concern flew from her and was replaced by a wide smile as she ran her fingers through his straw hair. Tyree blinked, his eyebrows drawing together. "So," she said conclusively, smashing her nose against his, "I win." She pressed her lips to his before releasing his face and scrambling higher up into the tree. "Come on," she shouted

down to him. "I had Karl hide our lunches way up top before
he left."

Tyree blinked.

Twenty-Four

Inhale, Morrigan told herself. Deep breath and focus.

Karl's bay window shimmered a weak lavender before Morrigan slipped through the place where glass had been moments before, and onto the earth on the other side. She then tapped the glass, which had reformed in a breath. It was difficult to convince an entity to take a brief intermission from existence and even harder to convince it to redon its earthly bonds. The glass tinged. Morrigan panted catching her breath and before the coming wave of exhaustion hit her, she stuffed one of the travel waffles she had brought into her mouth, savored the energy, and walked into the woods.

Crunching leaves, shivering branches, busy animals scratching holes into the earth after weeks of gathering. Autumn was good. Morrigan walked around the side of the cabin, noting the white walls, white blankets, white furniture as she passed in front of Viva's bedroom window. The emptiness. Everything appeared normal. It was Viva's room. There were no pentagrams drawn over the walls with blood–though, that would have made Morrigan more interested than worried. All of Viva's things were still there, just not Viva herself. Viva was currently huffing in the oak out front.

Morrigan remembered decorating Viva's room with Karl so many years before. She and Karl had envisioned a treasure chest with Viva's crib nestled in rolling hills of gold and jewels, and what did that girl ask for the minute she could speak? White. She had demanded everything white. It had to change. Karl had been heartbroken to change the room, the treasure hoard of Viva's room had been his idea after all, but he had said with a feathery shrug, it would just be an ivory chest full of pearls. Their treasure would endure, and Viva adored her pearly trove. Walking away from the window towards the encroaching woods, Morrigan recalled asking Viva: why white? So sterile, so nothing, so empty. The girl had shrugged tiny shoulders and claimed that no, it was freedom. Freedom to be anything at any time in her space. And who could argue with that?

The woods before her were cool and moist. Morrigan embraced the shade, removing another waffle from her pocket, taking a bite, and replacing it again. The air shifted between bony branches of naked trees. Roger's cave was not far from the house, and with autumn coming to a close, Morrigan needed to be sure that his cellar was fit for a king.

Roger sometimes woke in autumn, but at times not until winter extended his icy hand, awaking to decimation, to wintery dormancy. The stinging cold, the endless gray. From warm dreams to bitter waking. She did not have to imagine.

She could hear his thunderous snores from a mile away, and as Morrigan made her way towards the large cave she smiled. She and Karl had built the cellar directly into the cave. If more dragons had employed Mancy Morrigan for their hoard security, there would be a great many more dragons today, thought the mancy as she patted Roger's head lightly on her way back to the hidden hatch.

Walking down the echoing, stone staircase, checking for loose stones along the way, the mancy made her way to an intimidating door. It had a flat knob the size of Morrigan's head in the middle of it. Morrigan turned the knob with both hands, heaved the door open, and walked through. Morrigan couldn't be sure how many beings would actually attempt to break into a bear's treasure hoard, which consisted mostly of jerky, but the door calmed Roger's dreams, and Morrigan knew better than most the high price of peaceful sleep.

The cellar had been designed for Roger's particular needs; what would a bear often stuck awake during late autumn and winter need the most? Food, of course, warmth, and comfort. On a planet in the boney grip of passing death, the hunger for light and life consumes. An empty stomach gnaws.

On one side were cupboards filled with food carefully preserved and jarred by Karl, who had also, on the other side of the room, crafted a bear-sized roost that Roger used only in his waking season. Viva had insisted that a second smaller roost be set up for the Regums' regular visits.

The rest of the room was life. Morrigan had sprouted flowers everywhere, while Karl had convinced them, militaristically, to bloom gorgeously or go back out and meet the oncoming winter. Morrigan had painted the walls sky blue, carefully adding a few whipped cream clouds on each. Karl had flown Viva around for hours so she could paint the ceiling the same blue and in one lucky corner, a beaming yellow glow. What would a bear, waking to a world in icy repose, wish for the most?

Morrigan shook her head and pressed down on her temple. It was quiet.

There was only emptiness and silence. No. She shook out her whole body, pulled another waffle from her pocket, and with a flourish, the room sprang to singing life. Her voice echoed off the walls, song seeping into the floor, the flowers' petals opened in harmonized voices. Morrigan breathed.

Now she could work.

She checked the cupboards, humming every passing thought to the swaying flowers–how did one bear eat so much jerky? That cloud needed a touch-up. The items on her mental list were belted out, one after another. So much to do so much to fill up her mind. But there was silence always waiting for her in the depths of thought.

It was time to leave.

Get out get out get out.

Morrigan shook the slithering thoughts from her head and left the cellar behind. Patting Roger on his dreaming head as she exited the cave, she breathed in the sizzling autumn air. The path past Roger's cave was heavily wooded. The creek beside her hissed through its icy teeth. She walked the path.

Don't stray from it, she had told Viva. How many times? How many times had she told that girl? Wild, undomesticated nature does not bend. It does not compromise. It does what it pleases when it pleases. There is no persuading. No magic can sway its feral desires.

Karl

*K*arl's bay window, though small for his large frame, was comfortable. He had been making more and more magical things for the cabin—each one's completion earning a glittering smile from Lucy and an enormous groan from Morrigan. Mancy Regum was often out meeting with her clients, so Karl and Morrigan practiced mancying on their own during the day. Only on rare occasions now did they practice with the mancy herself. They practiced mostly in the woods while wandering, but sometimes they practiced in town while they waited for Lucy to finish up at the hospital. Lucy wasn't home very often, her job in town taking up most of her time, but when she came home after a day packed full of heavy hours, and Karl handed her a glittering wind chime made with the pebbles she gave him, a pillow the size of their coffee table, or a quilt put together with the hues of the woods, she would smile that smile. So, cushions and pillows, knitted wool blankets and quilts littered the main room of Mancy Manor. Karl had already filled his bay window with his creations, and *according to Morrigan the girls' bedroom was full too, but he adored that smile. And he filled with pride looking around the cabin at his accomplishments. So, Karl cooked, created, mancied, and he was happy.*

A full moon beat lacy blue rays through Karl's window. He lay in the beams and thought about his life now after only a year and some change in Mancy Manor. What he could do. What he knew. What he felt. Karl wondered if his grandmother had known how happy he would be.

Cutting through his reverie, a sharp hiss sliced through the air next to his ear. Karl jerked his body, twisting over the bench; he slammed heavily to the cabin floor. He groaned.

"Shhh!" The voice hissed again. "Let's go." A hand reached down and took his, and then dragged him towards the door until he could struggle onto his feet, stumbling after the leader.

When they reached the garden, Karl's feet were finally underneath the rest of his body, and his head whirred to catch up. "What—"

"Shhhh," Lucy turned back to him, tugging on his hand, and she whispered, "Mother has good hearing, so shhh."

He hushed, his breath catching in his lungs, trying to ignore his pounding heart as Lucy led him out into the midnight woods.

They were only on the path for a little while before Lucy turned away into the wild flora, ducking and curving. The moon beat down silver above them. Lucy's hand was locked in his, and he followed, tripping, branches reaching scratching his arms, face, legs, but he would always follow her.

The lake sparkled in the moonlight. It was impossibly still, reflecting the stars above it, and it was only when they had reached the closest shore, a breath away from the glassy waters, that Lucy stopped. She released Karl's hand, sat down, and dipped her feet below the lucent surface, breaking the water into shivering ripples.

He stared, but she didn't return the gaze. Didn't move. For a long time, he stared at Lucy gazing over the lake while the ripples at her feet stilled as though freezing around her ankles, as though transforming into a plinth for her luminous figure. Her: statuesque, slate blue radiating from her into the open, moonlit air. It was silent, and it was exactly where he wanted to be.

Lucy's voice broke the silence. "I'm leaving."

Karl's breath hitched. His heart dropped low into the burning acid of his stomach. "What?" He meant to whisper, but his voice croaked loudly.

"I was offered a job." Lucy took his hand and pulled him to sit next to her. "It's not far, but it's not here." He couldn't tear his face away from hers, blue and wistful, or maybe that was him. "It's a bigger town, there will be more to learn. It will be wonderful, and the mancy there knows my mother, so I'll be in good hands."

Karl cleared his throat, and in a voice like gravel he asked, "Did you tell Morrigan?"

"Not yet." She squeezed his hand. "I told mother this morning, and I'm going to tell Morrigan tomorrow. She will be... upset."

"I asked mother if Morrigan could come with me and study under the mancy there, but she said she's not ready, that she still has lessons to learn here," Lucy said, "But Morrigan won't like that answer." The water around Lucy's feet wobbled into shushing ripples. "I'll see her often. As often as I can. I'll come back here, and when the mancy says she's ready to apprentice with someone else, she can come to stay with me, at least for a season."

Karl's breath was short when he mumbled softly, "I could visit you."

Lucy didn't blush. She didn't turn away or laugh at him. She frowned deeply. Pulling her feet out of the water, Lucy maneuvered herself so she was on her knees, her face level with Karl's, and he couldn't breathe. Darker than slate now, her eyes were on him. Placing her hands firmly on either side of his face, so his eyes blurred slightly "No," she said, her brows creased further before she placed her forehead against his. "No. You're coming with me."

Karl's heart bucked and his lungs constricted. He would have started laughing, garish laughter that would gallop through the satin night. He would have, if Lucy hadn't kissed him then, deeply on the shore of the midnight lake illuminated by a silver moon.

Twenty-Five

Morrigan continued her way up the path, the growth of trees between her and the creek allowing only for an occasional peep of the rushing water. Outstretched arms of trees, some naked, others clothed in sharp needles, twitched in the wind. She opened her ears for birds, for wind, for beating rays of sun fluttering leaves. For anything.

It was quiet.

She stomped her feet and dragged each step out with a slam and scrape. She counted them—her steps—as she sang again her cellar to-to list and listened to her feet move, pebbles shifting under her weight, the crunching. There was a lot to do today. So much to do. No time to think. Don't think.

To her right, Morrigan heard the rapid tickticktick of a woodpecker drilling its needle beak into living bark.

She grinned. "Little bird," she sang, "that's not so kind, there's plenty of food around. Why do you need to hurt that tree? Circle of life, eat to live, but…" She identified the culprit and sprang up into the branches, the woodpecker flitting away in terror. Morrigan spread herself out in the branches like a lounging leopard.

"Now," she said, placing a finger to the wound the woodpecker had created. "You've got to stand up for yourself. They will never leave you alone if you don't fight back a little. Show some teeth." Her birdsong stroked the tree's bark and it hummed back a wistful ballad. Sappy, thought Morrigan as she closed her eyes and hummed along, she ignored the shadows in her mind, and dove into the pool of sound, swimming in the noise of the woods.

Karl

*K*arl and Lucy were leaving the next day, Lucy to start a position in a hospital in the next town over and Karl to apprentice with the mancy who they would be living with. Though it had taken ages, Lucy had finally convinced Morrigan that they should go to the lake to end the season right.

Morrigan had snorted with a box of the old mancy's herbs crooning on her lap, but after Lucy's persistent persuasion, Morrigan snapped the box closed, placed it carefully back on the mantle, and turned to them. "Fine," she said before leading the way out the cabin door. They followed in obedient procession as she navigated them through the wilderness, slashing at reaching branches and stomping over fallen leaves, to the lake. It was as isolated as always, a few scattered animal prints evidencing the only recent company. Karl toed the water before he dove into the icy silver. The water was so cold he couldn't feel his body swishing around below the surface.

Lucy watched in glittering laughter as Morrigan, from her steadfast seat on the bank, convinced waves to crash into Karl until he conceded the game. Morrigan then sprawled herself out letting the white sun beat down on her. Karl and Lucy could hear her sawing snores from the lake, and they held each other. They splashed and spun, diving, holding their breath, skin numb to the cold. It was too cold, Karl finally conceded between chattering teeth. Lucy kissed him, her lips an unsettling blue, and she ran her fingers through his wet hair before she waved him to the shore with a flourish and a splashing twirl. Not wanting to let go of her, he hesitated, but he was sure his legs would break off if he stayed in the cold a minute longer. Feeling burning electricity shiver up his body, he told her to come to the shore soon too, and he began to pull himself towards land.

Something pinched in his chest. He heard a sucking plop.

Morrigan, whose belly had been rising and falling slowly in time with her snores, suddenly sat straight up.

"Where is she?" she shouted to him, black and sharp.

"What?" Karl stammered. "She's diving, just playing around." He turned back, and it wasn't just that Lucy was gone. The surface was unbroken, unmoving silver glass.

Karl's mind didn't whirl. It didn't cloud or break into confused static. It turned to ice. He dove immediately under the water, eyes open and stinging; had it always been so clear under the lake?

Heart racing, a stampede of running, trampling hooves, he swam and swam and swam to where he and Lucy had been just moments before, but it was swimming through molasses. How was it taking him so long? Heavy and sinking throbbing, but they had not been this far out, the lake wasn't this big, stretching on for eternity, and he couldn't see anything but silver. He wouldn't breach. He wouldn't because if he did, he knew he would never find her. Ice. He couldn't leave this water. Drowning. His head throbbed and his pulse was in his throat, in every muscle in his arms and legs chest fingers eyes. Beating beating. He swam towards where Lucy must be, had to be, where he needed her to be. He couldn't—He had never felt so cold, Karl couldn't think, didn't know how to think. He pushed himself further, deeper and deeper deeper towards her, please be moving towards her towards Lucy. He saw himself, imagined himself grasping for her hand but he couldn't. Couldn't reach her. He was cold. Find her, he thought to the waters around him. Find her. Focus. Just focus. He was shaking, he was bursting, he was dying, he knew, but all he needed was to focus, to convince the magic around him to find her, it would be okay. His mind fogged, and he tasted thick warm honey drizzling from his mouth ears eyes nose, he couldn't focus couldn't think blazing golden spots like scales speckled his vision, he couldn't breathe swim survive and in the silver nothingness he was sinking into, only one thought rang clear through the fog. Lucy.

***

Heat. Fire. Boiling waters of fury. Karl's eyes fluttered open to see Morrigan. Her face was twisted, eyes alight, tears that he thought would turn to steam cascading down her cheeks. "What did you do." It was not a question. It was rage, barely contained.

Karl couldn't care because he needed to dive back in, to find her, find her, find her. His lungs burned and there was something in his hand, smooth and glassy, but he dropped it, whatever it was to the dirt, his only thought: Lucy. Stumbling to his feet, he ignored Morrigan's cries as he dove back into the water, knowing Morrigan did the same behind him.

They searched. Minutes turned into hours, how much time? How many seconds minutes hours? But the bottom of the lake seemed just the bottom of the lake and there was nothing there. Gasping breath, pounding lungs, cold blood. They searched. Until they didn't. Until they couldn't. Until they knew they had lost.

Night had snuck by them. It was dark. There shouldn't be stars, Karl thought, anger rising, as he sputtered on the shore now, soaked and shivering through streaming, furious tears. Wondering if he could go back and drown. He wanted to drown. Where was Lucy?

He rose to shaky knees. Not knowing not knowing anything, how could he think or feel or be? He couldn't. He wanted to scream, wanted to bleed, to swallow everything and burst into nothing, to die. He spread his fingers out wide on the lake's edge, water licking at his fingertips, tasting, mocking. He was empty, ruined, nothing. With a crack, a crack like lightning, like ravenous fire, like earth-shattering thunder, the lake's silver water began to shiver and evanesce, evaporating into the star-scattered night, leaving nothing. Nothing.

Nothing.

Karl collapsed; his face pressed to the newly dead nothingness. Through his tears, he saw the glittering of a small silver pebble, his breath hitched, and he couldn't breathe. He didn't want to breathe. He reached out and took the pebble, feeling it smooth between his fingers before clenching it in his fist, feeling all the pain in his body, he threw it with all his remaining strength, out into the void. There was nothing, no one, just a dead lake, empty of crystal water, of life, of everything.

Then he felt it. Searing pain. Deep. In all of him. Shooting, aching, blinding. Every kind of pain crashed into him with tsunamic force. He curled in on himself, bones cracking, muscles tearing. He was sure the hot blood gushing from his breaking body would fill the lake again. Still dead, but full. It was a golden pain and he deserved it. Didn't he? Couldn't he have done more? Shouldn't he have done more? Done anything. What was the point of being a mancy if you couldn't do anything? He wanted this pain; he wanted to fill the lake with thick, crimson blood and to drown in it.

Please let me disappear too.

But he didn't drown. Not in blood or tears or pain. A throbbing ache rolled over his entire body, and when his vision returned, he saw Morrigan standing over him, tears staining her sharp face, her eyes black and harder than he had seen them before. She wanted to kill him. She blamed him. She wanted to submerge his head underwater and hold him there. Fine. Do it. He wanted it too. But there wasn't water anymore; their lake was dead and gone. Karl tried to stand but fell to the ground. He tried to put his hands beneath him to push himself up, but—with agonizing horror—instead of hands, he had white, feathered wings, splattered red in the transfiguration.

Morrigan walked away, back into the woods, and with only pain as company Karl was alone with nothing.

Twenty-Six

The sun's rays stroked his downy wings, and Karl opened one eye halfway. His roost cupped him in its loving palm, the wool beneath him embraced his pearly body, he stirred slightly, feeling the shifting of treasures beneath the bedding. Sounds of sleep fluttered from Morrigan's room, from Viva's. Good, Viva was finally sleeping. Karl shook himself, loosing a few feathers, so they stuck out like punk rock chest hair. He chirped, remembering the school dance he had chaperoned with a glittering, pink mohawk at Viva's assertion that he couldn't chaperone because he wasn't "cool." He had been cool, he thought, though somehow, she had still been upset even after he had taught the kids his best dance moves. He tucked the askew feathers back in their proper place and stretched his wings to the morning.

He flew out the door and towards the Daisy House. Deep gurgling of coffee machines, that earthy rumbling, came from inside the garage. He floated through the smell of melting butter, through the yawning front door, landing gracefully on a perch in the tangerine kitchen. Clanging notes of heavy metal clicked on in a wink and Karl began to cook. Flour rose in breathy smoke, sugar mixed itself into fluffing butter, eggs cracked, and yolks ran.

As he carefully conducted the gustatory orchestra, he chuckled to himself. Tyree had never thought to hire anyone else but Karl. Strands of vanilla extract streamed past his glinting eyes with liquid ease. Karl was better, faster, and only required payment in various shiny objects: a few bottle caps or soda tabs here and there. A nice sparkling coin or two. He had also been the one to teach Tyree how to cook.

Tyree's company had always been one of manic comfort, Karl thought. The boy, (though a man, really) though fearful and shaking, button eyes wide with fear, always turned to wonder at every story Karl shared. At every invitation from the Regums. Everything. He had always joined them. Would you like to camp out for two weeks with us? Yes. How about inner tubing down the creek? Yes. Care to meet a large bear named Roger? Yes. Always without hesitation, though Karl felt the fear, Tyree agreed despite everything, despite fear. No matter how many broken noses, how many pulled muscles, bruises, or tears, Tyree didn't go anywhere. And Karl thought that they should make dinner together this evening. Something intricate, something new.

Then the fire alarm blared overhead, noting an umbra rising from the oven. Frantically, Karl tore the oven door open, removing a tray of blackened scones. Closing his eyes tightly, breathing and focusing, Karl waved a feathered wing over the tray. Focus. A few of the scones lightened slightly, but then blackened further and crumbled to pieces like ash. Focus, he thought, with a growl. Nothing happened. Magic couldn't save everything, he sighed. He turned up the metal blaring through the orange kitchen and started over again.

After Karl had made three more trays of scones, far exceeding his morning's first attempt, it was time for him to go back home for a bit.

Back at Mancy Manor, the speakers in his kitchen blared through the cabin, which he hoped would wake the sleeping ladies. It was waffles today, quick and easy, Karl thought, as he fought splashes of weariness in him. He shouldn't have tried reviving the scones. He knew better. He blinked sleepy eyes, catching a wooden spoon about to sneak out the window.

Morrigan was humming in the living room. Karl turned up his own music to drown her out. He needed to focus. Focus, focus. Oops, that was almost too golden brown, get out of the waffle iron now, onto the table, you know where to go. He thrust his beak towards the cushioned room and watched the waffle roll itself out of the kitchen. He had lost count, but Morrigan could take any extras to Roger, and so he conducted on.

Crashes of sleep slammed into Karl; his whole body shuddered. Just a few more, he thought. Then I'll rest. I'll rest. As he pushed visions of his roost—comfort sleep emerald treasure—from his mind, the sounds of controversy arose over his metallic music, over the noise of browning batter, of the hand mixer, over the muffled exhaustion. Focus, focus. He needed to get this done. To focus just a little longer.

A little longer came and went. Soapy sponges swirled through the kitchen in a flurry. And he was done. A door slammed, and Karl sank into his fatigue, pleased at the sparkling surfaces around him. Plopping down from his kitchen perch, he hopped clumsily to the living room, stumbling only once or twice until he finally nestled into an emerald, green pillow in front of the crackling fire. Through drooping eyelids, he watched Morrigan, whose ear was pressed firmly to the front door. Agitated, her face was red, eyes dark. "Karl, she's up in the tree. I know you're going to Tyree's soon but check on her before you go. And after you get back."

He cawed roughly and burrowed his face into the pillow—it smelled of cinnamon, and he felt a wave of tranquil slate.

Morrigan

*M*orrigan was angry. She was angry that Lucy was leaving, but she was mostly angry that she couldn't go too. She had pleaded with her mother, but the old mancy merely repeated that she needed more time to teach Morrigan. Deep down in her grumbling guts, Morrigan didn't think they would really be leaving tomorrow, they couldn't be leaving. Lucy wouldn't leave and Morrigan wouldn't have to cry, and though Karl had stolen her sister, she didn't want him to leave either. They would stay and it would all be okay, she thought as she sat on one of the many cushions that Karl had been mancying, which now carpeted the cabin floor. Morrigan opened a box of dried petals—pinks and oranges, yellows organized preciously—and she whispered. The petals came to life, humming comfort as Morrigan closed her eyes and sang along.

"Let's go," Lucy's voice rang through the flowery song.

"Go where?" Morrigan sang softly.

"*Lake.*" Lucy draped a jacket over Morrigan's shoulders. "*Mother's out and won't be back until after dinner, so come on.*" Morrigan sighed. Lucy was holding Karl's enormous, meaty hand and Morrigan crinkled her nose. "*Fine.*" She put the box back on the mantle with care and led the way out the door.

It was cold out for a trip to the lake. Normally, Morrigan and Lucy wouldn't be swimming this late in the year, leaves falling, breeze turning from soft caresses to snapping nips, but Morrigan would spend this day with her sister in whatever way Lucy wanted. Even if it meant Karl barreling along behind them.

She didn't wait for the other two but sprinted to the bank and sat down before the frigid waters. Lucy splashed her as she dove in; it felt like needles pricking her skin, and then Karl walked into the lake like a boulder, ripples running from him as though avoiding a devastating landslide. Morrigan smiled and caught Lucy's glittering eye before her sister dove downward, smooth and natural like a selkie as if the water was her second home.

Joy rang over the lake for a long time, but the shadow of oncoming loss was looming around the corners of Morrigan's mind, and so to stop the thoughts that were slithering ever closer, she spread herself out and thought of all the fun she and Lucy would have tomorrow and tomorrow and all the tomorrows after that when her sister didn't really leave, and with those tomorrows, she drifted off to sleep.

Morrigan was alone. Alone in the darkness. The woods were barren, trees made of bleached, cracking bones shuttered in a gnawing wind. A monster slithered. Morrigan took a step forward. She wouldn't be afraid. It couldn't make her. These were her woods. She would never run. Never leave them. Lucy was in front of her, skin blue and cold, standing between Morrigan and the draconic figure. Eyes of deep drowning sorrow she shook her head. Morrigan didn't understand. She stepped forward. The monster's long scaled neck cracked as it turned toward Morrigan. Dripping. Lucy didn't blink, only stared at her with those welling eyes, and when the thing opened a mouth like a black, toothy wound in a wide grin, Lucy opened her mouth too and vomited thick, silver liquid, which congealed on the ground almost immediately like glassy ice.

Morrigan's eyes snapped open, and she shot up in a breath. Her saliva tasted sweet, like golden honey. Behind Karl, who was now swimming towards the shore, Morrigan didn't see her sister. She wasted little time before diving into the water.

Lucy was there. Right there, right in front of her, she had to be. Morrigan could grab her arm if she could find her, drag her to the surface in a tight embrace and say you will never ever ever leave me. I'll go with you and Karl. I'll study with the other town's mancy. I'll help Karl practice because he's so useless at mancying. I'll be good, just take me with you. Don't leave.

Morrigan struggled, she sang out to the vegetation in the water, have you seen her? Have you seen Lucy? She was met only by silence. She begged the water, begged the debris that floated by her, begged any life, any magic, anything nearby to help her. Begged the vegetation nearby: find the mancy, find her and tell her to come. Help. Please help me find her. Silence.

She was sinking. The cold water gnawed dully at her frozen muscles. Downward and downward and downward she would fall until she dissolved into glittering silver. Please, she begged in a soundless plea to the lake. But it was silent.

Focus. She needed to focus. She couldn't focus. She would never be able to focus again. Never be able to do anything again if she couldn't find her sister. Her eyes burned and her chest throbbed in airless agony, but there in front of her, so close she blinked in disbelief, was Karl. His face was pale, black hair swimming like seaweed in front of his big, square face. Eyes open and clouded. He wasn't moving.

Focus. Morrigan surfaced for breath, resubmerged, and focused. She was exhausted, depleted. She couldn't think, focus, survive, but she needed to survive, needed him to survive so they could find Lucy. Morrigan fought her way back to the shore, urging the magic around her to ebb towards land, to carry her and Karl behind her, please help me. Carry me. Carry him. He's too heavy. It's all too heavy and I can't do it. Help.

They made it to the shore; Morrigan dragged as much of Karl out of the lake as she could, staring at him, fire building and building inside of her chest. He was breathing.

Tears welled molten behind her eyes, but she needed to focus. Morrigan dove back into the water to search, however long she needed to, she would search for Lucy forever.

She didn't know when Karl had woken up, when he had joined her back in the icy lake. But they searched. Minutes transformed into hours, in the hopeless abyss. Gasping breath, pounding lungs, cold blood. They searched. Until they couldn't anymore.

Night had snuck by them. It was dark. Furious tears broke through Morrigan. Body shaking uncontrollably, she could hardly see through delirious tears. How dare you. How dare you. How could he have lost her? She watched, blurrily, as Karl fell to shaky knees. What was he doing? How dare you, how dare you? Morrigan wanted to scream, wanted to bleed, to sink her teeth into his neck and feel the blood drain from him, to swallow everything and burst into nothing. She wanted him to do the same. He was nothing. She was nothing. There was nothing. Do something. Do anything. How did he not do something?

He was holding his arms out in front of him as if willing Lucy to run out of the lake and into them, but then he dropped, pressing his palms into the mouth of the lake, and Morrigan felt her steaming anger rise and rise. She watched tears pouring down his cheeks, hair clinging to his swollen face. Anger wept through every pore in her body, a black sludge. With a crack and a shimmer from Karl's hands, the lake began to drain. Morrigan's eyes flashed along every inch of the drying pit, searching. Nothing. There was nothing. Lucy was lost. She was lost. Karl collapsed in hot tears to ground. Morrigan stared at the dead lake, empty of water, of life, of everything. Morrigan was empty of everything.

Everything but rage.

She turned to Karl, shaking, drowning in fury. There was no focus. There was no thought. There was no Lucy. There was nothing. Morrigan pointed her gaze at the boy. The mountainous boy who took her sister away, who had the nerve to sob like he had lost, like he knew pain, like he could ever know. Pain. Morrigan held out her hand towards him. He would never know her pain, but he would know pain.

With obscene cracks, squelching, twisting, she watched as Karl's body broke and ground; Morrigan watched with dark, narrowed eyes as his bones splintered through flesh and crunched to pieces, and she could see pain. He would still never know. He couldn't know.

She watched as feathers sprouted from gore, splitting through seeping skin, as his nose broke and extended turning to hard silver. She watched, drowning in pain, and when it was done, Karl lay in front of her, pooled in feathers and blood, an enormous crow, white feathers red and sticky, breathing in shallow unconsciousness.

Morrigan walked away. Away from him. Away from this dead place. Into her woods, back toward Mancy Manor. Where she had nothing.

***

Mancy Regum found Morrigan along the path home. She sent her daughter back to the Manor and rushed up to see the obliterated lake to search for Lucy herself. She had found Karl, a mangled pile of crow, and after rigorous searching in, above, below, and around around around the former lake, had taken him back to the cabin, cleaned him up, and placed him gently in the bay window next to the fireplace. Morrigan's breath caught when her mother turned swiftly and grabbed Morrigan by the scruff of her neck and with decimating acidity said, "Heartless, Morrigan. Now he's your responsibility." The mancy was shaking. "Your curse is now your problem. And a stupid one at that. You set this trap for yourself." Morrigan had started to protest through tears she couldn't stop, but the mancy's grip tightened, and she did the strangest thing Morrigan could imagine: she pulled her daughter into a tight embrace and sobbed with her at the foot of the fire.

Twenty-Seven

Karl was tired, so tired, he breathed in his emerald pillow and exhaled slate, but he couldn't sleep, not yet. There were things to do, and if he closed his eyes now, he wouldn't awaken until late. He should've scrounged more from Tyree's earlier, but it didn't matter now. Karl shook his feathers out and rose. He took the pillow in his claws and tucked it into his roost bedding, inhaling memory's ghosts. Focus.

With another shake, he went to check up on Viva. She had fallen out of the tree plenty when she was young—how a kid could fall dead asleep propped in a tree was beyond him, but more often than he would care to share, he had found her like a baby bird, fallen to the earth and somehow still dead asleep, but children are rubbery and resilient. He did not want to find a grown woman broken and crumpled at the foot of the tree's generous trunk.

How was Viva still keeping him from sleep? He had assumed that would stop after childhood, hell, he would've taken post-adolescence or young adulthood, but it turned out, he ruffled, that children guzzled up sleep no matter how old they were. Maybe in her forties, she would let him rest.

As he fought his sleep, each beat of his wings like moving through gelatin, he flew overhead and noted Viva in her spot within the branches. He landed at the top of the oak where he had stood guard over her for so many years, before succumbing to a crashing wave, falling into slumber.

Twenty-Eight

Morrigan lounged in the tree for a long time, discussing the birds overhead, the quality of the soil below, and the oncoming winter. Morrigan chittered away to the tree she was sitting in. "You poor thing. You're not the only one who gets cold when winter comes." She counted out loud raising her fingers up and summarized, "Karl has twenty-four sweaters knitted for this winter and I'll be delivering next week. I'll be sure to drop one off for you. This year's color is blue—"

Silence fell like a hammer. Cold steel. The only sound, the cackling creek. Her heart twisted tight in her chest as she, holding on tightly to her sturdy branch. Below, basking like a Victorian maid spread across a fainting couch was Lucy. Vacant eyes fixed on the mancy, her lolling body edgeless and undulant. Colorless lips upturned in a mischievous smile. "Ah, it's you." Morrigan said, returning to her own repose, though her muscles remained tighter than they had been moments before. "Little later than usual." She ran a finger over the thick bark of her hosting tree, noting out of the corner of her eye, the specter's soft dissolve. "Anyway, blue is this year's color—not one of Karl's usuals, a little light for his taste, but the ones I've seen are nice. How does that sound?" Lucy had gone. Morrigan whispered under her breath to the thin, fall air. "She was never here."

It was time to go. Morrigan sprang from her branch. "I'll be back with a blue sweater, and don't take any more nonsense from those woodpeckers."

She stepped off the path. Further further away from the creek, deeper into the woods. As she hummed to herself, the breeze stroked her face, her hair, her everything, enveloping her in a cold embrace. Deeper and deeper into the woods, farther and farther from the creek.

Then the path ended.

About two miles away from the creek was a dead place. It wasn't a pool of asphalt for campers to park their vehicles—there was no trail near this place but the creek path, which was a ways away. It wasn't a field of brown, gasping grasses, it wasn't anything. It was nothing but dark earth, almost black, like the aftermath of a fire. It was a dead lake.

Their dead lake.

Morrigan pulled a waffle out of her pocket, took a bite, and replaced it. Breathe in. One step. Another. She wanted to turn around to run back to the path. Go home or hibernate with Roger for a season. The wind bit at her. Another step forward. And forward. And forward. Until the mancy reached the middle. The epicenter of their decimated lake, that empty earth, drained of everything, overlooked by surrounding, yet tentative trees, as though they were wary of the lifeless clearing. Morrigan fell to her back there in the center of their dead lake, and angelically, swished her arms and legs back and forth in the earth, that cold, ashy dirt. She did not close her eyes, but stared up at the gray sky, arms and legs stretched out over the black earth. Out of the corner of her eye, gauzy aureoles flashed. Morrigan didn't turn to inspect more closely. She didn't have to. She knew what it all was. She had seen identical shimmers from Karl's roost and large, tetradactyl-like prints blanketed the earth next to her. Morrigan sighed knowing he would never stop bringing treasures here for her. She ignored a thin, gossamer shade in the distance. She wasn't really there.

It was time to go home.

The shadow followed. It always did, always in the corner of her hard, obsidian eye.

Morrigan, consuming the last piece waffle from her pocket, rejoined the path, the creek running beside her cackling over smoothed stones.

It was too quiet.

Silvered

It started. A tap, tapping on the black, cabin door. It wasn't a scratching of claws or a pounding of fists. It wasn't a barge or a crash, but a soft and gentle tap, tapping.

Silence answered. Swelling in the dark of the house, a bloated, pulsing silence. Crawling into dusty corners, under bean bags and blankets, engulfing dust bunnies and crumbs.

Viva was awake. Silver silence bled under the door, sizzling as it met shards of eggshell, crushed charcoal, salt crystals, banishing. An argentine plume exhaled over the threshold. Over every threshold. Windows and doors and doors and doors. Everything was open and Viva was awake. She glanced around the room. Karl's roost was empty. There was no music from the sterile kitchen. The herbs were silent on the mantel and the mancy's room was empty too. Viva was alone in gooey silence and pewter breath. Alone, the word resounded through the muted atmosphere. Alone, it swirled in a musty breeze. Alone, brushing against her cheek, swishing through her hair, twisting around and around and around her. Viva drifted through the cabin, rolling a silver pebble between her fingers, seeing in her mind's eye everything that could be. Everything she had seen, everything he had shown her, him and her and him and nothing else, no one else, empty but for silver and gold, as the visions she had seen or perhaps had never seen and only wished for, but they were real, the only real, submerged her. Viva, ever veiled in the quiet, ever forgotten in the din, opened the midnight door.

His voice trickled down her spine: "Time to go." It oscillated dripping honey into the pool of her mind. Slicing through the black sheet of silence. A caramelized knife: "You are nothing here. No one cares here, no one notices. No one wants you here. You are alone."

Framed in the open door, haloed in ethereal light, Viva considered him. The face beyond the glass, the only face occupying her cloudy mind. She was nothing here, but there, beneath the rippling surface... Elusive but...Viva's knees buckled, and she sank down to the floor, before entry, the exit, the scent of the garden beyond crashing into her, but she shook it away. Her whole body wavered as she swept the banish away from the threshold and held out her hand.

He lit up the night as he stretched his arm into the cabin, taking hold of her, metal and warm, and her body shuddered at his touch, but she was ready, she tightened her grip, entwining her fingers between his, she was silver, and his smile was gold and blinding. The cabin behind her was cast into shadow. She longed for silver. He was so bright Viva's eyes watered, but she would not turn away. She pulled herself up. For him. For the self she longed to be. For silver.

Her heart beat as she strode over the threshold.

She walked in radiant light down a path she could not remember. She stumbled. Past foliage, stones, and trees she could not recall. She furrowed her brows at a sugary house to her left, not recognizing troubled eyes of dozens of gnomes, not seeing a slip of paper patiently waiting for her in the cauldron of a squat, ceramic witch. She knew only silver, only what could be beyond the surface, beyond the swelling ripples of what was, she knew only the auspicious hand in hers as they approached the bank of the creek.

The waters stormed over jagged rocks, miniature whitecaps foaming over slobbering rolls. She had done this before. He released her hand and stood behind her, heat emanating from him. Just a step over the edge, into a swirling moat. Into bliss, into silence, into a land where you will never be alone, where you will belong. The golden rays from behind her pulsed and flared brighter, hotter, as though he was about to ignite. Her body heaved with icy contractions, and her skin prickled. A drop of sweat slid down the back of her neck and over her spine. She felt his fiery hand on her back, and Viva didn't fall, but she so wanted to, drawn and drawn and drawn, pushed and pulled, sinking into the waters. His voice was molten now, deeper and more potent than she had heard before. Stronger, brighter, larger. Did she remember a before? Eyes glassy, she gazed into the waters to a place she knew. A place she had gone, had she gone, who had gone? In the waters. She fell forward, her body shattering the surface and she sank fast.

His lips pulled tight, revealing sharp white teeth, and he began to stretch himself out. His golden arms grew longer, glittering gold scales sprouted from the smooth skin of his body. His neck elongated, and silver spines like sharp stones ran down his curving vertebra, extending into a serpentine tail. His golden eyes glinted, taking in his reward, the newest addition to his hard-earned collection. His jaws unhooked and stretched into a reptilian snout, and his sharp, white teeth grew longer, sharper in a dripping grin.

She sank.

As she sank lower and lower toward his domain, his senses sharpened, his eyes, scales, body brightened, and his muscles mind power strengthened. In a breath of silver and a flash of gold, he dove into the waters and followed Viva downward, driving her to her eternal place with the others in the silver palace.

Twenty-Nine

Morrigan navigated her way back home the same way she had left, peeping into Viva's room as she passed. It wasn't night. Not close to it at all–Tyree would still be working at the Daisy House, and Karl would be there too. Viva would be in town readying the next day's adventure materials, so it shouldn't have been surprising that Viva wasn't in her room, but Morrigan's skin prickled when she saw the empty room. White bed, white walls, white everything white. Empty. Time, memories, concerns, and wishes spiraling, Morrigan saw Viva as an infant sleeping in a golden treasure trove, a toddler holding a miniature paintbrush dripping white– dripping, white–Morrigan shook her head and saw the five-year-old posing in a new backpack, the teenager refusing to open her door, the empty room void and waiting for college to end–Viva would come back. It was empty again. Morrigan's heart ached as she watched all her Vivas, their princess in her pearly castle. Shrouded in pure light.

But Viva wasn't there.

Across the room at Viva's door, a shimmer caught Morrigan's eye. Lucy's empty eyes were fixed on the invisible Vivas as well. Timeless memories collided and spun. Lucy appeared as frosted glass, now seated on the edge of a white bed, now shimmering in the desk chair, now gossamer in the doorway, each time watching Vivas who weren't there either.

Morrigan closed her eyes and walked on, sightless, choosing the blackness over terrific illusions of nothing. It was nothing.

There was no sound from the oak outside of her cabin. Viva had left the tree and must have gone into town, or maybe, Morrigan hoped, she was in the cabin, sitting in front of the fire, ready for an adventure.

Morrigan took a deep breath in, and the cabin door swung open. She reached for another piece of waffle, but her store had been depleted on her trip. Nonetheless, her tired muscles remembered to lift the banish jar from the entryway cactus and to spread it liberally over the threshold. Almost time to make some more, she thought to herself as she stepped into the cabin and collapsed on the first chair she encountered.

Morrigan

"*K*arl!*" Morrigan prodded him awake. "*Karl, let's go.*" He grunted and rolled away from her, his beak hitting the bay window with a ting. "*Karl, come on, we can find her. I know it. Mother is waiting on the path.*" He hissed at her and nuzzled himself up in his blankets. "*I talked to a woman from… Well, I don't know, but she's a mancy a few towns away, maybe even the town Lucy was going to go to—*" Karl snorted sarcastically, but Morrigan ignored him. "*The lady said that you can find ghosts for real. She gave me a list of the flowers they like, and mother and I planted rows and rows of them in the garden and throughout the woods a while back, some of them have already bloomed, so now we can search for her. We can find her. I know we can.*" Her voice broke, but she shook the tears out of her eyes. "*Let's go, we have to try.*" Karl faked a snore. Morrigan felt bubbles of annoyance rise in her. "*You've been sleeping in that window for a year, you can't even really fly yet, are you going to sleep forever?*" With a pang, she realized that he would. She* *knew he would, and she would too if her mother hadn't quit her advising job in town and stayed with them constantly. If her mother hadn't been taking Morrigan out to search every day. "Fine," she said finally, "We'll go ourselves."*

Karl sat dizzily up from his emerald pillow, rucking his quilt down his throat, and he cawed crushing gravel.

"We'll be fine. I've got the banish that mother has started making. You need to learn to make it too." Morrigan held up a large glass jar with black and white grains of something. She flipped herself around and marched towards the door, flinging it open. Arms filled with a jar of banish and a bouquet of moonflower, she wondered whether she should stay and sit in the garden, underneath the umbrella leaves of her favorite giant rhubarb. Could she curl up and sleep? Maybe if she stayed in the garden, she would sprout roots and start a new existence. No cares or pain, only flowery song.

Morrigan was about to settle underneath the gigantic perennial, when Karl kicked the door open and hopped outside, dragging Morrigan's jacket behind him. He fluttered clumsily up to her shoulder, draping the jacket over her and they set off up the path where the mancy waited, and where they would dive into the woods to hunt for Lucy's ghost.

Thirty

Morrigan awoke, heavy metal blared from the kitchen, where Karl was making himself busy. With heavy lids and a throbbing headache, Morrigan pulled herself to standing and walked toward the kitchen. "Where's Viva?" she asked the room above the metallic notes and simmering hisses.

Karl cocked his head at her and pointed his beak toward the garbage can where something charcoal-black still smoldered.

"Ah, okay," said Morrigan. "I see you've been busy." She walked away towards the back of the cabin. She made a mental note to set up additional appointments with sleep doctors in the neighboring towns as she knocked on Viva's door. She saw a red flash of Viva, five years old and missing and her pulse quickened.

She knocked again even though Viva would never have been able to hear anything over the kitchen din, then walked into the room. Whites and whites and whites, Morrigan scanned, only to see Lucy.

A shard of ice pierced Morrigan's heart and twisted, opening a red, weeping wound. She buckled over, holding herself up by the doorknob. Lucy. Translucent, waifish. Colorless body soused and dripping, clothes heavy, sticking to willowy limbs. The flesh—but it couldn't be flesh—slipping like wet paper over her skull. She was sitting delicately above Viva's empty, white bed, hands folded gently over crossed legs. With delicate hands, the skin shucking from white bone she toyed with something silver. Lucy, with a gaze like slate, opened her mouth as if to speak, and silver, oily liquid poured from her, down lifeless lips, chin, throat. Morrigan fell to her hands and knees and vomited.

Lucy's ghost didn't move.

Hands shaking, Morrigan rolled her palms gently over the floor. Over what? Over what? She closed her eyes. Raising her voice in a shout, but the music the music, there was music, sound, color, smell, and shouting, stomach churning, head spinning, turning, twisting. She dropped her eyes to the floor and saw below her hands, her knees, over the entirety of that pristine, white carpet were silver pebbles, smooth as glass, inside were gleaming images of Viva, translucent gray surrounded by shades of ghosts Morrigan didn't know.

The mancy peered up at the ghost, heart beating fast, keeping time with the pounding drums the guitar the screaming screaming screaming. Lucy held the pebble she had been rolling between her fingers toward Morrigan, but as she did, the ghost, the ghost Morrigan had been searching for all these years, the sister she had finally found, screeched in agony and turned to silver smoke, disappearing into the stone.

Morrigan waited for the pebble to fall and hit the floor, but the only thing she heard was a small splash and then there was silence and nothing. The room was white and empty.

***

Karl had awakened in the oak, groggy and frustrated, Viva was no longer perched below him, and so he had gone back inside to a silent house. Morrigan was asleep in the living room and Viva must have been in town preparing for tomorrow's adventure. He had begun cooking but gave up on his failed concoction and had suggested the rose-colored handset float off the base of Mancy Manor telephone and dialed the only number scrawled in permanent marker on the wall-mounted base. As he ordered the pizza, he heard Morrigan awaken, shifting and walking to the back of the cabin. Pizza was ordered, but there was no way Karl would ever serve pizza without fresh basil, so he flew out of the cabin and into the wild garden.

He flapped above the basil plant, grasping a few leaves in his claws. Every muscle in his body tensed and his heart stalled as he saw her just beyond the reaching tendrils of the garden. There. Waiting for him, angelic and blue slate, was Lucy. As he stared at her, the world turned silver. The mancy's unruly garden a gleaming metallic, the sky a sheet of unending iron, the path down the creek made of pebbles silver silver and silver.

Lucy was incandescent blues flickering there and nowhere like electricity in a storm, as though she could not sustain her state. A strained smile stretched over colorless lips as she shivered in the windless night, ghostly translucence.

Karl's body stuttered in the air before he fell roughly to the earth, but he was back in the sky again in an instant, flying towards her, remembering something of a dream he had once had. She blinked slate eyes as he neared her shimmering form, and she held out a silver pebble, smooth like glass, and in a cloud of gray miasma, in a shooting pain that sliced through him, she disappeared into the crystal depths. Extinguished, only the lingering pulse of slate remained. There was nothing left, and Karl's heart hitched as an icy frost formed over it through it around and around.

***

Tyree pulled the garage door shut with a heave. He had double-checked that everything had been turned off, that the door to his house was locked. He checked that he had double-checked. About to turn up the path toward Mancy Manor, he saw a dreamy glow coming from the witch gnome's cauldron.

He smiled. Viva had just needed time, a minute to herself to refresh and rejuvenate. The star-spangled witch eyed him with an expression he hadn't noticed before. When he got closer, peering apprehensively into the hat for the source of the glow, Tyree was surprised at the depth of it. He felt around, his note from earlier was no longer there, and there was no—oh. It didn't make any sense. Out of the hat, he pulled a small, silver pebble, glowing weakly in the moonlight. There was nothing else in the cauldron.

He studied the pebble, turning it between his fingers; in its depths, silver shadows, one shadow slightly resembled Viva's silhouette. Frowning, Tyree wondered what new game he was being asked to play, but he heard only the babble of the ever-running creek.

***

Morrigan couldn't breathe. She couldn't breathe couldn't breathe. The floor was shifting under her feet, the white walls pressed in, constricting, condensing, lost breath caught and choked.

Where was Viva?

Morrigan flew, lungs dry and bursting, out to the main room. The fire blazed, clangorous melodies blared from the kitchen. Morrigan's voice died in her throat as she called out.

No one was there.

The front door gaped. Had it been open the whole time? She hadn't noticed. Over the threshold, banish was scattered to solitary shards, evening was breaking in.

Morrigan, eyes stinging ears ringing, ran out the door.

She met Karl in the garden, his silver eyes were wide and when he saw the mancy, he cawed, voice cracking and led her down the path. They ran.

***

Tyree saw Morrigan and Karl sprinting towards him. His pulse quickened and his breath caught. Tyree waited for them, his bale of straw hair shifting in a breath of new wind. When they reached him, Tyree, not knowing why, held out the pebble he had found in the cauldron. The shadows danced within, around, around and around.

***

Morrigan gazed into the crystalline pebble in Tyree's hand, her eyes burned, and her muscles cramped, knees buckled. There, in the depths was

Lucy. It was Lucy–there was no doubt. The ghost Morrigan had been hunting for so many years was there within a silver pebble. The shade stopped and though there were no features, no eyes or face, she felt Lucy watching her in a moment of stillness. The other shadows danced around and around and around. A voice like that submerged– submerged in the depths of an icy lake–rattled in the mancy's head. It said, "The creek," and Lucy's shadow rejoined the others, as though pulled, in a spectral dance, movements languid like trickling streams of rain over a window. Lugubrious silence fell.

Morrigan, Karl, and Tyree flew towards the creek.

***

Viva had gone.

***

On the bank where Viva's footprints still walked disembodied into the creek, a cruel petroglyph on the muddy edge, Karl perched on Tyree's shoulder. The small pebble was secured firmly in his sharp, silver beak. The creek, impossibly still, impossibly silver. Karl wondered then, if Morrigan could turn him into stone–if she could please. Could she finally stop it, stop the bleeding of his fractured heart?

Stillness and silence engulfed them all until the mancy held out her arm. Karl flew to her and perched on the offered space, she held him in an obsidian gaze. He couldn't breathe, couldn't think, didn't want to feel as he shuddered on Morrigan's shaking arm. She placed a trembling hand on his head and said, "Breathe," she said through tears. "It's time." Morrigan turned to Tyree, "Tyree, would you please run home and bring us as much food as you can carry back? We're going to need as much energy as we can get." Tyree, heaving through effort and sobs, ran up the path towards the Daisy House.

Karl breathed. Morrigan breathed. Tears still fell down her cheeks. A swirling wind twisted around them. Morrigan said softly, "I don't know if it will work, even if we do it together, but we need to try so that we can find her. Focus, Karl."

The wind cracked and sparked as it wrapped around them. Purple flashes popped and sizzled while Morrigan, ushering Karl to the ground, sat with him, legs crisscrossed, both hands firmly on his white-feathered head. As the wind spun crackling and buzzing, the feathers beneath Morrigan's hands turned to black and down and black again, and some of the down barbs transformed into curling locks. The sound of breaking bones collided with the hissing wind, the electric bursts, the purple shimmering magic that the mancies spun together. Karl's beak broke down to a thin nose, and feathers fell to the ground–blood speckled snow, wings turned to fleshy, feathered arms, and thick trunked legs expanded from scaly appendages. After what felt like a lifetime, the wind died down, Morrigan breathed heavily, her body exhausted, her mind at its limit, she assessed the man in front of her. Gore-covered feathers stuck out over bleeding arms and legs. His thick, black hair was entangled in white feathers all encased a nightmarish face. A face reflected in a funhouse mirror, now sharp and beaked, now the boyish, square face he had long before, features all framed in feathers and black locks. Morrigan, breathless and tearstained, took Karl's hands and stared into the red, welling eyes of a man she had not seen for an eternity.

Tyree's racing, heavy footsteps neared and halted on the bank behind the mancies. Karl stood and turned. Tyree, eyes red and wide, mouth dropped in astonishment, held out a large bag of supplies. Karl took it and pulled Tyree into a full, feathery embrace. "We'll find her," he croaked with rusty vocal cords.

In silence, they broke apart and Morrigan winked at Tyree as she held her hand out to Karl, who took it. Together, they turned to the creek.

Morrigan and Karl stood at the bank of the creek hand in hand and one step at a time, they followed Viva's footsteps into the ever-burbling waters.

End

E.M. Chapel

Acknowledgments

During the writing of this book, it being in the middle of a global pandemic, I didn't do much other than swim around in my own soupy mind. In there, I reacquainted myself with all those positive influences, all those who have created for me that all too important sense of belonging and community.

To my most influential teachers, Mr. Carpenter and Mr. Sherman who bullied me into a love of writing and self-confidence, thank you for the guidance and please don't look two hard for typos.

To my students who are laughter, learning, and resilience itself. Feelings of isolation and insecurity are the constant companions of adolescence, so thank you for your steadfast authenticity, a reminder to me to be myself. I could not have written this without my students.

Kim thank you for readthroughs, the monthly virtual feedback, your steady logical input and ruthless feedback helped me to boil it down to what it is.

Flo, thank you for the beautiful cover art that still blows me away as well as all your help with editing.

Tisha and Megan thank you for your workshopping and encouragement.

Wendy, thank you for being my fairy godmother and providing all the magic and support that comes with that role.

And to all those other numerous positive lights I have encountered throughout this process, virtually, physically, or in memory, thank you.

The Weight of Silver

Author Bio

E.M. Chapel's debut novel "The Weight of Silver" kicks off her dream of releasing her writing into the world. When she isn't writing, she can be found in Seattle teaching high school-aged students, practicing martial arts, and reading, all with a cup of coffee in her hand.

Made in United States
Troutdale, OR
06/30/2023

10891985R00217